MEANJIN

MELBOURNE
UNIVERSITY
PRESS

Australia Council
for the Arts

THE UNIVERSITY OF MELBOURNE

Victoria
The Place To Be

ARTS
VICTORIA

palgrave
macmillan

Editorial by Sophie Cunningham

Welcome to the new look *Meanjin*. You'll notice a lot of changes. No contents page, for starters—that now sits on the back cover. Once I got over the shock of the idea, I agreed with my wonderful new designers, Stuart Geddes and Jeremy Wortsman, that it was, in fact, more practical that way. *Meanjin* will now be two-colour throughout with a four-colour section for the essays that demand it. Work will be divided into several distinct sections. Up front is a reprise of Clem Christensen's 'Newsreel' section for more current affairs and newsy pieces. That will be followed by a colour section in which *Meanjin*'s emeritus designer, W.H. Chong (*Meanjin* farewells him this edition and thanks him for six years of wonderful work), talks to us about books and book design, while David Nichols (in words) and Mia Schoen (in painting) defend the suburbs against more than a century of unwarranted snobbery. Our essay section ranges from lighter personal pieces, such as Andrea McNamara's discussion of growing up with footy (there's only one kind) as her second language—an essay I love despite the author's misguided passion for Collingwood, to Joseph Pearson's consideration of Don Watson's

American Journeys in light of the American primaries. Mel Campbell analyses the meaning of buying (and botching said purchase of) a leather jacket. Anthony Macris has allowed us to extract from his clear-eyed and moving memoir 'When Horse Became Saw', which describes his young son's descent into severe autism. Lynne Spender states the case for the copyleft movement, Andrea Goldsmith considers the intimacies of letter writing, John van Tiggelen hangs with the twitchers up in Cooktown and Carol Chan describes the lurch of calling both Melbourne and Singapore home. We continue our serialization of the graphic history 'Their hooks find hold deep in our flesh'.

There is lots of fiction to be excited about, including a piece by extraordinary young newcomer Abigail Ulman. Expect to hear a lot more from her in coming months and years. We've included previously unpublished UK writer Sandra White with her story 'Faith', and an extract from Luke Stickels novel, 'The Rise of an Urban Terrorist'— who says young writers aren't tackling political subjects? Mark Dapin, better known for his journalism, inhabits another skin in his story 'The Face of 1970' and we have a story from the master: Alex Miller's 'Salem Lodge'.

I particularly want to introduce you to Caroline Lee. In the June edition of *Meanjin* we ran the prologue of her novel, *Stripped*, and we continue with our serialisation of that work. You'll notice her section has its own design and pagination—for readers wanting to attend to the novel's unfolding over the months to come. *Stripped* is the novel of a true virtuoso and I want to thank Caroline for taking a punt with this unusual approach to publication. We're privileged to have her.

In our regular interview section I talk to Georgia Blain about the personal and professional complexities of life-writing, in the wake of the publication of her wonderful collection of essays *Births Deaths Marriages*. We also showcase, as we always have, Australia's best poets. These include—to risk mentioning only five of fifteen fine poems—the beautiful 'Lotuses' by Diana Bridge, 'What is Broken' by Melbourne's own speechwriter/poet Joel Deane and two impressive longer poems, from Claire Potter and Mark Tredinnick.

EDITOR
Sophie Cunningham

POETRY EDITOR
Judith Beveridge

DESIGN & PRODUCTION
Chase & Galley

COVER & SECTION ILLUSTRATIONS
Lachlan Conn

NEWSREEL ILLUSTRATIONS
Oslo Davis

EDITORIAL CONSULTANTS
Natalie Book, Richard McGregor
and Nicola Shafer

OFFICE MANAGER
Mary Kennedy

WEBSITE MANAGER
Anthony Hunt

VOLUNTEERS AND ASSISTANTS
Jess Au and Laura Kerton

ADVISORY BOARD
Louise Adler, Kate Darian-Smith, Mark Davis, Ken
Gelder, Deb Verhoeven, Chris Wallace-Crabbe,
Michael Webster, Angela Woods

FOUNDING EDITOR
Clem Christensen
(1911–2003; editor 1940–74)

Meanjin was founded in Queensland by
Clem Christesen in 1940. The name, pronounced
mee-*an*-jin, is derived from an Aboriginal word
for the finger of land on which Brisbane sits.
The magazine moved to Melbourne in 1945 at
the invitation of the University of Melbourne.
The University has continued to be the principal
sponsor of *Meanjin* in financial and non-financial
ways. In 2008 *Meanjin* became an imprint of
Melbourne University Publishing Ltd

SUBSCRIPTIONS
Contact the Meanjin office, or subscribe online
at our website.

ENQUIRIES
Postal address: Meanjin, 187 Grattan Street,
Carlton, Victoria 3053 Australia

CONTACT
http://www.meanjin.unimelb.edu.au
Fax: (+61 3) 9342 0399
Telephone: (+61 3) 9342 0300
E-mail: meanjin@unimelb.edu.au

Unsolicited manuscripts are welcome but
to be considered they must be accompanied by
a stamped, self-addressed envelope or interna-
tional reply coupon. A style guide will be found
at our website.

Minimum payment to contributors is $50
for poems, $100 for prose. Fees are generally
determined by word-length and will include a 5%
supplement to provide in advance for copyright
entitlements that contributions may attract
through the Copyright Agency Ltd (CAL).

Copyright of each piece belongs to the
author; copyright of the collection belongs to
Meanjin. Republication is permitted on request
to author and editor. Meanjin licenses selected
online publication through CAL.

Published contributions by academics are
refereed. See our website for details.

The views expressed by authors are not
necessarily those of the editor or publishers.

Typeset in a variety of faces designed by
Hoefler & Frere-Jones

Printed and bound by BPA Print Group
Distributed by Pan Macmillan
Print Post Approved PP341403 0002
AU ISSN 0025-6293

CORRECTION
In Wayne Macauley's essay 'The Other Way'
published in *Meanjin* Volume 67, Number 2, it was
stated that the Literature Board of the Australia
Council funds the Books Alive strategy. It does
not. It also needs to be pointed out that they do
fund the infrastructure of small independent
publishers: an idea which Macauley's essay
recommends without stating that it is already
Literature Board practice.

∘CONTRIBUTORS∘

LOUIS ARMAND (P 189)

is a Prague-based Australian writer and visual artist. His books include *Land Partition* (Textbase, 2001), *Inexorable Weather* (Arc, 2001), *Strange Attractors* (Salt, 2003) and *Malice in Underland* (Textbase, 2003). He is the editor of *Contemporary Poetics* (Northwestern University Press, 2007).

JAMES BRADLEY (P 200)

is the author of three novels: *Wrack*, *The Deep Field* and *The Resurrectionist*, and a book of poetry, *Paper Nautilus*.

DIANA BRIDGE (P 188)

Her most recent collection of poetry is *Red Leaves* (AUP, 2005). Her Translation Paper 'An Unexpected Legacy: Xie Tiao's Poems on Things' was published earlier this year by the Asian Studies Institute and the New Zealand Centre for Literary Translation. An essay on the China-based poems of Robin Hyde will appear in a book on Hyde to be published in September 2008.

MEL CAMPBELL (P 59)

is a journalist, editor and cultural commentator. A co-founder of quixotic poster-magazine *Is Not Magazine*, she now publishes a new Australian online magazine, *The Enthusiast*, and maintains a fashion research weblog, *Footpath Zeitgeist*. Mel enjoys drinking tea in copious quantities and fulminating against poor sub editing.

LAURA CARROLL (P 14)

lives in Melbourne. She teaches English at La Trobe University, where she is also completing a PhD on film adaptation.

CAROL CHAN (P 79)

is a student of anthropology at the University of Melbourne, and is currently spending a year in Edinburgh on exchange. Her writing has been published and performed in Singapore and Melbourne.

W.H. CHONG (P 18)

has designed most of Text Publishing's books since 1991. He was the designer of *Meanjin's* page template and its covers from vol. 60 no. 4 to vol. 67 no. 1.

MARK DAPIN (P 140)

is a features writer on *Good Weekend* in *The Sydney Morning Herald* and *The Age*. He has written for most of the magazines in Australia, from *The Picture* to *The Australian Financial Review* Magazine, and for British newspapers such as *The Times* and *The Guardian*. His short stories have appeared in *Penthouse*, *Woman's Day*, *Ita* and a couple of anthologies.

JOEL DEANE (P 190)

is a poet and novelist, as well as principal speechwriter to the Premier of Victoria, John Brumby. His second collection of poetry, *Magisterium*, was recently published by Australian Scholarly Publishing. He is currently finishing his second novel.

CORY DOCTOROW (P 14)

is an activist, science fiction author and co-editor of the blog Boing Boing: http://www.boingboing.net.

STEPHEN EDGAR (P 192)

lives in Sydney. He has published six collections of poetry, the most recent being *Other Summers* (Black Pepper, 2006). In 2006 he was awarded the Philip Hodgins Memorial Medal for literature.

KATE FIELDING (P 92)

develops innovative spaces for telling underrepresented histories in creative, playful and radical forms. She has filled research and public-history roles with Museum Victoria, National Archives of Australia, National Museum of Australia, Heritage Victoria, Koorie Heritage Trust, History Council of Victoria and—currently—the Warburton Arts Project based in remote WA.

MARIA FREIJ (P 193)

recently submitted her PhD in Creative Writing. Her theoretical work focuses on literary representations of melancholy and translation between English, Swedish and French. Maria has presented her work in Australia and Europe and her poems have appeared in journals and anthologies. She teaches at the University of Newcastle.

ANDREA GOLDSMITH (P 67)

has published five novels, most recently *The Prosperous Thief*, which was short-listed for the 2003 Miles Franklin Award. Her new novel, *Reunion*, a story of obsessive love, intellectual striving and untimely death, will be published by Fourth Estate in 2009. Her literary essays appear regularly in Australia and overseas.

BEN HARPER (P 8)

is an Australian composer, artist and writer. He has lived in London for the past three years, and is still adjusting to the concept of dual citizenship.

JOHN KINSELLA (P 191)

His most recent volume of poetry is *Shades of the Sublime and Beautiful* (Fremantle Press and Picador, 2008). His *Divine Comedy: Journeys through a Regional Geography* is due out in September 2008 (UQP and WW Norton). *Disclosed Poetics: Beyond Landscape and Lyricism* (Manchester University Press, 2007) and *Contrary Rhetoric: Lectures on Landscape and Language* (Fremantle Press, 2008) are recent volumes of his criticism.

ELIZABETH LAWSON (P 194)

is a widely published Canberra writer and poet who won the David Campbell Poetry Award in 2005. As a literary scholar she published *The Poetry of Gwen Harwood*, several editions of novels and many critical articles. Her art-history book *The Natural Art of Louisa Atkinson* appeared in 1995 and she was guest curator of the major exhibition 'Birds' at the National Library of Australia in 1999.

CAROLINE LEE (P 170)

is a writer and performer and in this edition of *Meanjin* we are running the second extract from her novel *Stripped*. She won the 2005 A.B. Natoli Prize for her short story 'the yo-yo' and has had stories published in *The Sleepers Almanac* and *Visible Ink*. The first draft of *Stripped* was completed with the assistance of the 2005 Marion Eldridge Award for Emerging Woman Writers. She can be contacted via her website www.carolinelee.com.au

ELIZABETH MCDOWELL (P 92)

achieved her Bachelor of Fine Arts, majoring in printmaking, at RMIT after completing her Bachelor of Arts in Art History at the University of Melbourne. Moving to the USA in 2003, Elizabeth worked as a Master Printer's Assistant for Akasha print studios in Minneapolis, before moving to New York City where she worked for Harlan & Weaver, Inc. in their intaglio print publisher workshop.

ANDREA MCNAMARA (P 52)

is Allen & Unwin's Commissioning Editor in Melbourne. Before changing careers in 2000, she was a freelance designer and lecturer at RMIT University. She commissions non-fiction titles for the trade, and is particularly interested in memoir, true crime, sport and humour.

ANTHONY MACRIS (P 85)

is author of the novel *Capital, Volume One*, which was shortlisted for Best First Book, Commonwealth Writers' Prize, South East Asian Section. He is a senior lecturer in Creative Writing at the University of Technology, Sydney. 'When Horse Became Saw' is an extract from a longer book of the same name that will be published in late 2009.

ALEX MILLER (P 151)

has twice won the Miles Franklin Award and is an overall winner of the Commonwealth Writers Prize. He is the author of eight novels, several of which have been published internationally and all of which are in print in Australia. His most recent novel is the critically acclaimed *Landscape of Farewell* (Allen & Unwin, 2007).

DAVID NICHOLS (P 92)

is a historian and Lecturer in Urban Planning in the School of Design, University of Melbourne. He is co-editor, with Keir Reeves, of *Deeper Leads: New Approaches to Victorian Goldfields History* (BHS, 2007) and over the last year has published on diverse subjects including the Mildura entrepreneur C. J. De Garis, lead singers in Australian rock bands and public buildings in private real estate developments of the early 20th century.

MANDY ORD (P 92)

is a Melbourne-based cartoonist and illustrator. She has self-published her own comic stories and her work has appeared in local and international anthologies. Her first graphic novel, *Rooftops*, was published by Finlay Lloyd in February 2008.

JOSEPH PEARSON (P 38)

lives in Melbourne, where he invents things for machines and humans. He has a blog at www.make-believe.org

CLAIRE POTTER (P 195)

was a Poets Union Fellow in 2006. She published *In Front of a Comma* (Poets Union, 2006) and *N'Ombre* (Vagabond, 2007). She lives and works in France.

DAVID PRATER (P 198)

is the Managing Editor of *Cordite Poetry Review*: www. cordite.org.au. In 2005 he was an Asialink resident in Seoul, Republic of Korea, where he pursued his obsession with PC Bangs. His debut poetry collection, *We Will Disappear*, was released in 2007 by soi3/papertiger media.

RON PRETTY'S (P 199)

most recent book is *Of the Stone: New and Selected Poems* (2000). Until he retired in 2007 he ran the Poetry Australia Foundation and was Director of Five Islands Press. He taught creative writing at the Universities of Wollongong and Melbourne. He has edited the literary journals *SCARP* and *Blue Dog: Australian Poetry*.

PAM SCHINDLER (P 201)

is a Brisbane poet and bushwalker who has also lived in Hobart. She works as a university reference librarian.

MIA SCHOEN (P 25)

lives in Melbourne. She divides her creative impulses between her painting—for which she has won numerous awards—and music (she plays guitar, drums, piano, and more) most notably through her band New Estate, released on the Low Transit Industries label. Her art is held in collections in Australia and internationally, and she is represented by Kozminsky Gallery, Melbourne.

LYNNE SPENDER (P 47)

is a writer, editor and digital consultant. Her most recent publication is *Between the Lines: A Legal Guide for Writers and Illustrators*. Having worked as Director of the Australian Society of Authors and the Australian Interactive Media Industry Association, she has a particular interest in the differences between print and digital cultures and is currently completing a PhD on 'Digital culture and the challenge to copyright law'.

LUKE STICKELS (P 159)

writes fiction and theory about politics, violence, peace, power and ethics. He started writing when he realised that culture can be made, and used, for almost anything. 'The Rise of an Urban Terrorist' is his first novel.

MARK TREDINNICK (P 202)

is an award-winning poet and essayist. His work has appeared in Australian and US literary journals. His books include *A Place on Earth* (2003), *The Land's Wild Music* (2005), *The Little Red Writing Book* (2006) and *The Little Green Grammar Book* (2008). *The Blue Plateau*, a landscape memoir, is due out in 2009. A selection of his poems, *The World in its Other Life*, appeared on disc in July 2008.

ABIGAIL ULMAN (P 132)

is originally from Melbourne and is currently a Wallace Stegner Fellow in Fiction at Stanford University. She has recently had work published in *The Best Australian Poems 2005*, *Hecate* and the *New England Review*. She lives in San Francisco and misses Australian junk food.

JOHN VAN TIGGELEN (P 73)

is a staff writer with *Good Weekend*, as well as the author of *Mango Country*, a book exposing the cultural underbelly of Tropical Queensland. He divides his time between Cairns, FNQ and Castlemaine, central Victoria.

SANDRA WHITE (P 146)

was born in Brisbane. She lives in London and is a journalist at *The Times*. She graduated with an MA in Creative Writing at Goldsmiths College, University of London last year. Her stories have been published in *Goldfish*, the Goldsmiths online journal.

NEWSREEL

BEN HARPER ON
WORLD CLASS ANXIETY

NEWSREEL ILLUSTRATIONS BY OSLO DAVIS

IT'S AN UNPALATABLE FACT THAT MANY OF the intrinsic qualities of our cultural identity, which we like to think of as unique to ourselves, are imports; transplants that have flourished in a foreign soil as they withered at home. I'm not romantic but even I like to pretend that Australian colloquialisms like 'dinkum' are entirely our own invention, and that their roots—in this case in Lincolnshire—are too obscure to count.

I also like to think, for better or worse, that our desire for a distinct Australian identity has led us to embrace our perceived failings, as much as our strengths, as cultural traits worth defending. We would like to think we are as famous for our nationalist apathy and our inferiority complex as we are for heroism and sporting prowess. For me, nothing symbolises that inferiority complex more than the frequent occurrence of that wonderfully meaningless epithet 'world class' when describing anything okay and Australian, be it an education system, an artist or a station wagon.

Like 'recyclable', the approving invocation of 'world class' is an expression of boundless optimism and infinite potential. As with many statements of optimism, it is also freighted with naivety and unconscious irony: the idea that if we strive and excel, we might just achieve enough to belong with the rest of the world. Beneath it lies the anxiety that our best isn't good enough.

In the Australian context, 'world class' has an attendant semantic miracle, being simultaneously more and less hubristic than the boast 'best in the Southern Hemisphere'. (Take that, Johannesburg! In your face, Buenos Aires! Eat dirt, Niue!)

I had always thought that saying something was 'world class' was an implicit plea to sit at the grown-ups' table; a distinctively Australian phenomenon. Imagine my surprise when I arrived in Britain to find the Mother Country bandying about the same uncertain boast. As in Australia, so in Britain: the term is common currency in the pronouncements of politicians, NGOs, pundits, and critics who should know better. Where did this phrase originate? Is it truly British, did they adapt it from Australia, or is it adapted from American marketing-speak?

Either way, the British have embraced it as their own. It suits their national stance of being somehow apart from the world, yet nebulously engaged with it in some discreet, behind-the-scenes manner: in other words, their relationship with Europe writ large. It reflects Britain's alliance with the United States and neighbouring European trading partners, and its simultaneous view of them as rivals. The magic phrase reveals how, like Australia, Britain entertains thoughts of being self-sufficient, yet tacitly acknowledges that it has been left playing catch-up. How Britain sees itself is the mirror of Australia's own dichotomous self-image: a small country subconsciously aware of its inadequacies while boasting of 'punching above its weight'.

It could be expected that a newer country inherits much of its character from its former colonial master, but Britain is now in the unusual situation where its political leaders are talking of reversing the relationship. In March, former attorney-general Lord Goldsmith published his government-commissioned report on British citizenship, in which he suggested Britain could be more British by being more like Australia. As reported by the BBC:

> Lord Goldsmith says a new British national day should be established by 2012 to coincide with the Olympics and what will be the Queen's Diamond Jubilee. It could operate in the same way as Australia Day, which is a public holiday on 26 January and is used to celebrate what it means to be an Australian.[1]

Like Australia, Britain has been questioning its national identity. Also like Australia, British leaders seeking to affirm a single, national char-acter have shown that they are unsure of their own country. They are unsure enough to look abroad for ways to bolster their sense of self. The British press and public response—almost completely derisive—to Goldsmith's report has focused mostly on his recommendation that feelings of national pride can be instilled by having school leavers pledge an oath of allegiance to the Queen. (Strangely, even people mildly in favour of a pledge suggested that instead of to the Crown, allegiance be pledged to the state, using Australian citizenship ceremonies as their model.)

The irony of affirming one's country's uniqueness by becoming more like another country was allowed to go largely uncommented on, as was the idea of Britain's national day being modelled upon a day commemorating another country's annexation to Britain. As an Australian, I suppose I should be thankful that the idea of Britain being expected to emulate one of its imperial outposts was spared the general ridicule with which Goldsmith's report has been greeted.

This bizarre idea that Britain should establish its own version of Australia Day also overlooks the fact that the holiday is not at all the unifying force the British naively assume it to be—geographically, socially or politically. This sticking point has not been noticed at all in the British media, neither in commentary against nor (less commonly) for Lord Goldsmith's proposal. Yet it would inevitably become an issue in the newly devolved Union, where distinctions between what is universally 'British' and what is only English are already points of contention. One of the major reasons for Goldsmith's report being commissioned in the first place was the perceived fragmentation of Great Britain into four separate nations. It seems that Goldsmith has optimistically identified Australia as a single, quasi-British state for inspiration.

The proposed British National Day shares another feature with the ways in which Australia's political leaders have sought to redefine their country. Beside the tenuous link to the monarchy (an institution just as remote from modern British values as it is from Australian), the national day also makes an equally tenuous connection with sport. In an attempt to find a common national ground that avoids any uncomfortable social, cultural or political debate, Goldsmith and his political cronies have resorted to sporting achievement as a stand-in for patriotism and national identity. This last concept is a relatively new one in Britain, at least compared to the extent to which it has been pursued in Australia. In Britain, the suggested substitution of sporting values for national values has been met with suspicion and revulsion, particularly among what the would-be populist public intellectual Professor David Flint has labelled in Australia 'the elites'.

As for pledging allegiance, such oaths are regarded by most as an American import, as alien to modern Britain as they are to Australia. More generally, Britain's true attitude to national identity is much the same as the one inherited by Australia. As a leader in the *Times* put it, 'Defining Britishness is rather un-British.'[2]

In response to Goldsmith's report, Alice Miles in the *Times* wrote: 'The idea of a national motto (or "national statement of British values", as they insist we call it) has already attracted derision on a glorious scale—and there's nothing more British than the refusal to be defined. *Times* readers chose as their national motto: No motto please, we're British.'[3] A few weeks earlier, Janet Daley had written in the *Telegraph*: 'British national identity is becoming more and more like the weather: everybody talks about it but nobody can do anything about it. And come to think of it, it is especially like British weather: so tepid most of the time that it is difficult to describe.'[4]

What is most interesting about these objections to Goldsmith's ideas—to an Australian at least—is that they come from the right of the political spectrum. British newspapers tending to the left or centre-left, such as the *Guardian*, gave a generally less reactive, more open-minded response to the questions of citizenship and identity raised by the report; whereas right-wing responses were unfavourable, effectively in defence of the laissez-faire attitudes towards national identity quoted above. In contrast, the Australian right has been busy for the last decade or so formulating an increasingly prescriptive idea of what 'Australian' means, a narrow definition centring on feel-good thoughts of diggers, battlers, bronzed Olympians, cockies and brave pioneers, the flag.

Since the 1990s, Australian governments and supporting institutions have served up this dumbed-down constructed identity, rejecting the conflicts and complexities that the world has brought to bear upon making Australia what it is today. Britain has built up a rich and nuanced understanding of itself, the legacy of a history of being good at accommodating such complexities. This makes it all the stranger to see Britain's Labour government entertaining plans to borrow this Australian model and impose a banal hurrah for sport and monarchy as the best means to appreciate its place in the world.

But a motive shared by both nations can be found. It is the perceived need to further withdraw from the world, to deny the shaping forces of globalisation, immigration and multiculturalism, and become resolutely inward-looking—turning one's back on the outside world while also loudly asserting one's mastery over it.

NOTES: 1. 'Pupils "to take allegiance oath"', BBC News, 11 March 2008. 2. 'Citizenship Test', Times, 12 March 2008. 3. Alice Miles, 'Citizenship: A British farce', Times, 12 March 2008. 4. Janet Daley, 'We don't need to define Britishness', Telegraph, 18 February 2008.

ISABEL ALLENDE ON
HALLUCINOGENS

WRITERS have been known to turn to all sorts of aids for inspiration, with drugs and hallucinogens ranking high on the list. Isabel Allende (*The Sum of Our Days*, *The House of the Spirits*) is the latest novelist to turn to powerful stimulants to overcome writer's block. While struggling to complete a trilogy of adventure books a few years ago, Allende decided to travel to South America to try a hallucinogenic called *ayahuasca*. The potion, which is made from jungle vines by American Indians, is meant to induce shamanic visions.

After drinking the brew, Allende was subject to terrifying dreams and memories, which left her retching, shivering and muttering on the floor for two days. She recalls facing demons and having her whole life flash before her. 'It was the most intense, out-of-my-mind experience that I ever had,' Allende said. She likens the experience to a certain kind of death: 'I was no longer a body or a soul or a spirit or anything. There was just a total, absolute void that you cannot even describe ... And I think that's death.'

Other notable writers who have turned to drug-induced hallucinations include Hunter

S. Thompson and William Burroughs. And, as for Thompson and Burroughs, the experience proved fruitful in its way. After taking the potion, Allende was exhausted but her mind was energised. She finished the three books—*City of the Beasts*, *Kingdom of the Golden Dragon* and *Forest of the Pygmies*—as she had promised her grandchildren she would. The trilogy is currently being adapted to film by the same producers of *The Chronicles of Narnia*. However, Allende is adamant that she will not be resorting to hallucinogens in the future: 'It was very revealing and very important and opened up a lot of spaces inside me. But I don't ever want to do it again.'

SOURCE: <http://www.telegraph.co.uk/arts/main.jhtml?xml=/arts/2008/03/23/st_isabelallende.xml&page=1>

JOSEPH HELLER'S

CATCH-22

'CATCH-22' has become the staple phrase for irony in the English language. Born of Joseph Heller's brilliant modern classic, the title beautifully captures the feeling of being caught in an impossible bind. But few readers know that they could just as easily be talking about being stuck in a 'Catch-18', which was the original title to Heller's debut.

Heller formed the idea for his first novel while enlisted as a bombardier in Corsica during the Second World War. Over the years, he found the first and last sentences of the story, and set himself the task of filling out the middle. Yet it wasn't until 1953 that he began the first chapter. That extract was published in *New World Writing* two years later, under the title 'Catch-18'. However, just before 'Catch-18' was to be published in 1961, writer Leon Uris also released a book about the Second World War, called *Mila 18*. Robert Gottlieb, Heller's editor, soon decided that the title should be changed to avoid confusion. 'I was heartbroken,' Heller recalled, 'I thought 18 was the only number.' A long numerical debate followed. 'Catch-11' was discounted because of similarities to the 1960 Rat Pack film *Ocean's 11*. Heller liked 'Catch-14' but his publishers felt it lacked a literary punch. Gottlieb finally picked the number 22: 'I thought 22 was a funnier number than 14.' He took two weeks to persuade Heller round.

The newly christened *Catch-22* was not an instant hit, selling a modest 25,000 copies. But a few years later, with the conflict in Vietnam becoming increasingly unpopular, a new generation of readers embraced Heller's work. Since then, more than 10 million copies have been sold, and the sharp, quirky humour of the phrase 'Catch-22' has found its way into literary history.

SOURCE: <http://www.telegraph.co.uk/arts/main.jhtml?xml=/arts/2007/11/18/sv_catch.xml&page=1>; <http://www.brooklyneagle.com/categories/category.php?category_id=12&id=19034>.

ROMANCE LITERATURE

IN NIGERIA

WOMEN in northern Nigeria are finding a new voice through a unique brand of romantic fiction. The books, known as Kano market literature, take a contemporary approach to life in a Shariah society. Muslim women are able to read about marrying for true love rather than social expectation, flirting with men and living in a polygamous family. With colourful titles like *Edge of Fate*, *False Love* and *Undeceiveful Heart*, the novels are proving extremely popular and have enjoyed print runs of up to 100,000.

Kano market literature is far from erotica, yet in the predominantly Muslim north the books have generated some controversy. Islamic leaders claim that the writings damage traditional practices by drawing on foreign influences, such as Indian Bollywood movies. The local emir recently conducted a ceremony where several of the books were burned.

Despite the candyfloss romance elements, it seems the novels are behind a greater social shift for young Muslim women. 'Women are not only writing for pleasure, no, we are writing because we are seeing what is happening in the society and we want a lot of corrections,' said Hasau local Binta Rabiu Spikin. Women have managed to take advantage of the boom in communication technology. The novels are produced cheaply as stapled pamphlets and sell for about 30 cents each. For many, Kano market literature signals an important increase in female literacy, as well as a desire to create a more liberal society where women can enter public discourse.

SOURCE: <http://www.theage.com.au/ articles/2008/05/06/12098396456 63.html>.

ANTI-PORN GROUP

CALLS FOR FUN TO BE BANNED

A **BOOK** about same-sex relationships has incurred the wrath of anti-pornography groups in Utah. Alison Bechdel's auto-biographical graphic novel *Fun Home* is a coming-of-age story about family and sexuality. Bechdel focuses on her own experience of coming out and her relationship with her closeted gay father.

Named 'Book of the Year' by *Time Magazine*, *Fun Home* was listed as part of the English curriculum of the University of Utah. However, the group 'No More Pornography' launched a campaign to ban the book after a student claimed to be offended by drawings depicting sex scenes. 'It's like they're turning their back and pretending graphics, depiction of oral sex, are not an issue', said activist Thomas Alvord.

The university has defended its curriculum, arguing that it is important to teach new and inventive literature in order to challenge and enrich students. PhD candidate Jennilyn Merton, who selected the book for the course, said that sexual experience is an important part of growing up and that the illustrations are not pornographic: 'I don't think [sexuality] should be something we hide from as part of the human experience. It also helps us understand the ongoing violence that happens around people's sexuality. If we can't talk about that, then I don't think we can be responsible citizens.' Under the university's religious accommodation policy, students are under no obligation to read the book if they find it offensive.

SOURCE: <http://www.ksl. com/?nid=148&sid=2952660>; <http:// qsaltlake.com/index.php?option=com_co ntent&task=view&id=489&Itemid=35>.

THE DECLINE OF

THE SEMICOLON

F RANCE is currently involved in an unlikely war. A grammar war, that is, over the humble and often misunderstood semicolon.

The dispute has inspired passionate debate across the French media. Favouring the contemporary English approach of short sentences and simplified grammar, some writers have argued that the semicolon, or point-virgule, is now redundant. French cartoonist and satirist François Cavanna claims it is 'a parasite, a timid, fainthearted, insipid thing, denoting merely uncertainty, a lack of audacity, a fuzziness of thought'. The late Kurt Vonnegut held similarly blunt views: 'Do not use semicolons. They are transvestite hermaphrodites, standing for absolutely nothing. All they do is show you've been to college.'

However, the point-virgule is not without its loyal defenders. Linguistic purists claim that the punctuation mark is a significant and subtle part of the French language, having featured prominently in the work of Hugo, Flaubert, Proust, Maupassant and Voltaire. The desire here is to prevent French from becoming too anglicised. Over the years, too many unwanted English phrases have muscled their way in—words like e-mail, blog, fast food, supermodel, takeaway and shadow-boxing. The fact that French is reportedly becoming less popular within the European Commission and the United Nations makes the need to preserve it all the more strong.

Yet confusion over the proper role of the semicolon is not reserved for France alone. In English-speaking countries people are frequently confused over its use. Caught somewhere between a comma and a full stop, the semicolon is more regularly seen as an e-mail emoticon than a well-executed punctuation mark.

SOURCE: <http://www.guardian.co.uk/ world/2008/apr/04/france.british identity>.

THE OXFORD ENGLISH

DICTIONARY

IN its heyday, the *Oxford English Dictionary* consisted of thirteen navy-blue bound volumes, complete with micrographic text and magnifying glass. The onion-skin pages contained definitions for every English word since the eighth century, including quaint and oddly poetic references to chickens as 'the young of the domestic fowl; its flesh'.

However, the OED is the latest publication to succumb to the pressures of digital media. The dictionary will no longer be reprinted in hardcopy, but will be available online to subscribers at OED.com. With the phenomenal rise of the Internet, web-savvy users are gravitating towards sites like Wikipedia and Dictionary.com. Australia's *Macquarie Dictionary* went online in 2003. It seems that dictionaries are now facing the same pressures as newspapers and magazines around the world to go digital.

The OED has had an iconic history. The first ten-volume set was printed in 1928, and was the result of seventy years labour by generations of editors and around 2000 volunteers. The compact editions quickly found a fond place in most households. However, lexicographers are currently busy revising entries and

adding new definitions, so it will be some time before Oxford University Press considers a reprint. 'We've only finished from volume "M" to "quit shilling",' said editor Jesse Sheidlower. 'We have about twenty years' more work to do ... Who knows what will happen with technology in twenty years? We certainly don't.'

SOURCE: <http://www.nytimes.com/2008/05/11/magazine/11wwln-medium-t.html?pagewanted=1&_r=2&ref=technology>.

MAUD NEWTON'S RULES FOR

NOT MAKING EDITORS HATE YOU

TALK to any editor in the publishing industry and chances are they'll have a story for you. That story will usually involve being harassed or pursued by eager would-be authors. After a rather disquieting run-in with a writer/stalker, blogger and editor Maud Newton shares some tips for not making editors hate you:

1) Never show up in person at a publishing company. Ever. Not unless a real person (and not an imaginary person in your head) has specifically made a date with you and asked you to come in for a meeting. Even if you are just well-meaning and happen to

be in the neighbourhood to drop something off, seeing an editor will make that editor feel incredibly awkward and more likely to hate you and your project. We lead crazed, frazzled existences and we don't like having to meet with people we are not expecting. Ever. None of us.

2) Don't call on the phone. Ever. Two reasons:

A. The phone is bad for us, because we can't choose the timing. If you email us, we can address your issue thoughtfully and when we have time to. Plus the phone is super awkward—I always feel backed up against the wall when someone I'm not expecting to talk to is on the phone.

B. The phone is bad for you. If you get us on the phone and ask for the status and we didn't like it, we're going to have to reject it right there, on the phone with you. Also, maybe we were thinking 'maybe' about your project, but now, since you've forced us to talk to you on the phone, we're suddenly thinking: no. Just. Don't. Call.

3) Do you have an agent? Then never, ever be personally in touch with me. I start to feel double teamed, and on top of that, I begin to question the relationship you have with your agent. The only time I should have any contact with an agented author before a contract is signed is AFTER I tell the agent I like the project and the agent and I arrange a mutually agreeable meeting or phone call. The author should never be involved in this.

4) Know what I acquire. If you send me your manuscript and it has nothing to do with what I edit, why should I do you the courtesy of wasting my very precious free time responding to you? Seriously. There are literally thousands of hard-working people who want to get published and have done the footwork. You are not special. You wanna get published, you do it too.

5) Do not harass my assistant. Ever. Her job is very hard. I've been there, honey. Just because she's as smart and savvy as she is does not mean she should have to deal with you and your mental issues.

6) Do not follow up the next day. Do not follow up the next week. You may follow up one month after you've submitted, but do so politely and in as inoffensive a way as possible. I'm softer towards the 'I just wanted to make sure all my materials were in order and to see if there was any other information you might need' approach. The 'Why haven't you looked at my manuscript yet? It's been over a month' approach? Yeah, not a favourite of mine, actually.

7) Do not leave me lengthy voicemails (although I suppose if you're calling at all I should just direct you back to #2). I just delete them without listening.

SOURCE: <http://editorialass.blogspot.com/2008/03/i-have-stalker.html>.

LAURA CARROLL ON

THE BILL HENSON AFFAIR

The swung torch scatters seeds
In the umbelliferous dark
And a frog makes guttural
   comment
On the naked and trespassing
Nymph of the lake.

The symbols were evident,
Though on park-gates
The iron birds looked
   disapproval
With rusty invidious beaks.

Among the water-lilies
A splash—white foam in
the dark!
And you lay sobbing then
Upon my trembling intuitive arm.
   —*Ern Malley, 'Night Piece'*

THE full scope of Kerryn Goldsworthy's and Chris Boyd's allusions in comments (at <http://sarsaparilla blog.net/?p=672#comment-350724>) to Detective Vogelesang's testimony in the *Angry Penguins* obscenity trial have just bubbled through to full consciousness.

Asked to explain why the two versions of the poem 'Night Piece' were obscene or, as he put it, 'immoral' ('I think they suggest sexual matters, and I consider they are immoral'), Vogelesang said: 'Apparently someone is shining a torch in the dark, visiting through the park gates. To my mind they were going there for some disapproved motive … The nature of the time they went there and the disapproval of the iron birds, make me say it is immoral. I have found that people who go into parks at night go there for immoral purposes … My experience as a police officer might under certain circumstances tinge my appreciation of literature.'

Yes, indeed.

The detective's sterling contribution to the annals of Australian comedy aside, it's worth remembering that Max Harris was found guilty of publishing indecent material and while it's melodramatic and inaccurate to say that the prosecution ruined his life, he was certainly a changed person afterwards. With hindsight, Australia only

damaged itself by so violently rejecting the openness to imaginative experience demanded (and offered) by modernism. And if history plays once as tragedy and once as farce, I can only hope that what we're witnessing here doesn't ultimately reveal itself as the former. If Revolting Rudd doesn't want to go down in history as the Vogelesang character, he'd better change his tune, although it may already be too late for that.

SOURCE: <http://sarsaparillablog.net/?p=674>.

CORY DOCTOROW

ONLINE CENSORSHIP HURTS US ALL

ARTISTS have lots of problems. We get plagiarised, ripped off by publishers, savaged by critics, counterfeited—and we even get our works copied by 'pirates' who give our stuff away for free online.

But no matter how bad these problems get, they're a distant second to the gravest, most terrifying problem an artist can face: censorship.

It's one thing to be denied credit or compensation, but it's another thing entirely to have your work suppressed, burned or banned. You'd never know it, however, judging from the state of the law surrounding the creation and use of internet publishing tools. Since 1995, every single legislative initiative on this subject in the UK parliament, the European parliament and the US Congress has focused on making it easier to suppress 'illegitimate' material online. From libel to copyright infringement, from child porn to anti-terror laws, our legislators have approached the internet with a single-minded focus on seeing to it that bad material is expeditiously removed.

And that's the rub. I'm certainly no fan of child porn or hate speech, but every time a law is passed that reduces the burden of proof on those who would remove material from the internet, artists' fortunes everywhere are endangered.

Take the US 1998 Digital Millennium Copyright Act, which has equivalents in every European state that has implemented the 2001 European Union Copyright Directive. The DMCA allows anyone to have any document on the internet removed, simply by contacting its publisher and asserting that the work infringes his copyright. The potential for abuse is obvious, and the abuse has been widespread: from the Church of Scientology to companies that don't like what reporters write about them, DMCA takedown notices have fast become the favourite weapon in the cowardly bully's arsenal.

But takedown notices are just the start. While they can help silence critics and suppress timely information, they're not actually very effective at stopping widespread copyright infringement. Viacom sent more than 100,000 takedown notices to YouTube last February, but seconds after it was all removed, new users uploaded it again.

Even these takedown notices were sloppily constructed: they included videos of friends eating at barbecue restaurants and videos of independent bands performing their own work. As Motion Picture Association of America chief Dan Glickman says: 'When you go trawling with a net, you catch a few dolphins.' Viacom and others want hosting companies and online service providers to evaluate all the material that their users put online, holding it to ensure that it doesn't infringe copyright before they release it.

This notion is impractical in the extreme, for at least two reasons. First, an exhaustive list of copyrighted works would be unimaginably huge, as every single creative work is copyrighted from the instant that it is created and 'fixed in a tangible medium'. Second, even if such a list did exist, it would be trivial to defeat, simply by introducing small changes to the infringing copies, as spammers do with the text of their messages in order to evade spam filters.

In fact, the spam wars have some important lessons to teach us here. Like copyrighted works, spams are infinitely varied and more are being created every second. Any company that could identify spam messages—including permutations and variations on existing spams—could write its own ticket to untold billions.

Some of the smartest, most dedicated engineers on the planet devote every waking hour to figuring out how to spot spam before it gets delivered. If your inbox is anything like mine, you'll agree that the war is far from won.

If the YouTubes of the world are going to prevent infringement, they're going to have to accomplish this by inspecting every one of the tens of billions of blog posts, videos, text-files, music files and software uploads made to every single server on the internet.

And not just cursory inspections, either—these inspections will have to be undertaken by skilled, trained specialists (who'd better be talented linguists, too—how many English speakers can spot an infringement in Urdu?).

Such experts don't come cheap, which means that you can anticipate a terrible denuding of the fertile jungle of internet hosting companies that are the primary means by which tens of millions of creative people share the fruits of their labour with their fans and colleagues.

It would be a great Sovietisation of the world's digital printing presses, a contraction of a glorious anarchy of expression into a regimented world of expensive and narrow venues for art. It would be a death knell for the kind of focused, non-commercial material whose authors couldn't fit the bill for a 'managed' service's legion of lawyers, who would be replaced by more of the same—the kind of lowest-common-denominator rubbish that fills the cable channels today.

And the worst of it is, we're marching toward this 'solution' in the name of protecting artists. Gee, thanks.

SOURCE: *This column was first published in the* Guardian, *<http://www.guardian.co.uk>.* Ⓜ

MEANJIN
IN
COLOUR

The Post-Gutenberg Prophecy

W.H. Chong

Lo!

In the very hour of the triumphant ascent to the peak in this golden age of book packaging, designers are troubled by a shivery vision: descending the same mountain top is the bald-headed prophet named Bezos, his slight arms full of the tablets called Kindle.

Kindle, and bastard kindling, will soon be in the universal possession of the diminishing literate, who will be able to download books and carry whole libraries around as we now carry our music in MP3 players. This post-print book will be a book of books. On a device no bigger or heavier than a paperback, our selections will appear on a light-reflective, page-sized screen that will transmit type just like paper.

Behold, within a generation's span, only illustrated books will justify the costs of printing—books that require the complex overlapping qualities of flickability, stillness and robust actuality: those dealing with art and pornography, cooking and gardening, maps and folio-sized references, comix and graphics and hobbies. All the titles we now see at the front of book stores will disappear—shelves will empty and A to Z will be framed in air. We will slipstream from analogue to digital, as books 'become a single liquid fabric of interconnected words and ideas'.

And woe betide us! For we shall no longer have the guilty pleasures of cracking a spine or dog-earring a page. No longer the fine judgement of hurling a book across the room, with its satisfying thump. No longer to grasp the measure of a novel by the heft of its remaining pages. No more underlining sentences or scoring exclamation marks in the margin. No more the auto-graphed object. Haptic turns optic.

Music graphics atrophied as 12-inch vinyl LPs spun into 12-cm silver discs. But books will shift radically from printed matter into ethereal files in a single shattered paradigm. And so it is that Marketing's dark artists will meet their nemesis—uncontrollable word-of-blog. In the new era of the PoGu book the text shall revert to spirit. Alas, and amen.

& Six Great Cover Ideas

W.H. Chong

1.
'If you want a great cover, get a great artist!'*

Graphic designers love typography, publishers love their type big; other folk prefer pictures—they hang them on their walls, they put them on their computer and mobile-phone screens. It says something about the Australian book design awards that they have never, in their entire 56-year history, offered a prize for the best cover photograph or illustration.

The cover image for *Eucalyptus* (1999), Murray Bail's classic fable, was made by the photographer Bill Henson. He shot this antipodean Ophelia one summer's afternoon in a Melbourne creek.

(*The same mantra as from my 2006 essay about album cover art in this journal, and why not?)

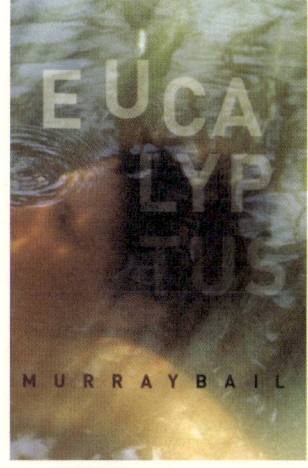

2.
Fiction is from Venus, facts are from Mars

It is a truth universally acknowledged by publishers and booksellers that the minority market segment known as 'male readers' will only purchase thrillers and books with facts.

When reading by necessity manuscripts of dramas concerning feelings, male designers are advised to recall their mothers and sisters. (In times past this audience was affectionately known as the Blacktown Mums, or the Brown Cardigans of Camberwell.) It remains a touching truism that readers of literary fiction remain, by self-selection, mostly women.

The Spare Room (2008) is Helen Garner's return to the novel after fifteen years of nonfiction writing. A story about the dying and the living, its depictions of the wild emotional relations between a carer and her patient are shockingly honest. For the cover it seemed right, paradoxically, to pinpoint an early, serene moment in the book. I painted three versions of the bougainvillea—the first two with a teapot instead of the cup. The cover type is also painted.

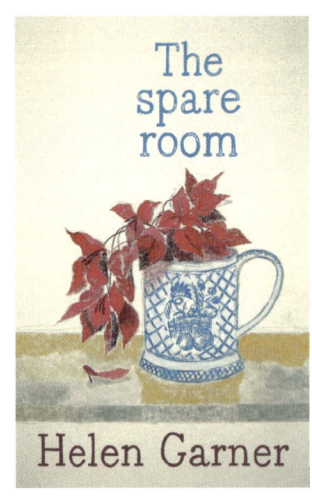

3.
A cover is the movie poster of the book

How does a picture propose a story? The poster image for a blockbuster movie is often a monolithic collage of characters and locations overlaid with expensively styled type and garnished with a punning slogan. An arthouse movie poster tends towards visual dispersion emphasising mood, and often suggests perversity or wit.

In movie parlance, a book cover makes a high-concept pitch; for example, *Harry Potter* crossed with *Sex and the City*. Tim Flannery's crucial debate-starter on climate change, *The Weather Makers* (2005), might be excitingly retitled by a Marketing Pug* as *Indiana Tim and the Planet of Doom*.

The nuanced photograph of the glass is by Fred Kroh.

(*The Marketing Pug is in charge of marketing and publicity. It occupies the centre of the plank between, in any variation, the Publisher and Publicity, and the Designer and Editorial. In any case, the Pug likes to take control, throwing its weight at whim to tip the seesaw.)

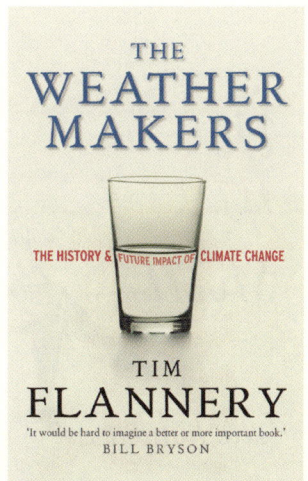

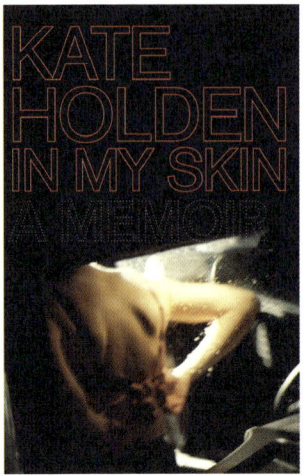

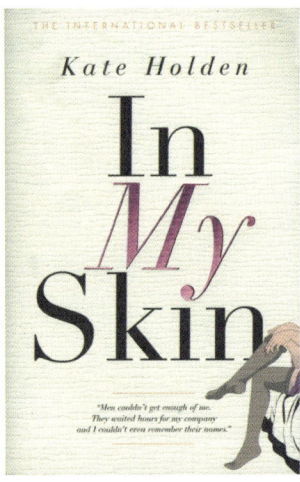

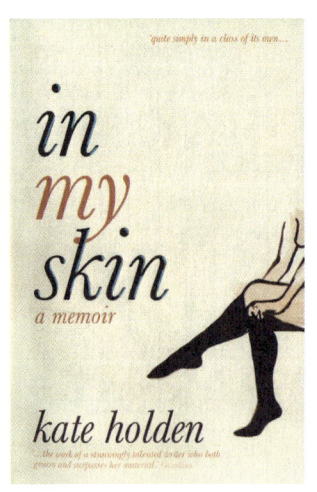

4.
I Go to R.I.O.
(Rip It Off)

In 1986 Milton Glaser, that most cultured intelligence among graphic designers, gave a lecture about the issue of originality in which he noted that while 'imitation and influence generally acknowledge their sources, plagiarism conceals them'. That was the year I got to use perhaps the first, tiny Apple Macintosh in an Australian workplace.

Since that distant time we have entered a world of sampling and allusions unimaginable to our analogue ancestors. If *hommage* is like a parody without the joke, and appropriation borrows other work as a quote, then book designers now are free to behave like shoplifters in the world's mall on the day the security staff have been raptured to heaven.

In My Skin (2005), Kate Holden's 'brutal' account of her descent into junkiedom and prostitution, first appeared to great success with a dark photographic jacket that featured the subtitle 'A Memoir' outlined as debossed pinpricks on the cover. The British publisher bought the design, which unfortunately didn't 'work' for them—that is, it didn't sell well.

For the book's next incarnation the Brits flipped the approach into absolute—and utterly inappropriate—chicklit, right down to the shiny pink foiled type (left top, design by Hoo-Ha). They sold lorry-loads. For our own small-format edition we thought (i.e. calculated) it might 'broaden' the audience to follow suit. Our embellishment was less exuberantly frivolous—the type is embossed in sober black foil instead (left bottom). My version of the chick legs kicked to life in a drawing session. I asked the model to pose theatrically, like a prostitute. She laughed, luckily.

5.
One ideogram is worth
a thousand words

The typographic ideogram is the orphan child of a Dadaist and
a shopkeeper, who ends up working in advertising disguised as
a poet.

   To fuse type and picture is the graphic designer's senti-
mental project. Milton Glaser's 1967 cover type (top) for Knut
Hamsun's astounding *Hunger* (1890) is the subject of my *hom-
mage* of 2007 (above). We were seeking an equally edgy audi-
ence for the remarkable young Welsh writer Rachel Tresize.
For *In and Out of the Goldfish Bowl* (2008) I photographed the
title as a *trompe-l'oeil* puzzle. And Mary Roach's witty report,
Spook: Science Tackles the Afterlife (2005) prompted me to fool
with the old automatic unconscious technique of *fumage*.

6.
'Some books have pictures, some pictures have books'

So remarked R.B. Kitaj, the late, great American painter, a notorious exegiser of his own complex picture dramas. Or, less gnomically, as the Nobellist Orhan Pamuk has written, 'When designers decide that *The Red and the Black* deserves a red and black jacket, or when they decorate books entitled *Blue House* or *Château* with illustrations of blue houses or châteaux, they do not leave us thinking they've been faithful to the text but wondering if they've even read it.'

Anna Funder was an unknown Australian writer in 2002, when *Stasiland* came out. A book about her encounters with East Germans near the end of the Communist era, the Australian edition has been reprinted many times, always with the cover picture by Luc Beziat. Yet it seems not to have been an obvious choice—even now I am asked by readers and book groups what it represents. But the picture picked the book.

I saw it and couldn't look away: it was an atmospheric, imaginary moment from that other world of the GDR (which would be so painfully limned in the 2006 film *The Lives of Others*). I imagine that the woman is named Veronika, the perversely glamorous door bitch at the steel entrance of the Stasiland club: but is she keeping us out, or her people in?

Funder's book won the biggest nonfiction award, the Samuel Johnson prize, and has appeared in numerous territories under many different covers. But when the Stasilanders, the Germans themselves, finally published their translation in 2004, the picture they asked for was of Veronika, the door bitch goddess of Stasiland.

THE UNCULTURED HERD AND US

~~~~~~

DAVID NICHOLS AND MIA SCHOEN DEFEND THE SUBURBS

'Suburbia' described a society which had neither a sense of tradition nor a spirit of innovation and change ... Much anti-suburban writing was derogatory rather than analytical. 'Suburbia' soon became a convenient explanation for a variety of shortcomings. It enabled the critic to condemn his society without explaining why it had failed to approach the high ideals of nationhood formulated by an earlier generation ...
    —David Walker, *Dream and Disillusion: A Search for Australian Cultural Identity*

Mia Schoen,
'Melbourne Storm 2'
2004, 10x15cm,
oil on panel

|

OUR HOUSE WAS BUILT IN 1972. Its previous owners were a couple who had bought it new: *he* had died and *she* was moving to a granny flat on her daughter's property in a new suburb almost twice as far again from the city. The house is on a street originally constructed at the edge of a scheme to turn a creek ravine into a stepped series of sporting ovals via the importation of thousands of cubic metres of rubbish. Our neighbours, who've lived here the full thirty-six years, tell us it was a great day in the mid 1970s when they finally saw the bottom of the tip—meaning the smell and, probably, social stigma of living so close to refuse was coming to an end. The ovals were given shape, but subsidence patches have put them off true; they remain, green open space, like much of the extended reserve two minutes' walk from our front door, no longer used for sport but only for dog walking, the occasional bloody trail-bike rider and the council's every-few-months mowing tractor.

And so now we, who were once committed to the CBD periphery and the live shows and coffee shops and galleries, now live twenty kilometres from the GPO, in a lower middle-class suburb founded in the mid-nineteenth century as a village, and developed over the next hundred years as an outer suburb at the rail terminus. It didn't really begin growing to any density until the 1950s, with the help of government agencies and then a couple of well-known developer-entrepreneurs. Depending on how you define suburbia, the suburbs beyond our house may well spread another ten Ks; it's certainly possible to walk through streets of houses for a couple of hours in some outward directions.

Mia Schoen,
'Jacana View 13' 2005,
11x15cm,
oil on panel

We bought here, first because we liked it, and second because it was about half the price of almost anywhere else we could have seriously considered. This was four years ago, in the midst of one of John Howard's barbecue stoppers, the furious increase in house prices. We now pay less on our mortgage than most of our friends do on rent.

We are in a suburban community and get on well with those of our neighbours we know. Whether we are genuinely *of* the community is hard to divine; it's possible, perhaps, that there isn't a community exactly but a collection of different associations based on age, ethnicity and other demographic details, overlaid and interlinked. I feel aware (not ashamed or proud, just aware) of my middle-class background and am uncertain whether we are slumming it—in the benign sense of that term, if there is one—or are perhaps early planters of the gentrification flag, alongside two friends in a similar income/education/class bracket who moved here last year.

What is perhaps most surprising about our relocation, however, is the reaction of people we know—not necessarily all 'inner-city dwellers', but perhaps most comfortable with that kind of identification—to this suburban location. It's a 25- to 60-minute trip between our home and the centre of the city, depending on the time of day and the mode of transport (public's quicker in peak hour; private at two a.m.). Yet the idea of removing to our domicile seems to many akin to crossing some alps into one of those little European duchies with its own stamps. One casual acquaintance asks me, whenever I see him in the city, how long we are in town and when we are going back (the inference being, I gather, that we will sometime load up our carriage with flour and stockwhips for four days journey). Others merely tell us we are 'so far out', presumably not in the groovy sense. Mia has at times been offered sympathy for her sentence in housewife hell. Most people we know had never been to our corner of the city until we moved there, and some still speak of it as if the reality of experience cannot dim the brightness of their preconceptions.

From this perspective, Mia and I—as entitled, surely, as anyone to take our place as members of the high-end urban 'creative class'—are just plain making an absurdist statement in living where we do. Suburbanites by choice, and in an unfashionable suburb at that, we have rendered ourselves amusing or unique anomalies. We should have been content always to live in tiny brick homes, with squalid makeshift gardens, for the privilege of being close to a hotel where good bands play, so we can walk home drunk: heaven.

II

Until very recently people have traditionally moved outwards. Until we came to where we are now, we had been renting in a lesser known region of the inner city, in a 1930s wooden house built by our landlady's father in a street the entire population of which, she told us on one of her uninvited visits, upped and moved to another rapidly developing fringe suburb in the 1960s. Allowing for hyperbole, this was no doubt how many postwar communities coped with the twin strains of community ties and aspirational pull; indeed in Britain during the creation of the postwar New Towns, whole neighbourhoods were transplanted to towns beyond the newly fashioned green belt. More commonly, young homemakers leapfrogging outwards into the expanding city edge would find community in shared demographics, interests and even a community spirit, predicated not on a love of suburbia per se but on mutual self-interest: issues surrounding home ownership, development (too much, too little, wrong type), recreation and socialising.

To define suburbia is to gather a number of suppositions under one umbrella and try to make them seem compatible. Australia, having often been lauded as the first suburban nation or as the birthplace of the suburb, usually nevertheless needs prompting to claim this honour. Of course, prehistoric cities had suburbs, as all cities since have had, so trying to tie this 'first' to any reality is merely to prop up a furphy. Perhaps there is more credibility in nominating Australia as the cauldron that conjured up the nineteenth-century leafy, middle-class suburb, even— considering its urbanisation emerged almost simultaneously with the railway—the modern commuter suburb. Perhaps it's better to resign oneself to the fact that 'firsts' don't exist. Yet it is plain that by the end of the nineteenth century suburbia was a flourishing art form in this country.

After the First World War, Australia also became the locus of a new type and style of suburb, one that would predominate throughout the twentieth century in some permutation or another. The garden suburb, in its genuine bastardised form (a miniature, conservationist version of the revolutionary garden city), was adopted and adapted with gusto by local planners along with a set of principles

relating to open-space provision, scenic road layout, block size and house orienta-
tion, and even preservation of native vegetation in some instances.

This is where the Australian suburb as we now know it really took root: in the
1920s high-end visions of Percy Hope and Carl Klem in Perth, Saxil Tuxen in Mel-
bourne and Walter Scott Griffiths in Sydney, Hobart and Adelaide—to name just
four serious proponents of this new-fashioned suburban design. Tuxen was a par-
ticularly versatile and driven planner, whose little-known story adds a lot to under-
standing of the twentieth-century Australian suburb. Not only was he a key partici-
pant in the (largely ill-fated) plan for Melbourne by its Metropolitan Town Planning
Commission of 1923–29, but he also lectured his fellow citizens, via radio and press,
on the appropriate appreciation of nature within the city; the use and provision
of transport; planning for housing all classes; the composition of street scenery;
and much more besides. His legacy as a surveyor/designer of suburban landscapes
lives on in subdivisions drawn up in his Queen Street offices over sixty years, taking
in demographics and terrains as diverse as Park Orchards, Reservoir, Coburg and
Mount Eliza. A skilled practitioner, he was as comfortable designing with the Vic-
torian government as a client as he was creating speculator's subdivisions for the
highly successful real estate agent T.M. Burke or, indeed, any other farmer/man-
sion owner/syndicate with land contiguous to metropolitan development who saw
the ripe time to sell. That many of his designs were barely on track to be populated
within his lifetime was clearly a minor consideration for Tuxen, who subscribed to
the common expectation among garden-suburb designers and advocates of his era
that these inherently logical and egalitarian town-planning principles would come
to be applied to entire metropolises. With this understanding, individual suburban
subdivisions designed to the 'correct' planning standards could be seen as forming
what Tuxen called in a radio address in 1927 'the mosaic of a great city'.

Tuxen's own interests after the onset of the Depression began to diverge to
more direct measures of societal improvement; he was a long-standing supporter
and associate of the Brotherhood of St Laurence until his death in 1975. Yet his
1920s groundwork was perfect for the community-based movements of the Sec-
ond World War and beyond—particularly those settlements with centralised shop-
ping and civic precincts and direct communication to transport—which is to say, if
he were alive today and a sufficiently sprightly 120-year-old, he would also be able
to tell the New Urbanists, that flourishing band of American designers borrowing
gleefully and haphazardly from early twentieth-century design to promote walking,
public transport and community, a thing or two about sustainable suburbs.

Slow urban growth in the 1930s and 1940s meant many of these places, like
their companion regions in other Australian cities, did not develop strongly until
the 1950s and 1960s, by which time a new, individualistic consciousness had
developed, and new modes of suburban life were being envisaged. Often, these
revolved around car ownership and use, and Australian cities' third major wave of
urban expansion was, as we are so often reminded, often under-resourced, par-
ticularly in terms of transport but also—as Whitlam saw and, in many cases, came
to remedy—in sewerage and other basic facilities. As an early-period Canberran,
Whitlam knew the frustrations of (sub)urban plans unfulfilled. Simultaneously,
the 'trendies', in many cases young people returned from European forays, were
gentrifying the inner city in the hope of reliving that experience of a nineteenth-
century built environment.

Mia Schoen,
'Jacana View 12' 2005,
11x15cm,
oil on panel

The sixties and seventies were not merely the routine unrolling of numb and unrestrained 'dead worm' designs to 'make cars happy' (to pinch, twice, from the New Urbanists' grabbag of catchy but slightly-off-the-mark phrases). Sometimes developers got it incredibly right: Ron Sloane's recruitment of planner Paul Ritter and architect Bill Kierath, for instance, to make the densely housed yet spacious Perth suburb of Crestwood in the 1960s. Or the Merchant Builders' and others' adaptation of cluster housing to retain natural bushland—just as their spiritual fore-fathers half a century earlier had attempted to do—with small housing lots, shared driveways and an emphasis on foliage and organic design. And the unknowns who designed our area, with open space a premium, unusual 'street pictures' (old town-planner parlance) and large, landscaped gardens. These are ideals many are still trying to recapture: the suburb's essence of the rural-urban mix.

III

To mangle a cliché, the more the attitudes to suburbia change within Australian society, the more they stay the same. A stroll through *Meanjin*'s back issues, as the journal both reflected the society and impacted upon it, stands as a gauge of change since the 1940s. The most typical attitude in the 1950s and 1960s is adequately revealed by John C. Alexander in 1962, during one of the magazine's regular trawls through (what it saw as the lack of) Australian intellectual and artistic endeavour. Here Alexander makes a casual allusion to our 'desperate suburban mediocrity', which understandably, for him, strikes a 'deep sense of horror in the heart of our more sensitive artists'. The ghost of early twentieth-century playwright and poet Louis Esson (who jovially cocked a snoot at the '*suburbs* ... the tabby-cat, and the garden hose, and slippers, and afternoon tea' but who also spoke darkly of a sub-urbia where 'all is repression, stagnation, a moral morgue') is heard loud and clear in mid-century *Meanjin* just as it was elsewhere in Australia. Peter Kirkpatrick, who quotes the Esson song above in his book *The Sea Coast of Bohemia*, also discusses in that history the view towards suburbia of the Australian bohemians of Esson's gen-eration. Citing David Walker's mid-seventies study of the early twentieth-century stride towards a national identity, *Dream and Disillusion*, Kirkpatrick typifies this attitude as creating two camps: 'the uncultured herd' of suburbanites 'and us'. This is, of course, often the core element of Australians'—even Australians who live in the suburbs—attitude to Australian suburbs.

The early 1970s sees suburbia-as-life-sentence *Meanjin* gems such as Judith Rodriguez's 1971 poem 'Afternoon suburb, framed by kitchen' (wherein the grotesque, wasteful and artificial suburban environment is at least one of the things described as a 'strange-featured, sly-pulsed residue of rape'). In the late 1970s a shift had occurred in treatment of the suburb as a (generic) place; Tim Rowse, in 1978, was far more benign, at least by dint of even-handedly discussing the biases of its harshest critics and a very sympathetic rendering of ideas from some of the smartest of its supporters, notably the Adelaide economist and social critic Hugh Stretton. Stretton—much like the abovementioned Ritter, though the two are very different in other respects—sees the best suburban environment as one crafted for children, families and the development of social intercourse and play. Ahead of his time, Rowse puts forward the now much more commonplace argument that to denigrate suburbia is to denigrate women; a huge shift from the conceptualisation of suburbia as misogyny writ in built form. The difference across this decade is marked, and it's Stretton's championing of suburbia, as well as his arguments on behalf of the domestic home's integral (though under-represented in official figures) place within the wider economy, which has made some of that difference.

Meanjin in the early 1980s—in fact, the first issue of 1980—included the redoubtable Craig McGregor defending suburbia as part of a pop culture palette: from 'love, work, family, sport' up to 'birth, fucks and death'. In response from the other end of the decade, John Tranter's poem 'Debbie & Co' name checks (like a later version of one of Barry Humphries' early monologues) all the commercial trappings—brand names and icons—of an afternoon at the 'Council Pool' where 'piss-tinted water slaps the tiles' but which, for all that, can't help being bucolic.

By 1990 we see Robin Gerster conducting an overview of 'The place of suburbia in Australian fiction'. Gerster titled his piece 'Gerrymander', for what he saw as collusion by those who would favour either the (central) city or the bush to exclude the suburbs 'and in effect ... the majority of Australians who live there'. Gerster had a rich field of satirists and haters to draw from: George Johnston, whose merciless railing against his home in Beverley Grove is that famous startlingly contradictory turning point of *My Brother Jack*; Patrick White; Helen Garner, who is admittedly primarily a critic of the suburbs only by the putatively subversive lifestyles in her fiction that infer the reverse of stifling suburbia (even if they are often nonetheless stifling) and so on. Gerster did not point readers in the direction of those who would explore suburbia with some sympathy and even, at times, empathy: John Morrison, whose stories were published in *Meanjin* in the 1960s; Glen Thomasetti, whose *Thoroughly Decent People* is a classic of its time (and remains compelling); or Christopher Koch's sublime novels *The Boys in the Island* and *The Doubleman*, which both paint sympathetic and exotic meanings into Hobart's postwar suburbia. This is particularly true of the former, wherein at night the lights of distant houses 'dance in a silent frenzy' and the outer suburbs resonate in fantasy with 'the sound of a tune ... a car's far hum in the deeps of night ... the cool country dark carrying the breath of those areas of otherness'. Here there is a primal attraction to the city's edge and its possibility.

In the almost two decades since Gerster's survey, numerous books have tackled suburban life with sophistication: for instance, Steven Carroll's trilogy of life in twentieth-century Glenroy, the wonderful Tim Richards and Hampton, or Wayne Macauley's marvellous *Blueprints for a Barbed-Wire Canoe*—a satire not of suburbia per se but of planning, bureaucracy and community tension. Yet even given these marvellous books and many others, in Australian stories any conception of the suburbs other than as prim, cardboard falsehood must be explained to a lurid extent. Because *everybody knows* the suburbs are a place where nothing happens and where nobody (interesting) lives.

Perhaps suburbia's greatest misfortune was that it was given a name. As a concept, it seems to be based not on what it is but what it is not: the filling in the sandwich between city and country, distastefully neither one nor the other. What strikes me as strangest about the approach of suburbia's critics is that it regards all suburbia, wherever it may lie (and this is, of course, a debatable subject) as the same beige graveyard of the imagination. Why bother discovering anything about the differences within a place that's not really a place at all, but a morass of indistinguishable places? Suburbia's critics remind me of my time as an undergraduate at the University of Sydney, where my fellow students who had never been to Melbourne were disturbed by the idea of a field trip to that place because 'it's just another city'. Anyone who thinks suburbia is all the same doesn't know what they're looking at, or just doesn't know what to see when they see, for instance, the crafted village squares of Caroline Springs in Melbourne, or the module model suburbs of Elizabeth, South Australia, or the huddled settlement of Rokeby, Hobart. A few years ago a very good Max Gillies show raised a laugh by introducing (Gillies' version of) Geoffrey Blainey as the author of a history of Camberwell: as if anyone but the most pissant historian would write a history of a middle-class suburb. As it happens, Blainey's foray into local history is an important book that suggests the larger story of an urbanising nation—and is a very worthy and readable account of a fascinating place. But it does not do, of course, to wax even slightly lyrical about places *everyone knows* are rank, and while I believe the randomly cited suburbs I mention above are worth knowing for their form and history and community and layout, I name them here in part purely because I know it's an impossible sell. Suburbs are, of course, rarely tourist destinations: indeed, they're seen as the opposite of nice places to visit people wouldn't want to live in.

Mia Schoen,
'Railway Place
Projection' 2008,
58x22cm,
oil and thread
on canvas

IV

As the environmental panic is becoming increasingly frantic, critics suggest that Australians, on the whole, lack the guts and imagination to cram themselves into something higher density and less wasteful. If suburbanites were a little more open to the idea that less is more—much as those privileged few in the inner city, where block sizes are tiny but café society is readily available—then we could pack more people into smaller cities, as they do in Europe. Public transport would become more viable (because there would be less choice about whether or not to use it), walking or cycling more plausible and various other services would be more efficient and cheaper. These notions all seem so eminently sensible, one wonders why the law wasn't passed yesterday to make it happen, and numbskull democracy by this estimation seems to be the only bar. Market providers of housing and housing estates will plead that consumers are simply not interested in anything more compact in new housing: the attitude seems to be that if you're going to live in the suburbs, and thereby accept some restrictions of mobility and/or access to the centralised culture of our metropolises, one thing you can have as compensation is a large block of land, and perhaps even a large house to go on it.

Recently I visited a prestige housing estate at the city's edge where attempts had been made to re-create a small block of inner-urban streets close to the new suburb's central shopping and civic heart. It had the air of urban infill that might have replaced, say, a factory in Zetland. Right down to the step-pavers at their side, these structures were designed to minimise a household's carbon footprint and, not irrelevantly, increase vendor profits handsomely. Indeed, while the block space was minimised, these terraces themselves were spacious to the degree that they often featured a luxuriousness of odd, inexplicable *unassigned* space. There are two ways to interpret this: either as a kind of tokenistic element of waste or as a means to offer individualistic appropriation or stamping. Either interpretation sheds light on the planner's, designer's, architect's, vendor's and commentator's habit of regarding the consumer/resident as a queer fish, prone to grabbing a cipher for something it thinks it ought to have, including a luxury of excess.

The condemnation of suburbia as environmentally wasteful is, to my mind, merely one more manifestation of 'uncultured herd' v. 'us'. It is entirely true that many suburbs are car-dependent, poorly planned, filled with energy-wasteful housing and too many ugly, litter-spewing McDonald's outlets. However, it is also true, now that the inner-city areas of Australian cities are the conspicuous consumption centres of our society, that while denser nineteenth-century areas of our cities might arguably contain greater potential for environmentally sustainable living, this is really only taking place piecemeal, predicated on individual conscience and motivation. Additionally, food has to be trucked in to the inner areas and sewerage and other waste transported away and treated; the hinterland is marshalled into service of the metropolis; the separation of people and their hidden-away support systems is reinforced. As commentators have noticed—the redoubtable Canberran Professor Patrick Troy among them, for the last two decades or more—greater density brings its own problems, not least issues of groundwater and stormwater run-off but also pressure on other systems. In any case the genuine dichotomy of those who would cajole the majority into higher density, at least at certain (one- or two-person household) stages of their lives, is that as much as they criticise suburbia as wasteful, the current style of home ownership is a core principle of this nation and, naturally, the reason many chose to migrate here. It won't go away without a serious struggle.

In 1932, Frank Lloyd Wright, an architect with a notable lack of interest in cities or their planning, put forward his conception for future living: Broadacre City. It was, in fact, only a city in the sense that it ... well, actually, it wasn't a city at all, though a number of social commentators in recent years have drawn parallels between Broadacre City and the occasional, accidental and probably temporary 'edge cities' at the suburban limit. Wright envisaged a new kind of living on large, agriculturally productive one-acre home sites linked by technology: cars on roads, and, at least in one artist's conception, privately owned helicopters for dad to get to work. Whereas genuine planners of an earlier era had hoped to combine the garden and the city in interlinked or adjoining open and living spaces, Wright saw the creation of sprawling, seemingly eternal smallholdings as the future lifestyle choice for Americans.

Wright was wrong, and that is not merely a pun. But some aspects of the dispersed mixedness of his vision accidentally have application in the present. The Sydney-based academic Ted Trainer, a visionary and, it has to be said, high-road idealist, has presented a bizarre but marvellous vision for future suburbia—the 'radical conserver society'—in his 1996 book *Towards a Sustainable Economy*. Here Trainer, in a scenario that is easily parodied but also for many surely attractive, paints a future suburban society in which roads (notoriously, a third of the land used in constructing cities) are pulled up for cooperatively managed agricultural land; barter and sharing predominate over waged work; and somehow—for many, this might well prove the hardest of all Trainer's tenets to swallow—a resilient community will develop from shared interest in local environments, harvests, construction and repair work, and the like.

Trainer's 'normal workday' in his conserver society includes hypothetical activities such as:

> 8 am ... Worked in home workshop; fixed chair; helped Mary repair bike. Walked to local library: watched ducks on pond ...
>
> 11 am ... Helped pack nuts in food co-op. Discussed local water catchment plan (we all vote next Saturday) ...
>
> 5 pm ... Bottled plums. Took surplus to neighbourhood workshop. Brought home some surplus carrots Annabel had left there. Browsed through thatching book: we do the goat house roof tomorrow. Chopped wood. Helped Mike shift the bees.

Arrived at from a base of what he sees as economic necessity, but surely also guided by his own idealistic preferences, Trainer's utopia is a mix between Amish society, a sharehouse fridge roster and William Morris's *News from Nowhere*. The shallow trappings of the consumer society will break down, says Trainer, as people realise it is more interesting and important to share Annabel's carrots (as I said, it is easy to parody—but that doesn't make it silly) than it is to, for instance, waste non-renewable fossil fuels on going on overseas holidays or, for that matter, importing exotic out-of-season produce from other parts of the world. Trainer's radical restructure dismisses as irrelevant the question of pursuit of 'the arts' and culture, the placement of which many of us no doubt would find of central importance to his new social vision; these will not change under the new regime, he says. He also announces firmly that there is to be no compromise: *this* is the sustainable conserver economy, and while there will be plenty of cherry picking, none of it will be made figuratively from the social cure prescription.

Whether anything like Trainer's conserver society takes root remains to be seen (and entails, of course, you, me and everyone we know heeding his call). But in one respect, Trainer and Patrick Troy are interestingly aligned: both see the potential for suburbia's reconfiguration as productive agricultural land. For Troy, this is a feature of suburbia that has gone into abeyance since the Second World War. For Trainer, it is a demonstrable fact that a mere portion of the average suburban block could support the adult who lives on it. Flat roofs, nature strips, parkland: all could become useful food-production spaces, and a practical, waste-free version of Wright's specious Broadacre City, a genuine blend of farm and town, could emerge.

Some local greenthumbs let their growing abilities spill out of their own quarter-acre block into surrounding reserves and lanes; a walk through most marginal open suburban space will reveal this truth. I blame old people with time on their hands, and too many gardening programs on television. Community building projects often harness the potential of gardens and crops to repair social bonds; in other places this appears to happen spontaneously, perhaps only sporadically, but nevertheless with dedication and no little skill.

V

I bring up this urban-agriculture solution in part because, like Troy, Trainer, Stretton and another academic I admire—this one a historian, Perth's Andrea Gaynor—I find it immensely appealing, just as I enjoyed William Morris's nineteenth-century tale of a perfect future society of craft-loving provincials. Trainer's vision seems to me to be a type of sci-fi at least *as achievable* as the higher density anti-suburban cities so often mooted today. While I would certainly not hate to plant a demon seed of radical societal change in your mind, assuming I am introducing you to Trainer and co., I do not wish to hijack the Trainerist line, but merely to observe this: suburbs are not, in their own form and style, wasteful and polluting (nor are they the sole habitat of the consumerist zombie). They are places of enormous potential. The denigration of the suburbs on environmental grounds is misguided; in many regards, it's the old culture war on the attack again, dressed up this time in a scientist's white coat.

I began with a quote from David Walker's book on the search to establish a national identity in early twentieth-century Australia. The writers and intellectuals Walker discusses were hostile to what they saw as a suburbia of complacent and selfish pettiness, where nothing was vivid or valid. I used it because, as is by this stage probably clear, I don't really think much has changed in a century. The denigration of suburbia is just another brand of Otherism, nowhere near as bad as racism or sexism (after all, suburbanites can still 'pass') but as pervasive. To say this denigration exists is nothing new.

But why does it still need to be said?

ESSAYS

EVEN IN KANSAS

JOSEPH PEARSON EXAMINES THE US PRESIDENTIAL ELECTION CAMPAIGN IN THE LIGHT OF DON WATSON'S RECENT ACCOUNT OF HIS TRAVELS IN AMERICA

Y*OU MIGHT REMEMBER HOWARD DEAN.* He's the former five-term governor of liberal Vermont, current chair of the Democratic National Committee. In mid January 2004, he seemed just inches away from becoming his party's presidential nominee. Polling thirty points clear in the key primary state of New Hampshire, running ahead all over the country. His unequivocal stance against the war in Iraq resonated with the activist base of the party, far more influential in the internet era than ever before. Via his website, ordinary people were donating small amounts in unprecedented numbers to the campaign. The phenomenon was evident enough to gain a name that entered the lexicon: netroots. With the support of his energetic believers and net legions, Dean had for months borne the mantle of frontrunner.

The winsome cornbelt state of Iowa had other ideas. In the angry public stoush between Dean and unionist candidate Dick Gephardt over the weeks leading up to election day in Iowa, both were casualties. Dean finished third in the caucuses behind John Kerry and John Edwards. Above the roar of a crowd that could hardly be heard on television, he bellowed a concession, and it sounded to America like a squeal. A month and two losing primaries later, he was out of the race. Kerry was the presumptive nominee. The Democrats closed ranks.

Nothing like that happened in 2008. Well, the frontrunner again came third in Iowa, but Hillary Clinton won a reprieve five days later in New Hampshire (following her husband in 1992, they called her the Comeback Kid, though in the face of post-Iowa polling she looked more like Lazarus). Thus the race see-sawed into February, to D-Day, Super Tuesday, when not quite half the nation declared their intentions. All expectations had been for a decisive day. It was anything but, honours were declared even, and the race ran on. Barack Obama won ravaged Louisiana and red Kansas, romped home in the beltway primary (DC, Virginia, Maryland), and completed February with a runaway victory in Wisconsin. Not only was he the frontrunner, most analysts also believed he had the nomination—but they would await the results of Ohio and Texas before crowning him.

The Democratic choice for president is inevitably an agonised one. Just as for Dean and Clinton, Obama's frontrunner status proved a curse. He fought Texas to a draw, winning on delegates but losing the symbolically important popular vote. He was trounced in Ohio. So Clinton claimed the day. The candidates rejoined a battle that had already continued a month longer than anyone projected. Now, yawning in front of a surprisingly attentive national audience, was six weeks without any significant contest. Pennsylvania, the enormous eastern swing state with demographics as diverse as cosmopolitan Philly and the northern ranges of Appalachia, would not weigh in until 22 April.

You have to appreciate that CNN talks politics almost twenty-four hours a day. The politically interested class in America, much larger and more varied than its

Australian equivalent, is omnivorous. To sate a terrible appetite, it has embraced the internet. In 2008, a butterfly can flutter its wings in the bayous of Alabama, be picked up on Marc Ambinder's blog and see a three-point dip in national polling. Six weeks without a contest became like a fragile truce, any misstep by the campaigns prefiguring disaster.

Into these simmering tensions, Republican research militia lobbed a grenade. Reverend Jeremiah Wright, the rambunctious pastor of Obama's Illinois church, had been captured on video shortly after the 9/11 attacks exhorting 'God damn America! God damn America!' from his pulpit. The video was replayed on all major news services for two weeks. It galvanised a section of the populace who had misgivings about Obama's sudden rise. His polling stagnated as Democrats wrung their hands over his electability.

Weeks elapsed while Obama painstakingly rebuilt his bridges. Then a few days out from the Pennsylvania primary, he spoke at a closed-door fundraiser in San Francisco. (It is important here to recognise that SF in the imagination of middle America is essentially a liberal pariah republic.) What he said became a scandal— dubbed 'bittergate'. The key passage is worth quoting in full:

> You go into some of these small towns in Pennsylvania, and like a lot of small towns in the Midwest, the jobs have been gone now for 25 years and nothing's replaced them. And they fell through the Clinton administration, and the Bush administration, and each successive administration has said that somehow these communities are gonna regenerate and they have not. So it's not surprising then that they get bitter, they cling to guns or religion or antipathy to people who aren't like them or anti-immigrant sentiment or anti-trade sentiment as a way to explain their frustrations.

In mid 2001 Don Watson wrote a *Quarterly Essay* on Australia's relationship with the United States, which took as its ruminative basis the Rabbit novels of John Updike and thus was called 'Rabbit Syndrome'. It invited a debate that, in 2001, was worth having—one that Australia does have, intermittently, when our warmth to the nation that aided us in the Second World War verges on servitude.

Unfortunately, the timing wasn't great. On 12 September, like the rest of the Western world, we were all Americans. By 14 September, our government had invoked the ANZUS treaty—the bedrock of the 'special relationship', guaranteeing that all member nations would act in the event that one of them was attacked. (Where for 'all member nations' read 'the United States' and for 'one of them' read 'Australia'—at least, that has been the prevailing wisdom for more than fifty years. Our eager reporting for duty stupefied the State Department.) In short, we'd all seen what happened in New York City and we were moved to extend our sympathy, our shock and real grief, and make an offer to help. In this heavy atmosphere, a wry, literary argument about the effect on the Australian mind of our close relationship to the States was unlikely to ignite.

Watson moved away from the topic, to take up cudgels as a language pedant for a couple of books. A few years later, 'Rabbit Syndrome' is still a powerful short analysis of this national pathology. Somewhere near the beginning, he wrote:

> The writer is no expert on American habits or history. He has made only brief visits to America and has never lived there. His knowledge of foreign policy is rudimentary. But for the apparent presumption of his writing this essay he begs to be excused. Like all other Australians he has lived with the Americans all his life.

1 Don Watson,
American Journeys
(Knopf, Sydney, 2008).

It sounded like a subversive apology, but in *American Journeys*,[1] Watson reveals it was also a personal regret. *Journeys* is a pilgrimage through much of the United States, conducted with keen eyes and a steady march, brandishing Tocqueville's *Democracy in America* in place of scripture. And what is an American pilgrimage if not a road trip? The map on the inside cover traces Watson's restless path by rail and road—such a studious sprawl of lines that political analysts might call it a fifty-state strategy, but for a few gaps in New England and the southern coast. Watson is no Sal Paradise, and neither is this a frat-boy road trip, careening from coast to coast with carloads of company. It's the solitary, even lonely adventure of a middle-aged man, leaning with grandfatherly attention into dining-car conversations, banging the wheel of the hire car and berating conservative shock jocks as the Midwest slips by, cultivating a romance with the automated voice recording ('Julie') on Amtrak's customer service line, racing though the heartland to get—not to Frisco or Hollywood or the Big Apple—to Yellowstone National Park.

A pilgrimage and a road trip: it's also a vox pop pastiche of America, conducted with the casual rigour of an expert. Watson learns from a fellow Amtrak customer that Dale Earnhardt Sr was the greatest Nascar driver ever—'Mean. But gentle.' An innkeeper upbraids him for an offhand reference to life evolving from the sea: 'I came out of my mother and father. And they came from Adam and Eve.' He exchanges alms for a Katrina survivor's awful account of the flooding of his hostel, whose elderly residents were given sleeping pills as the hurricane approached: 'Seven people drowned. Old people. They took the young and left the old to die.' A Mormon pulls out of the highway snarls of Utah to offer Watson help after he merely misses an exit; a New Mexico café owner, the wife of a professional rodeo rider, opens up to him about how hard it is to make ends meet. Between these scattered conversations and eavesdroppings, and Watson's voracious consumption of the local media, a picture of America emerges. Not the powerful or poseur America of our news, nor exactly the gritty, fast-talking, explosive America of our entertainment. This is something like Middle America, or the heartland as they call it—agitated by the great cultural issues, intensely where they intersect with religious beliefs (evolution, inequality, abortion, war, charity in the absence of government intervention), whipped up by religious leaders and conservative commentators, cast about by the economic downturn and the precipice of their debt, steely with the determination to improve themselves and find grace or success, leery of liberals but disenchanted by Bush, fierce in their philosophy and down-home in their manners. There is plenty of casual racism, usually couched in politically viable misgivings about free trade and the loss of job opportunities to migrants.

It sounds like the people Barack Obama was not surprised to find bitter. Exactly those who we might have expected to be bitter, having contributed the most sons and daughters to an essentially unjustified war, having stayed poor as tax cuts rolled in for the rich, having lost jobs in industries that (as both Obama and Republican nominee John McCain remarked during the primaries) 'aren't ever coming back'. Whose disaffection has been channelled into hot-button issues by clarion right-wing personalities, and away from real opportunities to improve their lot. From this distance, all the way across the Pacific, the oddity of 'bittergate' was not in its being said, but in mainstream media taking exception to it.

Watson's heartland was not quite the subject of Obama's misstep though. Broadly, the most vivid tract of America in *Journeys* spans the old South up to the heights of the Louisiana Purchase: New Orleans to Yellowstone. This disparate expanse voted marginally for Obama in the primaries. Parts of it are considered more favourable to Obama in the general election than for any Democratic candidate since JFK, although clearly most of it is safe Republican terrain. In the South, Obama eventually won over a wary black vote (they had vested political hopes in black leaders before, and seen tragedy), and more surprisingly the overwhelmingly white vote on the fringe of the Rockies. The target of Obama's remarks was the northern rim of bluegrass Appalachia, further to the east, a mountain region of mixed but majority-white constitution, compassing parts of Pennsylvania (which Obama lost to Clinton by 10 points), Ohio (also by 10), Kentucky (by 35), West Virginia (41) and Tennessee (13). It tails into regions of North Carolina, Alabama and Georgia in the South, which Obama won, but these mountainous reaches are tiny fractions of the population of those states. Unless there's a rout these are all relatively safe for McCain in November. The Appalachian campaign battalions will converge on Pennsylvania and Ohio.

Probably due to Amtrak's logistical preference for skirting high-country, it's a region Watson doesn't really get to visit. One way to characterise the mindset of this area, not quite north and not quite south and not yet midwest, comes via the polling analysis website <fivethirtyeight.com>. The US Census asks for an ethnic classification from all respondents, with tickboxes for all the most common nationalities. Seven per cent ignore these boxes and write in 'American'. <fivethirtyeight.com> mapped out the geographic concentration of these Americans (you might call them rednecks). That darkest swathe is Appalachia.

If another name were needed, you could say it's Rush Country. Perhaps that's unfair: Rush Limbaugh has a national audience for his radio show, the highest-rating radio show in the United States over the course of twenty years. It's not reasonable to say he's ignorant—he is canny and alert to the sensitivities of his audience— but his moral demagoguery has the whiff of ignorance, and it sure sounds like redneck radio. 'It is difficult', says Watson, 'for a halfway reasonable person to drive in a straight line while listening to Rush Limbaugh.' Yet again and again Watson returns to it; and if not to Limbaugh, then to Fox Network's Sean Hannity, who is something like Rush without the charisma, or to the radio preachers like Hank Hanegraaff, the Bible Answer Man. It animates him, this 'great contest for America's soul', carried out over the ubiquitous but surely waning medium of radio. It makes his stomach churn and endangers other motorists, and though these nemeses are entertaining, you occasionally wonder whether Watson's passion is well spent. There are liberal initiatives, such as newfound Air America and the venerable NPR, that seek to redress the balance. There's television, where if not exactly unbiased, opinions are arguably less uniformly preposterous (Hannity, on Fox television, is paired with a 'liberal' by the name of Colmes, if only to pay lip service to Fox's 'fair and balanced' motto). And then there's the internet, inhabited by conservative luminaries such as Matt Drudge—and yes, Rush Limbaugh has a presence—but indisputably the neighbourhood of a Democratic guard: Markos Moulitsas, Arianna Huffington, Josh Marshall, Ambinder, Atrios, even Colbert and Stewart, and on and on. Fund-

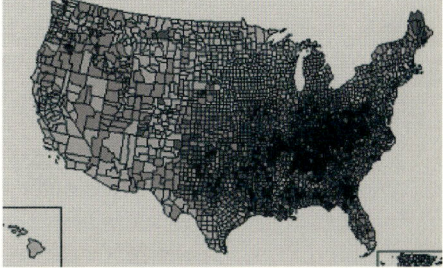

Distribution in the United States of respondents in the Census who wrote in 'American' instead of selecting from a range of ethnic backgrounds. Source: the website <fivethirtyeight.com>.

raising numbers in the primary season revealed the partisan disproportionality of the internet readership. The contest for America's soul is well over two centuries old, and conducted on many planes, employing many strategies.

Still, Limbaugh is especially difficult to ignore. When net lingo is commonplace we'll call him a 'griefer', one who delights in agitating the enemy, or really anyone who doesn't agree with him, or anyone at all. In February, recognising that the primaries had delivered an early Republican decision and an unexpectedly torrid Democratic contest, in a year of many positive auguries for the Democrats come November, he launched something called Operation Chaos. In the remaining open primaries (where a registered voter can choose to cast a vote for either party's nomination), he told his audience not to simply rubber-stamp McCain; instead, cast a vote for Hillary. This after ten years of spitting vitriol in her direction. The point, he explained, was to keep the Democratic contest alive, to give Obama and Clinton as much opportunity to destroy each other's reputations, without the GOP having to lift a finger.

It's arguable how much impact the operation had. There aren't many open primaries on the calendar, but two of them are Texas and Indiana. In both cases, Clinton won the popular vote by just a few per cent—a margin perhaps small enough for Limbaugh's 'operatives' to have pushed the result in Clinton's favour. But exit polls were ambiguous on the subject. And in both Pennsylvania and Ohio, where Hillary really staked her campaign, closed primaries were held, requiring that voters register as Democrats in order to vote for a Democratic candidate. It was her wins in these states that propelled her campaign into June, when finally 'the math' caught up with her.

Ultimately, despite the easy egregiousness with which they goad American liberals and visiting Aussie bleeding hearts, Limbaugh and his fellow commentators are something of a distraction. Like most purveyors of immoderate opinion, they preach to the choir. How the choir came to be is the more interesting question. Why is there such a mainstream audience for discussion at the extreme of public opinion on matters such as immigration, abortion and war? A convincing answer begins with the Goldwater campaign for the presidency in 1964, which failed but, in the governmental expansiveness of LBJ's Great Society, discovered disaffected Democratic voters in all sorts of unlikely places— like, for instance, the Solid South ('solid' because it was resolutely Democratic, and had been since the Confederates were defeated by GOP founder Lincoln). Nixon surfed the wave of this disaffection, in large part the concern of small-town citizens about the increasingly amoral and apparently mutinous youth culture of the late sixties, all the way to the Whitehouse. In 1972 Nixon gathered these voters into the blunt instrument with which he bludgeoned liberal George McGovern in the general election. His staffer Kevin Phillips labelled them 'the emerging Republican majority' in a book of the same name. In the 1980s, their ranks swelled with low-income earners in every state of the union; these latest apostates were dubbed 'Reagan Democrats', and though the schism did not prevent Bill Clinton eventually ascending to the presidency, still they were largely responsible for the 1994 'Republican Revolution' that delivered him a hostile Congress for the remainder of his time in office.

It worked, this new 'conservative movement', because there were people at ground level galvanising support from these unlikely bases. The Cold War environment led to a conflation of unionism and labour politics with the mortal foe, and there was a substantial drop-off in working-class self-identification from its New Deal heights. The employed but unwealthy voting bloc began to fragment. Conservative whisperers, organisers, leaders, preachers and authors took the old, seductive mythology of America as the 'land of opportunity' and used it to sunder the working class. 'Improve yourself!' was the edict; the subtext was 'climb into and up the middle classes'. Few white Americans would answer to the charge of working class now; indeed, the term is hardly ever used in the media or every-day conversation. In this election campaign, every viable candidate has directly, sympathetically and without a trace of irony addressed his or her message to 'the struggling middle class'.

The middle class is struggling in large part because it voted for a succession of governments that have failed to deliver it any respite. Reagan and Bush Jr were unabashed in their promulgation of 'trickle-down economics', which with increasing abandon took the form of tax cuts for the rich. The American workforce has been on the defensive since the oil crises of the seventies, when for many industries importing became cheaper than manufacturing. Little has been done to reform or replace US primary industry. Given the disparity between low-income voting patterns and governmental reciprocation, you might arrive at Watson's conclusion, that 'Americans believe things that are not true and vote for their exploiters'.

What is motivating these voters, if not the self-interest on which their democracy is founded? It's probably the 'issues': the hot-button controversies that disproportionately dominate American political discourse. Civil rights and the status of minorities early on, along with the traditional Republican injunction against big government, which by the middle of the century was growing rapidly—although it certainly did not shrink towards the end under Republican tenure. Then there was the need to win a war against the Evil Empire, which had the nukes to bury North America and end the world. Latterly, and most effectively, it has been the 'moral' controversies, where that label normally implies the presence of religious dogma in the debate. The list of these controversies includes the *Roe v Wade* decision on abortion, the teaching of the theory of evolution, responses to Islam (the militant terrorist network that inexplicably 'hates freedom') and of course the constant threat of homosexuals getting hitched under the auspices of the state.

In short, a large percentage of the electorate that might be predisposed, in a calculus of self-interest, to vote Democratic seems instead to be voting Republican to quell its insecurities—anxieties the conservative movement does not so much address as amplify with great sympathy, and which the Democratic Party has so far proven powerless to dispel. This is the larger question that Watson begs of his hosts: Why, in the great democracy where the desire of all citizens is to better their condition, are the big topics of the day not globalisation or education or health or wages or poverty, which impinge directly on their prospects of success, but abortion and gay marriage, which for the most part don't?

It's an argument in danger of succumbing to the classic anti-American pitfall, which sees US citizens as fundamentally ill-informed and irrational in their approach to politics. Watson cavorts along this precipice, and some of his formulations (such as the 'exploiters' quote above) seem offensively simplistic. Still, a couple of pages earlier he explains that informed American voters know more about their democracy than anywhere else in the world. And it's because, in part, the American political system can handle a debate about these things. Watson's argument, and mine, and Barack Obama's, echoes that of Thomas Frank, the author of *What's the Matter with Kansas?*, which remained on the *New York Times* bestseller lists for four months in 2004. Detailing the particular composition of his home state, the middlest state in the union, Frank portrayed the social conservatives pushing these 'values issues' as pawns of the traditional economic conservative base, because they fight the battles that have already been lost: Darwin will never be ejected from the classroom, a constitutional amendment prohibiting gay marriage will never pass. They bring the anger that gets a demographically significant segment of the electorate out to vote, but when the election is won, survivalism kicks in and the leaders tread water, getting to the next election and picking up points attacking 'elite liberals' for attempting to break the stalemate.

The chess terminology might not be out of place here, because the argument is perhaps excessively black and white. You won't get as far as you might think in American politics by crediting the people with limited awareness. There clearly are sections of the media that do reduce complex problems to 'something less challenging than the thoughts of Captain America'[2] and there is a unique frenzy-of-the-moment that few in the media can resist—encapsulated by 'bittergate', which was sinking Obama one week, forgotten the next. There are notable examples, like Willie Horton in 1988 and the Swift Boat Veterans last time around, where drummed-up scandals may have fatally wounded presidential candidates who were otherwise viable. But Americans have shown over and over again that they are not locked into their prejudices, that they are willing to reshape their allegiances but not without reluctance, and with what appears—from the bird's-eye view of millions upon millions of votes—to be serious consideration.

I'm about to contend that the 2008 elections for president and seats in Congress will break many of the patterns on which we recent observers of US politics have been inculcated. It's not just in the absence of Bush and the silence of the neocons, but in the unusual characters of both McCain and Obama, and it goes far deeper than either of them. It's not all in one direction, however. Again, the reactions to Obama's remarks in San Francisco are instructive. He was paraphrased everywhere as saying that midwesterners cling to their guns and their religion. The politico-historical argument was inevitably lost. The geographic precision was blurred. The Second Amendment got caught up in it, naturally. But the real 'problem' was a black candidate, middle name of Hussein, with an educated manner and a wildly incandescent pastor, speaking at the citadel of coastal radicalism, lampooning the faithful of the heartland.

Will the Christian Right turn out for McCain as they did for Bush? It's hard to say. Without question, however, religion will exercise an influence over this campaign like few before it. In the primaries, Huckabee suggested that the constitution should be brought into line with 'God's Standards', Romney batted back excessive fascination with the sanctity of his undergarments, and Clinton somehow prevaricated on whether Obama was not a Muslim. And they were the orthodox candidates. Then there's Reverend Wright. McCain, too, has been tarnished by his religious associations, seeking out the endorsement of Pastor Hagee (for whom Hitler 'hunted' the Jews in fulfilment of Old Testament prophecy) and accepting the same of Pastor Parsley ('America was founded with the intention of seeing the false religion of Islam destroyed'). McCain was courting the Christian Right and the faithful congregations of Ohio, both of which he'll need in November. Under

2 To quote Watson doing a great injustice to the Marvel character, who in recent decades has been singularly provocative on the subject of patriotism

pressure he eventually denounced the pastors. That they were even wooed, that Wright's preposterous sermons were replayed endlessly on television and radio, that both candidates are down in Florida arguing who is the better friend of Judaism, all speaks to the thorny importance of religion in present-day US politics. The extremes seem to have folded into the middle; faith is now the dangerous frontier of a political system that has prided itself on the separation of church and state. In everything that comes after this point, religion is the wildcard.

If there can be a measure of America's capacity for reinvention and renewal, a reminder of its restlessness, it might be found in this observation by Watson in *American Journeys*, likely written late in 2005: 'It's hard to imagine anyone now promising what Robert Kennedy promised that year, and just as hard to imagine the crowds who turned out to cheer him all across the country: in the rural South, in the cities, in the ghettoes, even in Kansas.'

Not three years later, Obama's unexpectedly good showing in Indiana confirmed what had been widely suspected since late February: he would be the Democratic Party nominee for president in 2008. The media embraced it, and everybody knew it, though Hillary waited a month to make it official. The remaining handful of states were dead rubbers. But unlike previous cycles, where dead rubbers had seen reduced turnout and voting that (like the post–Super Tuesday Republican contests) could be easily recognised for rubber-stamping or fringe protestation, the fervour for the season continued. In Portland, Oregon, a week later, and a few days before their mail-in primary concluded, Obama drew a crowd of seventy-five thousand people to an outdoor rally. Seventy-five thousand! It's occasionally seemed easier to land Superbowl tickets than a seat at an Obama stadium gig. Not that anyone's sitting. And the phenomenon hasn't been limited just to Obama; Hillary drew massive crowds throughout the contest, and even at her concession speech, thousands were turned away.

Part of the enthusiasm derives from the slate of candidates: the studious former First Lady and a visionary African American, competing for the right to take on the decorated former prisoner of war. Of course there are plenty of citizens caught up in the Hollywood storyline. But greater energy stems from the sense that a series of fault-lines that have increasingly divided the country are being sealed over by this campaign, that the red-state/blue-state divide, which by 2004 seemed like a sectarian cold war, is crumbling in fits and starts. McCain and Obama are tussling over independent voters, taking a different tack to the Karl Rove philosophy of energising the base, and both could lay some claim to post-partisan political outlooks, if the term weren't mostly meaningless in an active Western democracy. McCain has had to back-pedal from his monicker as a maverick to prove his Republican heart, and he will have to wear the charge of Bush Mk II from Democratic campaigners, though it's not entirely a fair one. Obama has a surer base, although he too has to mend the rifts of an arduous primary season. He tends towards reconciliation, even to the detriment of his political fortune, as when in January he found himself under pressure in Reno, Nevada, for telling a newspaper's editorial board that 'the Republicans were the party of ideas for a pretty long chunk of time' and that 'Reagan changed the trajectory of America . . . in a way that Bill Clinton did not'. They were reasonable, even illuminating observations, but Hillary, campaigning to a more traditional wisdom, turned them to her advantage.

That doesn't mean this will be a feel-good election, but America is changing. 'Change', it turns out, has become the dominant theme. It's a remarkable indictment in a string of indictments upon the current administration that all contenders on both sides fought for due recognition as the 'candidate of change'. As foreigners, we've been perplexed by this oddly empty-sounding war-cry—what change, in which direction, towards what? It sounds like 'anything has got to be better than this'. But there's no doubt that it has resonated with broad swathes of the populace, and that Obama's 'Yes we can'—could it be more quintessentially American? How could you doubt his patriotism?—has the effect of a tribal chant. Vitally, and strangely, this election has the hallmarks of the first post-boomer election, to be fought between two candidates who fall on either side of the generation that has dominated politics for decades. It might be too early to celebrate the end of that hegemony: already the likely candidates for 2012 were born in the immediate post-war years, and even this election, since boomers have no candidate in the race, their votes will be prized by both parties. But there are other dynamics. For the first time in a long time, young voters are an active, not a passive, force. States that have been forsaken to the other side since 1992 are back in play.

Obama and McCain, as figureheads, seem in their disjuncture from the candidates preceding them to presage a new political era. But if they do, the origins of this new era predate their nominations by at least a half-decade. For McCain, it comes out of the steady leak of seats in Congress, which turned to a landslide in 2006. He owes some of his political fortune to it. The discard of 2000, without greatly extending his résumé, and getting eight years older, became the nominee of 2008 because the Republican electorate looked at their less revolutionary options (Guiliani, Romney, Thompson), and realised they would not survive in the present climate. Obama too, in some ways, is the product of Howard Dean's failed campaign and the changing dynamic that 2006 wrought. His use of the internet, while almost matched by Clinton, has dwarfed McCain's efforts so far. The formidable Republican war-chest has been rendered paltry overnight. For every stadium speech Obama gives, the real advantage he gains is in the flood of small, renewable donations via the web. This is the lesson Dean learned, perhaps accidentally. America is large enough that if you harness the dreams of ordinary folks, cautiously, they'll propel you far further than you imagined.

It can be argued that the 'emerging Republican majority' is dwindling. Even Kevin Phillips, who named it, did not expect it to hold for much more than thirty years, and it's long outlasted that. That doesn't mean Obama's a safe bet, and the elevation of McCain to the Republican leadership is some indication that they understand the new terrain and are up for a fight. The adventures this primary season of Ron Paul, a libertarian whose policies recall an ancient GOP that upheld the Monroe Doctrine of wilful isolation, of America first, have shown just how far Republican believers are prepared to journey in search of new ideas. The coming months will provide an engrossing contest for New America, after 9/11 dunked the nation back into the twentieth century, and old battles with old battle-plans have rumbled through all the years since. Forget the hanging chads: America's twenty-first century, and thus to some extent the world's, awaits November's decision.

COPYRIGHT
FREE RIDERS

LYNNE SPENDER ASKS HOW EFFECTIVE TRADITIONAL COPYRIGHT LAWS CAN BE IN THE DIGITAL AGE

HERE IS MOVEMENT AT THE COPYRIGHT STATION. The word has passed around that the digital content 'colt' has 'got away'. The movie, music and publishing industries are sending their top lawyers to rein it in. In spite of their having convinced government and the legislature that the fences should be stronger, higher and locked with new technological protection measures, the colt has escaped. Many potential 'free riders' are more than pleased.

Since digital technology enabled all forms of expression to be digitised as ones and zeros that could be transmitted anywhere in the world to anyone with an internet connection, the incumbents of the copyright industries have been aware of the threat to their businesses. They have known that digital technology and ever cheaper access to the internet were likely to result in their content being copied without permission or payment and that this presaged the loss of control of the market for commercial content.

Their response was to call 'Pirate' and 'Theft'. The industry bodies representing the American content industries lobbied national and international law-makers to strengthen copyright law and to extend the period of copyright protection to seventy years after the death of the author for individual works or ninety-five years from publication for corporate (Disney)-owned works. Jack Valenti, CEO of the Motion Picture Association of America (MPAA), who was for many years the spokesperson for the Hollywood movie industry, embarked on a campaign to demonise the internet as an economic and moral threat. Basically, his argument was that if the law were not changed to better protect American content, the internet would destroy the movie industry (and the billions of dollars it brought to the economy) and become the lucrative lair of pornographers and organised crime.

According to some critics, Valenti was almost single-handedly responsible for the construction of file-sharing as theft, making what might have been seen as a new cultural phenomenon into a legal issue about the protection of personal property. The recording industry attached itself to his coat-tails, and the Record Industry Association of America (RIAA) started its own anti-file-sharing campaign. First it sued Napster, a file-sharing technology (which was closed down) and then twenty-thousand of its customers, most of whom paid a hefty fine rather than pay even heftier fees to a lawyer to defend them. The book-publishing industry jumped on the piracy bandwagon. They may have been unsure of the effect of digital copying on books (who wants to read a book on a computer?) but they were very certain of the threat it posed to scientific and academic journals from which they made huge profits. With much rhetoric, if little action except to offer huge discounts to supermarkets to move large print runs of bestsellers, to offer even less palatable contracts to midlist authors and to increase the price of subscriptions to rarely read journals, they willingly joined the copyright maximilists in the fight to keep control of the print marketplace. If copyright is good, they seemed to think, then more copyright must be better.

The reaction of the content industries was understandable. Since the 1710 UK Act of Anne, the producers and distributors of content have been well protected by copyright law. At that time, they were granted a monopoly to exploit the works they controlled for a period of fourteen years, with the possibility of extending the protection for another fourteen years. The time limit was imposed to ensure that there was a balance between their interests in being rewarded for their enterprise and investment and the public's interest in having access to works as they moved out of copyright and into the public domain.

Ostensibly also to reward and provide an incentive for authors (who of course had no power unless they had a contract or a deal with a publisher), this balanced regime worked reasonably well while there was a distinction between accessing, using and copying a work. The law could be adapted to include new rights such as translation, abridgement and serial rights. Within the analogue world, it could even, at a stretch, accommodate new technological media such as photographs, tape recorders and CDs.

As these new products were tangible and their reproduction was both visible and expensive, most copying could be controlled most of the time. Thus book owners could not 'copy' their books but they could read, lend, scribble on and even resell them without breaking the law. Not so in the digital world of intangible zeroes and ones, where every access and use is arguably a form of copying. To access the image of a work on a computer is to access a reproduction or a copy. E-mailing it to a friend involves copying the copy. Browsing, borrowing, sharing, reading, downloading, printing—all involve a reproduction and, under the prevailing principles of copyright law, every one of those activities becomes a potential breach of the law.

A decision might have been made, at what copyleft writer Siva Vaidhyanathan calls the 'digital moment', to view digital reproduction as qualitatively different from analogue reproduction. New laws could have been devised to preserve a balance between the rights of the copyright owner and the rights of the user. Because digital works are intangible and non-rivalrous (that is, the use by one person does not prevent use by another) and because the ease of digital reproduction turns 'supply and demand' economics upside down, policy-makers might have conceived a different approach based on a different notion of economics and the public good. At its simplest level, this might have been an intuitive system based on distinguishing between commercial works and non-commercial works. Or it might have involved the delineation of what Jessica Litman calls a 'free-use zone', an area of use for which individuals don't need to ask for permission to creatively repurpose and reuse digital works. A place where they could lawfully 'rip, mix and burn', as Apple briefly encouraged its users to do with ipods.

But the decision was made instead to strengthen copyright law. Law- and policy-makers determined that if content providers were to be attracted to the new digital environment, the law should be modified to offer at least the same level of copy protection for digital works as it had for analogue works.

In the countries that are signatories to international copyright agreements, this new level of copyright includes such long periods of protection that no copyright works being created now will enter the public domain in any of our lifetimes. When they eventually do, and providing the period of protection is not again extended when Mickey Mouse is next due to become copyright free, users may still not be able to access them, even for 'fair use' or 'fair dealing' purposes. This is because they may also be protected by Digital Rights Management (DRM) systems that technologically encrypt or 'lock' the works. Under what are called 'anti-circumvention provisions', the international legal regime now makes it a criminal offence to break the locks or to manufacture or sell any device that could be used to break the locks, even for non-commercial or educational purposes.

Dmitry Sklyarov, a Russian PhD student and employee of Elcomsoft, found this out the hard way when he gave a paper at a 2001 conference in the United States. His topic was Adobe's e-book security systems and when he had presented his paper, the FBI arrested him, presumably at the behest of Adobe. He was charged under the anti-circumvention provisions of the Digital Millennium Copyright Act (DMCA) with distributing a product designed to break Adobe's anti-piracy code. The charges against him were eventually dropped but not before he was obliged to provide US$50,000 bail to secure his release from custody.

Tarleton Gillespie, a fellow at the Center for Internet and Society at Stanford Law School, says that this encryption is a dramatic intervention into communication and culture. He says it allows film and music distributors to govern not only whether we copy a work, but also our private uses as well. DRM can stop users from reading, borrowing and sharing locked works, even if they own them. Ask anyone who has tried to play a region-coded American DVD that simply wont 'read' on an Australian DVD player.

What we have now is a copyright system that has drastically disturbed the balance between protecting the property of content owners and allowing reasonable access by users to a public domain of new works. Lawyer James Boyle, among others, has noted a parallel between this situation and the privatisation of the agricultural commons during the agrarian enclosure movement, where common land was appropriated and fenced off for the exclusive use of its owners. This first enclosure movement of common land took centuries to effect. The 'second' enclosure movement of the intellectual commons has been effected in the last twenty years.

Pitted against this enclosure movement is an array of organisations and individuals who have argued that it is time we rethought copyright law. Some are concerned at the monopoly control of the content owners and its impact on society—especially on free speech and democracy. The Electronic Frontiers Foundation, for example, has been at the forefront of legal battles to defend free speech and users' rights in the digital environment. Richard Stallman, an early software programmer, was appalled when the early computer-software-sharing community was commercialised and software was no longer a tool to be shared for the common good. Often referred to as the 'father' of the free software movement, he developed what he called a 'copyleft' licence, an 'all rights reversed' system that allows software to be used and adapted, providing any new adaptation is also released free to the public. Similarly, the Open Source software movement, which relies mainly on the unpaid contributions of developers, makes software source code available to the general public with few copyright restrictions.

Others critics focus on the 'chilling effects' of copyright law on creativity and innovation—which are now so much more dependent on permission and payment to the owners of privately owned and 'locked' copyright works, including software.

In response to what he saw increasingly as a 'permission' society, Lawrence Lessig founded 'Creative Commons' (cc). It is a flexible licensing system that operates within copyright law but which offers a choice of cc licences that provide a range of protections and freedoms for creators, including making their work available in the public domain. Forty-three countries have their own cc licences: millions of websites and creative works of scholarship, music, film, photography, literature and courseware are now available under the cc licensing system.

Others despair at the law itself, which they say is arcane, anachronistic and no longer respected by the millions of people who continue to download music and movies from the internet. Australian authors surveyed in 2007 admitted that they knew almost nothing of the provisions of the 560-page Australian Copyright Act. They certainly did not understand the anti-circumvention provisions. Not that it mattered much. None of them could afford the $5000 or so to pay a lawyer to take legal action.

But perhaps the most interesting objections come from those who have looked at the economics of the current copyright regime. They point to significant changes since the digital moment. Cory Doctorow, a Canadian blogger and science fiction writer, has trodden the path of numerous musicians who have put their work online, for free. Like many of the musicians, he found readers downloaded his work, but sales of his books also increased. And he was offered much more money to write and to make public appearances. Turning conventional supply-and-demand economics on its head, he pointed out that on the internet it is obscurity, not piracy, that is the problem. The better known you are, the better chance you have of using some of the new internet business models to sell your work.

Rupert Pollock, an academic at Cambridge University, undertook a study in 2007 of what he calls 'optimal copyright'. He used a theoretical model to establish the optimal period of copyright protection and found, first, that it falls as the costs of production go down, as they have with digital technology. Second, by studying new and existing data on recordings and books, he asserted that the optimal term for the greatest rewards was about fourteen years. This, ironically, is the term of protection originally offered to copyright holders under the first copyright law in 1710!

It is also nine years longer than the term recommended by the Swedish Pirate Party, a political party formed in 2006 to reform copyright law. Their platform, which has gained considerable support in Scandinavia and other countries, suggests that a five-year term is appropriate for copyright protection. Founder of the party Rick Falkvinge says this allows for a period for commercial exploitation of new works, which can then move into the public domain and form the basis of 'the greatest public library ever'. He points out that the commercial life of cultural works is staggeringly short in today's world and he questions why anyone needs to make money seventy years after their death.

None of this carries much sway with today's copyright owners who have most to lose by reforms to the law that loosen their control of the still profitable entertainment and information markets. And it does not appeal very much to intellectual property lawyers, nor to copyright organisations such as the Australian Copyright Council (ACC) and Copyright Agency Ltd (CAL). When public hearings were held into the effects of the intellectual property provisions that Australia would be obliged to adopt under the Australia–US Free Trade Agreement, ACC and CAL were vocal in their support for strengthening copyright laws and extending the period of protection.

But as philosopher and lawyer Eben Moglen says, our current copyright laws are 'impossibly burdened'. And there are now several generations of what Axel Bruns calls 'produsers', people who have actively engaged in creative collaboration, file-sharing and social networking on the internet. Many of them are still idealistic about the potential of digital technology to contribute to a more democratic society and a richer culture. Many of them have a more universal sense of ownership of knowledge and information goods than their print-based counterparts. It is possible that their values and practices—often outside the commercial marketplace—will force a change to our inherently contradictory copyright laws that aspire to serve the public good through a system based on private gain. In the meantime, they live in a parallel creative universe where file-sharing, far from being a moral and economic threat, is a predictable reaction to the serious imbalance introduced by twenty-first-century copyright laws. It is not surprising that digital natives might see free-riding on the escaped content colt as a reasonable cultural and economic response.

SPEAK-ING A SECOND LAN-GUAGE

ANDREA McNAMARA finds a central place for football in Melbourne's cultural mix

On 20 September 1958 a huge crowd turned up to the grand final at the MCG to see two powerhouse clubs compete for the honours. Collingwood won, against the odds; flag favourite Melbourne was hoping to clinch four in a row and break Collingwood's record for consecutive premierships, from the 1920s. It should have been a crowd of 97,957 people but it was one short of that: my mother stayed home in suburban Melbourne and listened to the game on the radio. I was born eight weeks later, and it was all my fault she wasn't at the 'G.

Still, plenty more to come, she might have thought; after all, Collingwood already had twelve cups in the silverware cabinet and there was no reason to doubt the powerful club's ability to win many more. Little did she know that it would be a 32-year wait, with nine grand-final appearances yielding only bridesmaid honours before pulling off another big one in 1990. I was thirty-two by then. That time, my mother was at the 'G, and I listened on the radio.

I googled to check the attendance that day in September fifty years ago, but otherwise I don't need to look up any history books to tell this story. It's part of my family history. In fact, it's the only family history I know, apart from the basics of who my ancestors were—well, there's some doubt about one great-grandparent but, so far, no-one can be bothered with the exhumation of information. I know that my maternal grandfather, born in 1901, left school after grade 7 and did a plumber's apprenticeship at the Flinders Naval Base. He worked with men who caught the train to Melbourne from Bittern on the Mornington Peninsula to go to the footy. The games were probably mostly played in the paddock that is now part of Yarra Park, next to the MCG. Those men barracked for Collingwood, and, when he was old enough, my grandfather came up to town for matches too. When he moved to Melbourne for work, football became part of life and the rest is my history. Grandad's younger sister, Mary Unthank, my great-aunt, can verify the black-and-white legacy—she's alive and kicking at 102, still barracking for the Magpies.

They say that a baby's temperament and intelligence are influenced by what they hear in the womb and that classical music in particular can stimulate the unborn baby's alpha waves. Babies can hear clearly from about twenty weeks; this means I started hearing things around the time of round one, 1958. I would have been lolling about in amniotic fluid with a soundtrack of football in the background for about five months of the pregnancy. I would have heard the teams announced on the radio late on Thursday night, and the match played on Saturday afternoon. No opera, no lullabies, just 'Good Old Collingwood Forever'.

In the winter months, the weeks of my unremarkable Melbourne childhood were bookended by mass on Sundays and footy on Saturday afternoons. In summer, cricket was background noise, along with the lawn mower. We lived in the leafy-green eastern suburbs. My dad was a primary school teacher (he barracked for Richmond) and my mum did clothing alterations to help pay for our good education. I was the eldest of four girls; we went to Catholic schools. We were like a whole lot of other families, nice and ordinary.

But when we went to the footy at Victoria Park, we entered another world. Usually our group was some variation on Grandad, Grandma, Mum, a sister and my uncle, Johnny, and we parked the Holden at Campo's place—he was a mate of Johnny's who lived a few blocks from the ground. I remember this quite clearly because the back streets of Abbotsford were so different to our Californian bungalow, set in the middle of a block on a wide street. Campo's single-fronted house seemed to be almost falling down, and there was no backyard, just a small space out the back off a lane, where a car could just fit. After the game, we'd often have to sit in our car while Grandad and Johnny had a few beers with Campo. This was the other side of Melbourne; it was like seeing the city's underbelly—before the word was a TV series. It was semi-industrial, cramped, inner city, grubby, gritty and it reeked of football.

I look back on Victoria Park with a kind of beer-infused nostalgia. I remember standing on cans or maybe an esky, craning to see, or sitting on hard narrow benches—like church pews without backs—and being embarrassed by my mother barracking too loudly. Filling in the scores obsessively in the *Footy Record* and loving every minute of the game. Learning the language of barracking: 'Baaaaaalll!' and 'Holding the maaan!' Knowing the players' numbers off by heart. If I look at photos of One Eye Hill from the 1960s and 1970s and put them up against family shots taken in our backyard, it's hard to believe Victoria Park was part of our otherwise squeaky-clean life.

Fast forward to 1990. I'd become less interested in footy in the late eighties as it had gone national and become big business. I was part of an arts scene, and I still hadn't worked out that art and sport were not incompatible. This was partly a hangover from school, where I chose art over sport. Not that it was exactly a choice. I was always picked last for any team, stuck in goal defence in netball because I was bigger than everyone else. To quote Dennis Cometti, I had the mobility of a traffic cone. And it was partly because in the 1980s I was a bit up myself.

So, in July 1990 I was working in the Cook Islands, on Rarotonga, for a couple of weeks as part of the AESOP (Australian Executive Services Overseas Program). Although the program was usually the domain of retired professionals, my then business partner, Matthew Flinn, and I had been asked to volunteer our services to assist a struggling T-shirt printing company to improve the quality and quantity of their output. Within the first couple of days, we were invited to a barbecue with all the other vollies. The average age was around sixty.

Matthew and I were standing awkwardly with a group of nice ladies and gents when I spotted a familiar face across the way.

'Is that Brian Dixon?' I asked.

'Yes,' said one of the nice ladies. 'He's a volunteer in sport administration. Do you know Brian?'

Not personally, I didn't. But he was an ex-footballer who had coached North Melbourne in the seventies and he'd been a minister in parliament for a time so he seemed familiar.

'So you're from Melbourne?' she asked. 'Who do you barrack for?'

Well, one thing led to another and suddenly I was having a conversation. Brian eventually came over and we talked about what it was like to play in five winning grand finals for Melbourne in the fifties. We talked about Thorold Merrett, Ray Gabelich, Ron Barassi and what it was like to lose to Collingwood, in the year I was born.

Hours later, we left. Matthew had been mostly an observer, looking on with cultural bemusement. To him, we might as well have been speaking in tongues. There we were in a tropical paradise, at an Aussie-style barbecue—we were thousands of kilometres from Melbourne's winter and he'd had to listen to footy talk for hours. And it was clear that I had unexpectedly enjoyed myself.

'Since when did you speak football so fluently?' he asked. Since Brian Dixon was winning grand finals.

Probably because of the Brian Dixon connection, I paid a bit more attention to the footy for the rest of that season. On Grand Final day, 6 October 1990, my parents were at the 'G. I spoke to my mum in the morning, wishing her well. I listened to the game on the radio, with increasing interest as victory seemed possible. I felt the tingles up my spine when Darren Millane held the ball high as the siren sounded. You'd think I had barracked for good old Collingwood for a hundred years. When I spoke to my mother that evening we joked about closure. The next day, I drove over to Victoria Park; I wanted a sniff of the delirium and to revisit that other side of Melbourne, the bit that was part of my history. I didn't actually go in, but it wasn't because I was too up myself; in fact, I felt like I'd come back down to earth. I knew what my one-eyed, colour-blind, hungover bretheren were experiencing and it wouldn't be long before I was back in the outer.

n 1996 I spent a couple of weeks working at Tiwi Design on Bathurst Island, north of Darwin. I'd never been to black Australia and I felt very naive and extremely white when I arrived at their workshop to start developing some new textile prints. On day one, on the short drive through Nguiu, I was taken aback by the poverty and crude living conditions. I had no idea where to start with the program I was supposed to run—I felt like I'd need a year to acclimatise and adjust my expectations. After a clumsy introduction to the artists, I retreated to the security of the office to type up a list of things we'd need to order from Darwin.

Tim the bookkeeper, a silent type, was in the other corner.

'You from Melbourne?' he asked, after a while.

'Yep.' Wanting to add, 'That's why I'm so out of my depth here,' but I figured that was obvious.

'Who d'ya barrack for?'

'Collingwood,' I said without hesitation.

'I went to school with Billy Picken,' Tim told me.

'I loved him!' I said. 'Number 25,' I added, almost to myself.

I could tell Tim was still proud of this connection with the high-flying idiosyncratic champion who had retired from Collingwood in 1983. Tim went on to explain he'd won a scholarship to Assumption College, Kilmore (once known as 'the football factory'), and so had Billy. They were there for different reasons, but their friendship was forged forever, through footy. It turned out there was a big black-and-white following up north.

Needless to say, the ice was broken and we were off and running. And once more, I loved footy for being my second language. When one of my visits coincided with their footy season (which runs in the 'off-season' of the AFL comp) the spectacle was amazing. Kids, dogs and chaos everywhere but such good fun. It's just possible that football might one day be the language that brings black and white Australians together.

At the end of 2006, Melbourne was pronounced overall winner in the search for the world's top city for sports events. The survey was conducted by London-based research firm ArkSports, and Melbourne rated particularly highly for the level of public interest in sport—apparently it was 'never far from prominence in a city that boasts an impressive and broad cultural calendar'.

If you've lived in a place all your life it's hard to know what defines it. Many of my friends left to go overseas as soon as we finished university in the late 1970s, looking for something they couldn't find in Melbourne or even Australia, but I liked it here. I didn't think much about what I liked thirty years ago, but it certainly wouldn't have been sport that came to mind if I'd been put on the spot. If I think about it now, though, I would say that Melbourne is defined by its cultural mix, and the mix is determined by having a huge sporting precinct so close to the CBD, yet it doesn't seem to be dominated by it in an ugly way. Sport has never been seen by this city's architects as something to be ashamed of.

For many Australians, the MCG, the 'people's ground', is the epicentre of sport in this country; it's the home of cricket, football, the occasional sell-out soccer friendly, host of the 1956 Olympics and the 2006 Commonwealth Games. It's a couple of long bombs from a sophisticated city centre, where there is a plethora of amazing bars and restaurants, and great shopping. It's a city that has embraced sport to such an extent that a second stadium was purpose-built at the other end of the city, and a third one is to be constructed on the other side of the 'G. The sports precinct is completed by the National Tennis Centre, and the whole thing is linked to the city by Birrarung Marr, a new park that has just slipped into our language as if it's always been there. The thing is, if you hated sport, you'd still like the parklands that surround the city.

The MCG is an icon. It's what makes people ask you who you barrack for when you say you're from Melbourne. It's a password to conversations that you might not otherwise have, where you find a common language in the most surprising places.

I n August 2005 Allen & Unwin hosted a 'meet the authors' night for international guests Harlen Coben and Michael Connolly. Making conversation, I asked Coben what he wanted to do while he was in Melbourne. 'I want to see what makes this place tick. Where do you suggest I go?' He'd put me on the spot, and before I realised what I'd done, I was taking him to the football, at the 'G, outside, on a winter's night.

Suffice to say that, much to his surprise and that of his Sydney-based publicist, Coben shared a cab to the 'G with several other people who were also leaving the Melbourne Writers Festival cocktail party early to go to the footy. I was already there so I could get us a possie near the Collingwood cheer squad—far enough away not to be part of it, close enough to get a good eyeful. The game was between Collingwood and Port Adelaide, and I explained the intense rivalry between these two clubs, one of which believed it had the God-given right to the black and white stripes and the other that believed it had been denied those colours at elite level, despite its longer club history—in South Australia—as the Magpies. Coben was intrigued that the supporters were all allowed to sit together. He commented on the number of well-dressed and underdressed people in the same area, the mix of men, women and kids. It was a night of great hilarity—try explaining the rules of a game you've been watching from birth, and for which you have accepted every idiosyncrasy, to an American sports nut who wants to understand *everything*.

We walked back through the gardens and had a late drink and bite to eat at the Supper Club, as far removed stylistically as it could be from the MCG Southern Stand. There were footy scarves there though—if you're in the know, you see them. As we walked him back to his hotel, Coben commented, 'I like this city, it's hard to pigeon hole. I'd love to come back.' And his assessment of the game? 'It's brutal and beautiful. And what a venue.' At the time, the 'G was undergoing major reconstruction but it still exuded an eerie power.

And I remember thinking that next time I'm in an unfamiliar place, I'll make sure I go to a sporting event, even if I don't know the rules. A sporting crowd is a great measure of a city's ticker.

n 2005, another sport was embraced wholeheartedly by Melburnians with the arrival of the A-League. Not that soccer was new to Melbourne, but it hadn't exactly been accessible to the masses. It must have been a successful marketing campaign because after just one season I jumped on the Melbourne Victory bandwagon. I liked the idea that it was about barracking for *Melbourne* as a team and that the season ran in the AFL's off-season. And I was curious as to whether I could pick up the rules of another ball sport. By the time John Aloisi sent Australia to the World Cup on my birthday in 2005 I'd been to several Melbourne Victory games and was starting to appreciate that it was all about nuances and strategies, so different to Australian Rules where it's all in-your-face. But I liked the way the crowd was integral to the entertainment. I was ready to learn the language of the round-ball game, the beautiful game—but I stopped short of calling it 'football'.

When Melbourne Victory won the premiership in the second A-League season, I was there. I really don't like missing grand finals. The losing ones supposedly make you stronger. Look at Aunty Mary—she's survived more losing grand finals in her lifetime than it should be humanly possible to endure: twenty-three at last count. But being there when your team wins is the best feeling and great fun. Watching Archie Thompson's five goals, I was sold. I loved the chanting and being part of a crowd with a common purpose.

If you know the words to one sport, you can easily learn the words to others but I'll always barrack for Melbourne, whatever the competition. But walking across the bridge over the rail yards at Telstra Dome on my way home from a soccer match is not the same as walking home across the land that my grandfather stood on to watch the team I still support, some ninety years later.

MY FAILURE AS A LEATHER JACKET PERSON

MEL CAMPBELL explains why she took her failed purchase so personally

Some months ago I decided to buy my first leather jacket. I figured it would be a good investment: I'd look cool and be warm in winter. However, the monstrosity currently hanging in my wardrobe was a terrible buy. It is ill fitting and looks terrible whether it's buttoned or unbuttoned. I paid far too much for it and, far from feeling hip or stylish, I feel horribly ashamed every time I wear it. But there is an upside. It is warm in winter.

It's slightly embarrassing to admit you've been vanquished by an item of clothing. Why should I feel so powerless in the face of aesthetic decisions and consumer activities I ostensibly control? After all, it's not as if I was forced to buy it. But leather jackets are what consumer behaviourists call 'high involvement' purchases. For a start, they're expensive, so there's pressure to 'get it right' when buying one. The marketing term 'post-purchase dissonance' describes that sinking feeling of having 'got it wrong' and wasted pots of money.

Leather jackets also carry layers of symbolic meaning accumulated through their various appearances in popular culture. Furthermore, their inescapably animalistic, tactile nature makes them very intimate and emotionally charged to wear. This all adds up to a kind of mental smokescreen for the potential buyer, clouding any rational attempts to weigh features and benefits. As I discovered, it also makes buying the wrong leather jacket seem like a misjudgement of someone's character … or even a flaw in your own.

While consumer behavioural theory imagines shopping as a process of uncanny orderliness, many commentators, in the academy and the popular press, depict clothes shoppers as *disorderly*. 'Maxing out' their funds on emotionally charged 'retail therapy' and forming frenzied scrums during sale time, shoppers are unable to explain their attachment to fashion's arbitrary dictates, accepting without question that trends are there to be adopted. Some media narratives even suggest that using shopping to realise an 'ideal self' is immorally narcissistic, since it necessarily involves the exploitation of workers and the environment.

I would argue that leather jackets are simultaneously ordered and disorderly purchases. So in this essay, I try to pin down some of the ideas swirling diaphanously about leather jackets by retracing the steps of my ill-fated purchase. Which of the leather jacket's many connotations spoke most to me? What did I notice about the leather jackets I saw other people wear? And what version of myself did I hope to present in my new jacket? What follows is deliberately peripatetic: I wander past the same ideas in different ways, much as a shopper might return to several shops again and again to re-evaluate each different potential buy in the context of the others. Perhaps this might help us gain some purchase, so to speak, on how shopping responds to cultural imperatives and moulds individual identities.

REBELLION AND INTIMACY: LEATHER-CLAD TRANSFORMATION At the beginning of the twentieth century, the leather jacket was a practical, protective garment for motorists, aviators, police and the military. This lent it connotations of both adventure and intimidation, and that play between freedom and constraint lies at the heart of the leather jacket's subsequent iconic status within subcultures and wider popular culture. Indiana Jones wears an intrepid explorer's battered brown jacket, while the Nazis and Communists who would subdue him wear structured, disciplined leathers. The 1970s jackets worn by the Black Panthers and early Crips gang members collapse the duality, making their wearers appear simultaneously anarchic and threatening.

The image of the leather-clad rebel, which vroomed into the popular imagination in the form of motorbike-straddling Marlon Brando in *The Wild One*, marries the freedom of the open road with the menace of the outlaw. While motorcycle clubs had existed throughout the twentieth century, the early outlaw biker gangs were comprised of Second World War veterans whose experiences of wartime horrors alienated them from the comfortable materialism of postwar America. They transposed many military traditions, such as camaraderie, gallows humour and group iconography, to their newly founded motorcycle clubs. For instance, several squadrons and military units in both world wars had been known as the Hells Angels, with distinctive logos that members proudly displayed on aircraft, banners and tattoos. There's a similar slippage between the leather aviator jacket and the motorcycle jacket, which took on a talismanic role among outlaw bikers, displaying their allegiance via embroidered logos and patches.

Leather also has a long history in fetish wear. The styles of leather clothing used in bondage, discipline and sadomasochistic sexual practices draw largely from underground homosexual 'leatherman' culture. With their emphasis on ultra-visible ultra-masculinity, postwar leathermen considered themselves outlaws from both straight culture and gay culture, which at the time emphasised either 'passing' as heterosexual or a flamboyant sense of camp. Early gay leather clubs operated similarly to outlaw motorcycle gangs, adopting similar clothing and iconography, and many of them became outlets for exploring kinky sexual practices.

BDSM practices added a sexual frisson to the tension between freedom and constraint that leather had already connoted. But leather is a good symbolic fit in these cultures for another reason: as animal skin, it covers (and strategically reveals) human skin, while mimetically suggesting another kind of nakedness. Fetish magazine *Skin Two* is named after the notion that fetish wear forms a second skin: it creates another way of experiencing one's own body and of admiring the bodies of others, in which the fetish garment is integral to aesthetic and corporeal pleasure. In tight-laced corseting subcultures, for instance, the fetishised garment itself *creates* the body, and the sense of self, that is being celebrated.

Unlike most leather fetish wear, leather jackets are not worn next to the skin. Instead, they act as protective outer garments, carapaces against real and symbolic onslaughts. Yet they are still strangely intimate. For a start, they mould to their wearers' shapes, creasing or stretching to accommodate their movements. But you don't just wear a leather jacket; you also surrender to its wealth of sensation and weight of cultural meaning so that, in a way, it wears you. You and your jacket share stories and adventures, as well as being a source of spectacle and speculation for onlookers. In the minds of strangers and casual acquaintances, you become inextricably linked with the jacket. You become a Leather Jacket Person.

Popular culture also views leather jackets as catalysts for transformation—

perhaps because they're animal skins. There's a wealth of European folktales in which humans are cursed to take animal form, requiring specific conditions to reveal their 'true' selves. Other tales feature animal skins worn as disguise or penance that ultimately bring their wearers status and happiness. In the French fairytale *Donkeyskin*, a princess in exile disguises herself in the skin of her father's prized magical donkey to work as a scullery maid. The story is propelled forwards by the strategic donning and doffing of the skin. Meanwhile in the German tale *Bearskin*, a desperate soldier makes a pact with the devil to wear the skin of a bear for seven years, and ultimately marries the only one of three sisters who can stand the sight of him. In these and many variants, the animal skin symbolises the same tension between freedom and constraint, revelation and concealment, that the contemporary leather jacket dramatises.

As well as continuing to mine the rich iconography of rebellion, leather jackets in contemporary cinema act as a metaphor for realities and bodies in flux. The *Matrix* trilogy contrasts the weird homespun T-shirts worn in the 'real world' outside the Matrix with the severe, stylised black leather trench coats worn to fight inside it. The subtly different repertoire of blood-red leather jackets sported by the charismatic Tyler Durden underscores the growing surreality of *Fight Club*. Fresh as a daisy from her coma, the Bride in *Kill Bill* slays her enemies in a cheery yellow leather motorcycle jacket. Distressed mutant Wolverine favours distressed brown leather in *X-Men*; while a cyborg assassin's acquisition of clothing from a leatherman of convenient Arnold Schwarzenegger proportions has become one of the *Terminator* franchise's key motifs.

In my everyday world, unthreatened by mutants, devils, psychopaths or killer robots, how was a leather jacket going to transform me? Back in the mid 1990s, I had been that most gormless of Leather Jacket People: the Teenage Wearer of Dad's Old Leather Jacket. Like many a teenager before me, I thought myself mighty tuff and groovy as I strutted through the mall, but it never really left the realm of dress-ups. I don't think I ever really felt transformed by those jackets, and I certainly had never craved another one. That's what made my sudden decision to buy one so odd: I saw a rack of variously styled jackets in a chain store, and thought to myself that (in marketing parlance) it was a low-involvement purchase. The price was low enough for me to cut my losses if I chose poorly.

But still the choice lay ahead: which of the available styles to pick? It took me a week or two of musing, discussing leather jackets with my friends and observing leather-clad strangers on the street to negotiate this semiotic minefield. I longed for a leather jacket, a chrysalis: an unformed and symbolically 'clean' garment that would incubate a fresher and more glamorous version of myself. But from the range of garments I could see in the shops and in public, it seemed I must allow the leather jacket to 'wear me'; to mould me in the image of other Leather Jacket Wearers. The Sleek Bourgie, with softly gleaming leather in a conservative cut. The Rock God, with retro-style blazer. The battered, baggy blouson of the Scruffy Academic. The fitted, cropped, hooded bomber jacket of the Insouciant Hipster. The Quirky Matron's deliberately wacky coloured leather. The motorcycle-style Clubbing Doofus, with flashy, contrasting racing trim. The IT Goth's ankle-length trench coat.

Ultimately, I bought the least iconic style in the store. Hip-length, with a Peter Pan collar and puffed sleeves, its overt girliness offset the toughness of the black leather, maintaining the leather jacket's essential tensions while refusing the weight of its accumulated cultural connotations. In this jacket, I felt, I could be myself. I was wrong.

LUXURY AND GLAMOUR: LEATHER-CLAD FETISHISM Sharon Zukin's 2005 book *Point of Purchase: How Shopping Changed American Culture* devotes a chapter to following a 29-year-old New Yorker, Cindy, on her quest for 'the perfect pair of leather pants'. Over an entire year of combing department stores, upscale designer stores, small, hip boutiques, high-street chains and, finally, discount leathergoods merchants, Cindy refuses to compromise her vision of the high-waisted, straight-legged pants she wants. This makes the going tough—at the time, fashion favours low-waisted flares.

The leather-jacket buyer faces the same dilemma as Cindy. Despite their expense, leather jackets are still fashion items. They might fall hopelessly out of style before their owners have worn them enough to justify their cost. One way to circumvent this dreaded dagginess is by purchasing a 'classic' style that won't date as quickly. 'Leather is such a classic thing,' insists Cindy. Zukin initially treats this pronouncement with scepticism:

When I was her age, in my late twenties, I never thought that leather pants were classical. In those years, if you wore leather pants, especially black pants, people thought you were some sort of a sexual fetishist—or, at the very least, that you didn't mind being stared at for flaunting a well-honed pair of thighs. Recently, however, leather pants have changed their image. If you wear them with a cashmere turtleneck and a houndstooth jacket, they look simple, rich, and casual. They represent the 'classic' American sense of comfort with a materially satisfying life. (pp. 89–90)

Leaving aside the somewhat alarming sartorial spectacle conjured by Zukin, she does open some interesting possibilities by invoking leather's connotations of material satisfaction and success. What Cindy (and Zukin) really means by 'classic' is 'luxurious' and 'glamorous'.

Luxury involves an object or experience that isn't a necessity, but is intended only to bring pleasure, ease or comfort. Expense can make a leather jacket extravagant, but the way it delights the senses is what makes it luxurious. It's quite marvellous to consider that a purely utilitarian garment intended only to encase the body can also provide intense corporeal pleasure. Leather jackets feel wonderfully soft and supple to the touch; their scent is unmistakable and their subtle sheen echoes the sleekness of a well-fed, happy animal.

Leather is casual, too, because luxury is a feeling of leisure. As Gwen Stefani sings in 'Luxurious':

Working so hard every night and day
And now we get the pay back
Trying so hard, saving up the paper
Now we get to lay back

Here, luxurious things are simultaneously enabled by labour and relief from labour; they are inextricably linked with languid enjoyment and freedom from economic considerations. In this way, working enables the consumer to afford a leather jacket, which then casually advertises that its wearer doesn't need to work.

Glamour, meanwhile, has a contemporary meaning of mystery and allure, but in its original sense from the Scottish *gramarye*, glamour meant 'magic, enchantment'. In a pithy 1998 essay entitled 'Fetishizing the fetish', American sociologist Matt Wray argues that the attribution of some kind of magical power to a particular object is the most primitive and still most powerful meaning of fetishisation. It's this magic we invoke when we speak of finding 'the perfect' iteration of some garment that will somehow invest us with glamour. Cindy's obsessive, drawn-out search fetishises the leather pants she seeks, but the sex-fetish connotations of leather are a red herring here. Rather, Cindy's mythologised leather pants act as a receptacle for her dreams of being glamorous.

I wanted the luxury of a leather jacket that was pleasurable to wear, and in a dim, non-specific way I hoped it would enable me to become more glamorous. But I had never imagined this luxury and glamour to inhere in a particular 'perfect' leather jacket. With relative pragmatism I'd simply selected from the contents of a single shop, telling myself that it would be all right if it turned out to be a bad buy, because I hadn't invested too much of myself (or my money) in the purchase. But it turned out I was implicated, whether I liked it or not.

Wray argues that the media focus on the psycho-sexual dimension of fetishism has come to crowd out other ways of conceptualising the fetish—especially Karl Marx's critique of commodity fetishism. Whether it's because of the increased visibility of sex in official discourse, the cultural influence of psychoanalysis or the individualism that leads us to turn our erotic gaze on ourselves, he writes, holding up consumer goods as the solutions to our problems makes us 'lose sight of and forget the processes of exploitative production which create commodities in the first place'.

I still cringe when I remember the first time I wore my new leather jacket. At a friend's birthday party, I was chatting with Nathan, an acquaintance who runs an independent fashion label. Appraised by his industry-savvy eyes, I felt naked ... but not in the intimate sense of feeling comfortable in my 'second skin'. Rather, Nathan seemed instantly to recognise the scope of the disaster: the jacket's poor fit, low-quality leather, and design that, he noted, was a rip-off of some more reputable label whose name I instantly forgot in my shame.

As I turned away, crestfallen, Nathan tapped me on the shoulder and pointed out that I had forgotten to remove the protective tissue paper covering from two buttons on the back of the jacket. This is an act of fashion illiteracy right up there with not realising you can remove the 'Wool/Cashmere Blend' label on the sleeve of your new winter coat. Nathan made some throwaway remark about how it was important to give the kids in the Chinese factory something to do, and I felt like the worst kind of schmuck. I had squandered the indentured labour of Chinese teenagers on *this*.

Now my mistake had dawned on me, I re-enacted the purchase over and over in my head like some recurring nightmare. The insufficiency of my leather jacket had left conceptual room for that mythic 'perfect' jacket that I could still buy; this was retroactive fetishising. Eventually, I slunk back to the shop where I'd bought it, the offending jacket rolled into a ball and tucked under my arm so nobody could spot its telltale resemblance to its fellows on the racks. I'd bought my jacket on sale and considered it a bargain. But when I entered the shop, to my horror I noticed it had been reduced to half the price I paid.

In a frenzy of post-purchase dissonance, I contemplated buying the damn thing over again, getting it right this time. I tried on another jacket one size smaller. Yes, it did fit better. My jacket was still new enough to return to the shop. I could totally do this. But then a sick, heavy feeling of self-loathing seized me. What was the point? It seemed obscene to get so worked up over what was ultimately an unnecessary luxury.

In *Point of Purchase*, Zukin writes that the shopper's sense of shame surrounding their narcissistic quest is a *gendered* self-loathing:

> The more sophisticated and self-aware we [women] are, the more we try to distance ourselves from our urges for commodities—or even to laugh ironically about them. Deep within our belief in sexual equality lurks a severe distrust of our aesthetic urges—our unworthy urges for goods. (p. 91)

It's not as if women are the only ones to make ill-judged purchases. (My dad recently bought an electric warehouse pallet stacker. As far as I know, he doesn't spend time in anything resembling a warehouse.) But a female consumer must bear the moral as well as the intellectual weight of her buyer behaviour, struggling against the 'commonsensical' idea that her shopping is irrational and emotional. Yet the more she attempts to evaluate and justify her purchases, the more obsessive and fetishistic her behaviour seems. When purchase decisions fail, a woman is more likely to blame herself—and if her leather jacket was a bad purchase, she, by extension, is a Bad Leather Jacket Person.

Like a fairytale prince punished for hubris by being transformed into a hideous beast, I wear my leather jacket almost every day. But as I constantly remind myself, all is not lost. It's cold outside. My jacket is warm in winter.

CLANDESTINE COMMUNICATIONS: LETTERS BETWEEN FRIENDS

ANDREA GOLDSMITH REFLECTS ON THE ILLUSIONS AND PLEASURES OF LETTER-WRITING

A *T THE AGE OF TWENTY-ONE* I bought a cheap airline ticket and flew to London. I left behind the expectations of friends and family and an entrenched sense of duty. And I left behind a boyfriend—I'll call him Dave—a fellow who was well past his use-by date.

It was a particularly cold winter that year in London. Ice formed around the cracks in the window-pane of my room and I needed to dress for bed. I rationed the coins I put in the gas meter for the heat, I rationed my baths because of the rationed coins—and also because a bath shared by several strangers is not an attractive proposition to a compulsive cleaner. I sat alone in my room at the top of the house and as the weeks passed, Dave, the main reason why I left Australia, came to occupy the centre of my life.

Within a month my letters to Dave had become a daily occurrence and the high point of an otherwise skimpy existence. I managed to write him into a perfect presence and myself into a love to rival young Werther's. I wrote on Wedgwood-blue, onion-skin paper in a small and careful script. I loved the sponginess of the paper, the rise and fall of my pen riding the dimpled surface. Writing my letters was as physical as playing the piano, and sensual like Chopin or Scriabin or the second movement of the *Pathétique*. The more I wrote to Dave the less effort I made to meet people or find myself a proper job. By the end of the first month I had convinced myself that the main purpose of my London trip was not to further my career as a speech pathologist but to give myself time to write. So I instituted a tight budget and settled down to letter-writing and fiction. In retrospect they were much the same.

I wrote to Dave for hours every day, I wrote my feelings and most private of thoughts, I wrote my hopes and expectations. And as a 21-year-old idealist who desired nothing less than perfection, I wrote at length about my philosophy of life. And when I wasn't writing I read books of great loves: *The Sorrows of Young Werther*, *Women in Love*, *Portrait of a Lady*, *Anna Karenina* and *Madame Bovary*. I read as many Iris Murdochs as I could find in the second-hand bookshops of Charing Cross Road and all five of Doris Lessing's Martha Quest books.

Passion marked the fully lived life and I was awash with passion as I sat alone in my room reading great books and writing my letters. I wrote myself into a passionate future with Dave where Life was writ large and bursting with books and our two gifted children and the sorts of discussions that I imagined Jean-Paul Sartre had with Simone de Beauvoir, and Martha Quest had with whomever was sitting around her breakfast table. When I put my pen down I would imagine these conversations, I would actually speak them aloud as I sat alone in my freezing room at the top of the house.

As it happened, while I was writing my way into an idealised future with Dave, he was having it off with his very real and present biochemistry partner. Such a betrayal would never have occurred to me. My Dave was, after all, my creation, the product of my imagination, and my imagination was in service to me. It had no interest in the real world, it had no interest in the real Dave. Dave was simply a cipher in the life I longed to have.

And that is how it might have remained except my imaginings were made public in letters that were dispatched day after day across the world to a man who, being otherwise engaged, probably did not even bother to read them. When I returned home Dave was as he had always been, pompous and arrogant, smelling of Clearasil and Aramis, and far more interested in himself and his biochemistry partner than in me and my passions.

Since the debacle of Dave, I have been wary of correspondence with lovers and would-be lovers. The lover's imagination is a fool for romance. That personal, confidential and seductive first-person voice of letters—both one's own and one's beloved's—is irresistible. And the letter-writing lover, so fastidious when it comes to removing the soiled bits of self, is never less than fascinating and adorable. When it comes to a lover relationship, reality does not stand a chance against the imaginative possession of letters.

How different it is with letters between friends. The self-serving monologue of the distant lover becomes a conversation in a letter to a friend. It is as if the feelings of the distant lover become concentrated and caught in the fact of separation, while the feelings of the distant friend are far more dispersed, encompassing new places and people, fears and delights, risks and discoveries, and accompanied by a desire to share. A friend does not have to convince of her desirability as a friend, but the lover, particularly the new lover, is compelled to keep adding to her credentials. The friend being certain in the friendship can communicate and share, the lover whose position is a good deal more precarious has to show greater discretion. And the leisurely solitude of letter-writing so in thrall to the narcissism of the lover inspires the sort of reflection and intimacy that deepens real communication with a friend.

One of the two enduring correspondences of my life began in 1989 with a contemporary from my high school who moved permanently to London after matriculating. We were not particularly close at school. Only when I made contact with her many years later on a trip to London did our friendship begin, developed and enriched almost entirely by letters. F is a historian of the eighteenth century, a document scholar whose work takes her into the letters of the long-dead. When first I met her in London, apart from her struggles with British Rail—she lives in Kent and commutes daily—she might well have been living in the eighteenth century. The modern world was anathema to her and she preferred to let it pass her by. Consequently she was very thin—Sainsbury's was too severe a challenge for someone better equipped to deal with Queen Anne's kitchen.

I'd never known anyone like her. In her letters to me, long letters arriving every two to three weeks, she would write about her work, her views on human foibles, on the city and the countryside, on contemporary life. She had strong and critical opinions on everything from microwave ovens ('Unnecessary and unnatural') to sex ('Sex is not a twentieth century invention; the English court could have taught Freud a thing or two') and the increase of crime ('We live in a fallen world'). She revealed an existence that was foreign and fascinating, and through her letters she invited me in.

My own world view seemed so prosaic when compared with hers, but through her letters she convinced me otherwise. I was her intimate friend, she wrote, the only one she had. She once told me she knew immediately when one of my letters had arrived. There would be the sound of the letter slat opening in her front door and the slap of letters falling to the floor. 'Your letters fall with a unique sound,' she said.

Our correspondence continues to this day, although it is experiencing marked fatigue. While the incessant groan of maturity demands the quiet reflection of letters more than ever, after work, family, friends, a smorgasbord of entertainment, regular exercise and the infinite attractions of cyberspace, there's little time left for letters and even if there were, one is far too aroused for the calm, quiet stillness of letter-writing. Too often I resort to e-mail and cheap telephone calls—Skype is out of the question given that F's computer was purchased in the computer age's equivalent of the eighteenth century. But it is not the same. Our letters gave us a special entry into the other's life and thoughts, and much of the time I remained unaware of the ordinary vagaries of my friend's days as she remained ignorant of mine. But phone and e-mail love the quotidian, and the kitchen-sink narrative manages to insert itself even when you try to keep it out. These days when we communicate, F and I skim the wide surface of our lives; rare is the deep lunge that used to characterise our letters. And the friendship has changed. And yet on those rare occasions when I do write her a proper letter, the sense of an intimate and unique connection comes rushing back.

The other enduring correspondence was with Andrea Stretton, who died suddenly and far too young in November 2007. Over a period of fifteen years Andrea and I exchanged letters, although not regularly as I have with F. We wrote when there was confusion or emotional upheaval such as those long months in 2001 when Andrea's mother, Dulcie, and my father, Arthur, were seriously ill and dying. And Andrea, who knew so much more than I about the visual arts, would write to me about painters and sculptors. And often when stymied on my current novel I would write. Why might she want to read yet another novel that drew on the Holocaust? I once asked. And another time I wanted her views on novels peopled by strong and unlikeable characters. Andrea had an ancient wisdom and a staggeringly accurate intuition. Her letters would come to me, several pages of her large, neatly sprawling handwriting hurtling to the end of the line. The writing would become more energetic as the letter progressed, as she, Andrea, welled up like ink through the nib of a pen.

And I always wrote to Andrea when a novel was finished. She was one of my first readers. I have just finished my new novel, *Reunion*, and the pleasure is not the same without her.

Then there were our London letters. Both Andrea and I were unabashed Londonphiles. When Andrea launched my third novel I gave her an illustrated book of London I had discovered in a second-hand bookshop. It carried the best marks of age—no vegemite or red-wine stains, just a gentle dimming of the colours and print, a nice loosening of the binding, and the pepper and age smell of old paper. We both regarded it as a treasure. We loved London and whenever one of us was there we would write to the Andrea back home to include her in the wonders of the place. We always planned to enjoy London together one day.

My own handwriting, although neat and even on the page, is difficult to read. I try to make it legible—I consider it an act of hostility to send hard-to-read handwriting to anyone but a sworn enemy. Andrea loved my letters—which I regarded as evidence that she loved me. She treated them like a long slow meal, she said, taking particular pleasure in deciphering the hard-to-read words.

During the brief illness that preceded her death, Andrea asked that friends of hers not living in Sydney write to her. I had flown to Africa just prior to her diagnosis and I arrived home the week after her death; I did not even know she was sick. But had I known I would have written her a letter that took us to London on the trip we never made, that had us walking the Bloomsbury streets together, searching out the blue plaques on the houses of our favourite writers and thinkers, having a sandwich lunch in the garden squares where Virginia and Leonard walked their dogs. I would have written us strolling through Regent's Park and Kew Gardens, and tramping across the heath to Keats' house to read 'Ode to a Nightingale' under the plum tree in the garden—not the same tree under which he composed the poem, but a very good likeness. And off to the Courtauld to view our favourite Kokoschkas, then to the NPG and the National Gallery, and a day wandering through the smaller galleries in Soho. And to the theatre in the West End, and other productions in hard-to-find locations and later the two of us standing on the platform of an otherwise deserted tube station talking, always talking while we waited for the last train to whisk us home. I would have written us at concerts at the Barbican and the Victoria and Albert Hall and a special exhibition of bibliophilia at the London Library. In my last letter to Andrea we would have made the trip to London we had always promised ourselves.

Writing letters is a means of discovery. Writing letters is always a writing down into the self at the same time as it is a writing to the outer other.

Writing letters is to oppose forgetting. You write into memory, stamp and engrave it, and then send it to someone else for acknowledgement and safe keeping. Every letter reminds: *I am alive*.

Writing letters is intimate, just between me and you. And handwriting—always idiosyncratic, spontaneous, the personal and revealing fingerprints of a valued friend. Every letter proclaims: *I appreciate you*.

And letters with their resonant first-person perspective are authoritative. Saul Bellow begins his great novel *Herzog* with Moses Herzog alone in the countryside deserted by his second wife, who has run off with his best friend. Herzog is wallowing in squalor and writing letters to people known and unknown, from dear dead Mama to dear living Mr President:

> *Dear Mr. President, Internal Revenue regulations will turn us into a nation of book-keepers. The life of every citizen is becoming a business. This, it seems to me, is one of the worst interpretations of the meaning of human life history has ever seen. Man's life is not a business.*

Herzog is telling the president how it is. Herzog is all-powerful in his letters while the rest of his life is running amok. He is writing letters as a means of convincing himself he is not wasting his life. He is writing letters in order to avoid taking other more difficult but ultimately more constructive action. He is writing letters while time rolls forward without him. In this sense his letters are not unlike those I wrote to Dave.

Life hurtles along with work, family, friends, meals, travel, movies, concerts, the theatre, a rally in Fed Square. Texting, e-mail, blogging, telephoning and online chat fit so much better with the hectic pace of contemporary life than the long, slow absorption of letter-writing. These days if people want to plunge deeply into the self they go to a therapist; as for plunging deeply into another, in an ethos where the immediate gratification of self dominates, this is not a common desire. Rather than fill an hour or two with writing a letter, we would prefer to fit three or four activities into the available time. Letter-writing conjures up processes such as stewing, fermenting and brewing, and a languid and mellow atmosphere. Letter-writing is communication's equivalent of 'slow cooking' and few see the point of it any more.

As letter-writing is confined to the storehouse of history along with illuminated manuscripts and sewing by hand, more is lost than the actual physical object. A way to deeper self-knowledge, an occasion to rummage around in the imagination, an opportunity to refine thoughts and ideas, and a way of privately and significantly connecting with someone else. I don't want to give up e-mail or texting or the telephone, but I want the full immersion of letter-writing as well.

And I want to go to the letterbox and find among the mail an envelope with my name and address in a handwriting I recognise. I want to see the familiar scrawl of sender details on the back flap, to feel the squish of several sheets of paper, to acknowledge that thump of anticipation as I walk inside. I want the lovely ritual of withdrawing to a comfy chair with a fresh mug of coffee and my letter, reading through at first quickly and then more slowly, savouring the burn of just me with my friend and nothing to intrude on our clandestine and highly charged tryst. And later slipping the letter into my wallet so that as I ride the tram and shop for dinner and attend meetings, I feel through the presence of the letter the real presence of my absent friend.

And I want the pleasure of responding, when alone with my own thoughts and with no barriers to imagination, to memory, to secret hopes and pungent yearnings a voice from my own deep consciousness becomes ever more audible. An hour or two with no-one looking over my shoulder, no-one to restrain my arm as it moves across the page, nothing and no-one to temper my thoughts and desires as I communicate to another person in that intimate and confidential way which is the special province of letters, and in that act letting them know they matter even though they are far from my everyday life.

In the latter part of the nineteenth century in the port of Shanghai a man boarded a boat bound for California. He carried with him a valise of handwritten letters. He was an amanuensis. For several months he had visited the homes of people whose relatives had emigrated to America. While he transcribed, brothers and fathers and sisters and mothers told their stories and revealed their private thoughts and vented their love and loneliness. Months later, in homes across the state of California he read the letters aloud to homesick Chinese families. He would answer their questions and transcribe their replies and later, with his valise again full, he would board the ship for China. This guardian of letters, a true memory-keeper, travelled back and forth between Shanghai and San Francisco several times over two decades. Each round trip took about a year.

COOK-TOWN'S SECOND COMING

JOHN VAN TIGGELEN on a flock of bird watchers

Around lunchtime on Valentine's Day this year, a stooped, balding, bushy-browed chap named Traj drove from his house at one end of Cooktown's main street to park under the mango tree at the other, down at the wharf. Traj lives in the scrub with three cats, three dogs and the ailing Mishka, whom he nurses with daily ministrations of oats, cuddles and flyspray. Mishka is forty-two, which is very old for a horse. Although Traj, short for Tragedy, was given his nickname forty years ago because of his real name, John Kennedy, it seems to have stuck to him for all the sad, disaffecting reasons that see a lot of lonely men drift north, far north, to Cooktown.

Valentine's Day waxed hot and heavy. During the torpor of the Wet, swinging by the wharf is a Cooktown custom; everyone likes to 'do a wharfie' because it's something to do, and there's a chance of a breeze. Also at the mouth of the Endeavour River that Thursday was a group of orange-vested council workers on their lunch break, eating fish and chips under the mango tree and surrounded by a small flock of expectant gulls. As Traj got out of his car, he followed the men's gaze to where some gulls were dive-bombing another sitting on a lamppost. It was a paler, much bigger gull.

A chip poked from its massive black bill.

'Holy Jesus, have a look at the size of that!' Traj said. But then the men already were. Big critters have always been appreciated in tiny Cooktown. Big pythons, big crocs, big groupers, giant geckos and big cats—panthers mostly, but locals say there are sandy-coloured mountain lions out there, too. Traj himself has seen a big cat, 'black as a billy-goat's arsehole', as have several of the lunching workers on the wharf. But no-one had ever seen a big gull.

Traj and the orange men conferred briefly. The verdict was unanimous: the gull was a) big, b) hungry and c) 'not one of ours'. Traj is Cooktown's wharfinger, aggrandised in the local manner to harbourmaster. As the collector of mooring fees, Traj felt the newcomer was his responsibility. He scuttled off to the parks and wildlife office about fifty metres away, next to the fish-and-chip shop, to tell the ranger. 'There's a giant gull down there,' he said, pointing. 'It's panting a lot and looks hot and bothered. I reckon it might be from Antarctica. Or Tasmania.'

The ranger promptly took some pictures and e-mailed them to head office in Brisbane. No-one down there had a clue. Ornithologists were consulted but they, too, were stumped. It was an adolescent gull in winter plumage, they surmised, from the Northern Hemisphere. One thought it might be from Alaska. At twelve minutes to midday the next day, a Friday, as the gull was guzzling its second labourer's lunch of chips and batter, the following e-mail appeared on a national newsletter of 'hot' bird sightings: 'There is a juvenile gull *new* to *Australia* at the Cooktown wharf *now*.'

To twitchers, a subgroup of bird watchers who are obsessed with the length of their species lists, the report was the ultimate come-on. Within minutes grown men were calling sickies, googling gulls, standing up loved ones for the weekend, booking flights to Cairns as well as hire-cars for the four-hour drive from Cairns to Cooktown. It didn't matter that no-one knew what species it was; that could be sorted out later. The main thing was that it was entirely 'tickable'—of the four or five species in the running, none had been seen in Australia before.

The first twitcher, from Newcastle, arrived in Cooktown that very night, at three a.m., having braved flooded causeways and 200 kilometres of unfenced road through pitch-black cattle country. He stayed till lunch. Half a dozen twitchers followed over the weekend, and scores more in the next fortnight, from as far as Adelaide, Melbourne and Perth. The first Big Twitch of 2008, as bird nerds knew it, represented an off-season tourism boom for Cooktown's barrel-scraping restaurateurs and guesthouse operators. 'I call it the Big Wharfie,' says Rex Button, who, from his Cook's Landing Kiosk, observed about one hundred 'twitchy types' swinging by the mango tree. 'That gull's been very good for business. For next year, I'm thinking I might bring out a penguin.'

O utside the suddenly confluent spheres of Traj and bird tragics, the arrival of the gull went unheralded. Living in Cairns, the first I heard of it was five weeks later when a friend from Hobart rang to ask if I felt like a trip to Cooktown. Angus being Angus, I guessed instantly there were birds involved, but he was coy about the gull. In the twenty years I'd known him, Angus, a fisheries biologist, had made a concerted effort to temper his twitching tendencies. 'I just like to watch,' was his line. It was my line, too. But I knew he maintained lists. I knew he consorted with other bird nerds. And I knew he went on 'seabirding' trips, where birders hire a cray boat and head into the wild blue yonder in the hope of adding oceanic species to their terrestrial tally. The biggest giveaway to Angus's urges, however, was the vehemence with which he repressed them. 'Twitchers are gung-ho, like hunters,' he used to tell me. 'It's a macho thing. For them it's all about the chase and the competition, and not about the bird.'

I've argued this point with Angus. The twitchers I know—all right, I've done a little consorting in my day, too—are nothing like hunters I've met. Twitchers are unnerving in a different way. Like train-spotters, or teaspoon collectors, the base instinct manifesting itself isn't hunting but gathering. Even so, it's still not about the bird.

I told Angus I had a free weekend in a fortnight. There was a long pause. 'That's too late,' he said. 'I need to go *now*.'

Then it all came out. About the gull; how he'd itched to join the Big Twitch but had held himself back; how the gull didn't seem to be going anywhere; and how the longer it hung around, the more he longed to tick it. Almost every day for the past month he'd gone online to check for updates, potential flights and fresh gull pictures. He was losing sleep over it, he said.

'Angus, it's okay,' I said. 'Give in and come out. Stop living in denial. You'll feel much better.'

'All right,' he said. 'I've relapsed. I'm a twitcher. I'm a hunter.'

'Gatherer.'

'Hunter.'

'So you really just want to "tick" this gull?'

'Yes.'

'You don't care how it got here?'

'No.'

'You don't care that it is young and lost and lonely and probably being picked on by local gulls?'

'Definitely not.'

Two days later, a new, out-and-proud Angus arrived in Cairns. On the brief walk from the plane's steps to the airport hall, he brandished his binoculars to twitch a crimson finch on the grass by the tarmac. Lugging the bag with his telescope and other twitching paraphernalia through the car park, he rubbernecked shamelessly at anything winging overhead. The man was giddy with possibility. He had vague plans to stay a week but told me this would depend on the execution of his twitching strategy—he'd compiled a target list of species and mapped their likely haunts. Birding intelligence is highly specific: Angus was to find the rare blue-faced parrotfinch, for instance, in the very trees by the very clearing along the very mountain track where he'd been told to look for it. Twitchers neither amble nor go sightseeing; they march and they tick. *Veni vidi tici*, goes one tragic's motto. And so the new Angus and I hightailed it to Cooktown.

B y this stage Traj, who does up to ten wharfies a day, had seen the gull every single day for almost six weeks. Initially it looked tired and off-colour, but its diet of greasy chips, battered fish and fried chicken seemed to fortify it. The other, smaller, gulls soon learnt to keep a respectful distance. 'Whenever someone sat down with their tucker, it would come hurtling in to send the other gulls packing,' says Traj. 'They wanted no part of this bastard.'

The gull quickly developed a routine. It roosted on a nearby lamppost, breakfasted on crumbs at the nearby Cook's Landing Kiosk and then hung out at the wharf, where fishermen might toss it leftover bait. People grew rather fond of it. The bird reminded them of a huge groper called Barney, who, until his mysterious death a few years ago, also used to alternate between the wharf and kiosk, forever getting hooked and released, feeding off scraps and even rolling over in the shallows to allow Rex Button, the kiosk owner, to clean the algae off his belly with a broom.

Jack Degney, a kiosk regular who lives on the river, recalls how Barney was hooked by an English tourist. 'He was jubilant, shouting, "Check it out, man. Check it out!" So four locals went over and said, "Mate, you're going to let him go, aren't you?" He said, "No way." They said, "Mate, you are." Then they decked him.'

Degney says the gull can expect similar protection. 'It's our gull now, so we'll look after it.' Traj is doing his bit: 'She worried me at first, I must admit. The birdos said she was the rarest bird in Australia, and here she was toddling across the road to get a drink of water from a puddle after people had been feeding it salty chips. Some of the locals roar along here. A couple of times I had to gee her along so she wouldn't get run over.'

Traj followed the debate about the gull's identification with interest. In the first week, each of Australia's top five twitchers (it was their 802nd, 776th, 768th, 767th and 756th bird respectively) came to tick it, yet it would be another week before they knew what they'd ticked. At the time they wrongly told Traj it was a Mongolian gull, a form of the Eastern Siberian gull. One of them let Traj look through his telephoto lens. 'That lens must have been two foot long. Christ almighty, it could have bought a bloody four-wheel-drive. But still they couldn't tell what gull it was.'

The final identification had to be left to experts based in Norway, England, the United States, Japan and Hong Kong, working from detailed photos. They determined—though not unanimously—that it was a young, female Slaty-Backed Gull, which breeds in Siberia and winters in Japan, Korea and China. The poor thing must have ridden every storm and boat going to get past Taiwan, through the Phillipines, across the Equator and around Papua New Guinea. Global warming may or may not have been a factor: on the one hand, the warmer it gets, the less far a bird should need to migrate in winter; on the other, global warming may mean global storming. Regardless, some Cooktowners don't buy it. They prefer a local theory that the gull is a mutant bird that landed in toxic waste at the local dump. 'The government knows this,' a man who performs his wharfies on a yellow scooter told me. 'All this stuff about it being from Manchuria is just a cover-up.'

As we neared Cooktown, Angus became jittery. He'd stocked up for the trip with a bag of crystallised ginger sweets, which he'd decided tasted like toilet cleaner, yet now he was chain-munching them.

We sped past waterlily lagoons, melaleuca-lined rivers and magnificent lookouts. Whenever I slowed down to take in a view, such as of the Annan River Gorge or the other-worldly Black Mountains, which appear to consist solely of black boulders, Angus would stare ahead stonily and say, 'The gull, the gull.'

We drove unseeing down Cooktown's picturesque main street. The Endeavour River lay glinting in the sun. At the wharf, a team of men was replacing the decking timbers. Their machines were very noisy. No-one was fishing. No-one sat under the mango tree. And there was no gull.

Angus leapt out of the car and made for a small jetty. He peered up the river, down, and across to the other side. Still no gull. In the water below us swam a school of fat mullet and some slender garfish. A large yellow-banded batfish lurked beside a weedy buoy rope. I pointed it out to Angus. 'Fish shmish,' he muttered. 'Stop trying to distract me.'

I left Angus at the river's edge, next to a crocodile warning sign. At the fish-and-chipper I was told the gull had been sitting on the adjacent lamppost that morning. The post was covered in guano. Further up, at the river kiosk, Rex Button said he'd fed the gull just hours before. 'He's a beaut bird, twice the size of anything else. You can't miss him. He likes it here; he's not going anywhere.'

I went looking for Angus to let him know the gull was around. I found him in the mangroves, being attacked by sandflies (midges). He was grumpy, and suspicious. 'These people run tourist businesses,' he said. 'Of course they're going to say the gull is here.'

We hailed a very hairy man doing a wharfie in a rickety ute. 'I haven't seen the gull in three days, not since the weather fined up,' he said. 'I'd say it might have pissed off. But if you're into birds, look behind you. That sea-eagle just plucked a fish from the river. Beautiful, that is.'

Angus did not give it a second glance. An hour later, we returned for a second wharfie. Still no gull, though the *Cooktown Local News* was chuffed to spot Angus, bedecked as he was in his khaki gear, floppy hat, telescope, waterbag and binoculars. 'We've been meaning to snap one of you twitchers for ages,' said the paper's reporter, Sarah Martin. (Angus made that week's front page.)

On our third and final wharfie we were in luck, sort of. Angus had spotted a dot on a distant sandbank that appeared larger than several surrounding dots. He set up his telescope, leant down and, 'Yes! Yes! Yes! Hel-lo Miss Slaty-back!'

He let me look. It was a gull all right, preening itself. It was pale and motley, not slaty-backed at all, because Miss Slaty-back was in winter smock. I was underwhelmed. As Great Moments in Natural History went, it needed a crocodile to rear up from the river and snatch it. But Angus was deeply, deeply satisfied. 'It's a tick,' he said. 'A very "speccy" tick. That bird is hot, hot, hot.'

NOTE

The Slaty-Backed Gull stayed in Cooktown for forty-nine days—one more day than Captain James Cook did when repairing his ship from reef damage in 1770. No-one knows where it has gone.

MOT-ION SICK-NESS

CAROL CHAN finds herself torn between two cities and two cultures

The road to where I live is long. To get there I must pass through a small, quiet playground from the bus stop, a little alley along a drain, and traverse two smaller housing estates.

At the bus stop, I felt impatient, though I was not in a hurry. A little girl chewed on a sugared doughnut, and her grandmother carried her furry schoolbag while stroking her hair. A young schoolboy ran out into the middle of the road, and yelled to his mother, 'Ma-mee! No car!' He ran back to the bus stop and flashed us all a cheeky grin. A boy had died a few years ago along this very road: he had been jaywalking. The mother looked weary and dishevelled as her son ran back onto the main road and waved his arms in glee.

'You want to die, is it? Get back here!' his mother yelled. 'I didn't buy insurance, you know!'

I wondered if I could somehow insure my body against its reactions to moving away from Singapore and then returning. It was reacting in strange ways: I felt dizzy, nauseated, on the verge of a potent fever. I could be on a Mass Rapid Transport train, and the speed would send my head spinning. The shopping centres made me claustrophobic; sometimes, even my favourite foods at *kopitiams* (coffee shops) made me sick to the stomach. Walking around Ang Mo Kio central or Orchard Road made my head hot and my mind a blank. Though restless, I felt drained of energy and grew attached to longer hours of sleep. There might be an injection for this homecoming sickness. If we could pop anti-malaria tablets to build up our immune system against the disease before we set off on our tropical vacations, I was positive there must be some sort of pill I could take for this sense of displacement.

At first I thought it must be the weather: I was very warm but unable to perspire. My body could not expel the heat trapped within, and it felt stifling. It made me think of fish swimming inside a very small jar of murky water. It was understandable that my body sensed I was back in Singapore: I was eating different foods now. *Meepok* (noodles) instead of cereal for breakfast; *zi char* (rice with side dishes) and not canned tuna for lunch. Even coffee and tea were different: *kopi* had the sweet smell and comfort taste of condensed milk; *teh tarik* (tea made with condensed milk) was 'pulled' to froth cup by cup instead of relying on a barista's steaming wand. My skin used to peel and crack in the dry Australian air, but was now healthily moist in Singapore's humidity.

Places smelled addictively the same and reminded my body where I was, lest I forgot: the small grocer's shop in my neighbourhood smelled of fresh local *kaya* bread and glossy magazines; the MRT carriages smelled of mixed perfume, perspiration, take-away hawker food and the tropical rain. I soon found myself humming to songs that used to haunt my childhood in Singapore: from Faye Wong to Bananarama's 'Guilty', to the score from *Les Miserables*, which my mother always played in the car.

I took a taxi to the doctor's the next day.

I used to take the trams or walk everywhere in Melbourne city. Everything seemed so close and accessible. Here, I had become dependent on taxis, being somehow too impatient for the already efficient buses and trains. I had also developed a fear of buses and trains. It was inexplicable how I often found myself on the wrong MRT line, heading in the direction that propelled me further from my destination. For some time I felt that the bus company had a conspiracy against me: they redirected my familiar bus route one week without my knowledge. I ended up waiting for the same bus no. 70 for an hour, thinking: I got stood up by a bus.

As I was being driven around the city-island, I begun to notice how green the roads were, and how they resembled a jungle of sorts. The island was littered with huge rainforest trees and palm trees that hid the people from the sky, or rather, the sky from its people.

'Go where?' asked my driver.

The car radio was tuned to Gold 90FM, which played oldies. Singapore had an old soul but a new, botoxed face. She was keeping up with the times, eager to be like her peers who were forward-looking. But, as a columnist in the daily paper ironically or aptly named *Today* observed, Singapore really belongs to the 1980s. Wednesday nights are ladies' nights, when the nightclub Zouk is most packed due to the popularity of its 'Mambo' nights where people of all ages groove enthusiastically to corny disco music. It is silly, fun and, above all, liberating to live in the past so wholly and loudly. Shopping malls and hotel lobbies play heartbreaking love songs from the eighties and early nineties. Singapore must come across as being heartbroken and rejected, a pining lover.

'So-and-so clinic, please, uncle,' I said.

'We don't go by CTE, okay? They've got ERP,' he explained.

'Okay, but quickly.' I haven't learned to drive, and didn't know much about highways, except that they were designed so people could get to where they were headed more quickly. The irony was that highways in cities were mostly jammed with too many people heading in the same direction.

'Miss, you got visit the museum or not?'

'Which one?' For a small, young country in its mid forties, we had too many museums. It made us seem sentimental, nostalgic, with a penchant for all things historic and ancient. The truth, however, was that we had fallen in love with the future, and needed to tuck the past away in storage, in order to make space for the new.

'The new one, national museum ah.'

'Oh, the one near Plaza Singapura.'

'Ya, very interesting, have one exhibition on old hawker food, like *kok-kok mee*.'

I thought of my grandmother, who had called me the day I landed, and insisted on making traditional Chinese *soon kuehs* for me: steamed rice cakes filled with radish and minced meat. I did not have the heart to tell her that I had never liked these *kuehs*, would rather eat an egg sandwich; also, that I no longer ate meat.

Later, the doctor enquired about my discomfort. He took my heart rate.

'I've got a sore throat, think it's going to get worse.'

'Open your mouth and say "Ah",' he said.

I did as he asked. 'Ahhhh! It hurts when I speak.'

'Then don't talk so much the next few days, okay?'

That was not going to be difficult. While at the university in Melbourne I often had to search excruciatingly for things to say. It was strange: in a foreign country, I felt alienated from my body and mind. In the mirror, I looked slightly deformed, or not as I'd remembered; I could not think as I used to, thoughts did not come as easily, and I was less certain of my views and beliefs. As the good doctor scribbled instructions for the nurses who were waiting outside, I told him about my giddy spells. 'I often feel like I need to puke, too.'

'Nothing very serious,' he assured me, smiling. 'Just a period of adjustment. Must be the weather. Now I'll just give you some pills to reduce the nausea.'

'These will cause you to feel drowsy,' the nurse at the counter later warned me. Oh no, I thought, I'm sleepy enough as it is. But I did as I was told, and slept the following week away. Each time I awoke, I felt like Rip Van Winkle, as if I'd slept for years and years, and forgot my dreams in deep slumber.

The time had come for me to meet my relatives after a year's absence. I had postponed this visit for too long; my strange illness would not go down well as an excuse this time. I arrived at my aunt's place, where the extended family gathered. Each relative took my hand and gave me an overall evaluation, a family report-card.

'Your face is a bit chubbier, but your body's the same. You look healthy. Good!' said the oldest uncle, my mother's brother.

'You haven't lost weight,' mused the youngest aunt aloud suddenly, while we were in the middle of a group discussion. Then she added quickly, 'But you haven't gained weight either, I mean.'

'I thought you would gain weight!' exclaimed another. 'You're still the same, hor.'

I squirmed under their scrutiny, and quickly felt an eating disorder develop in those few hellish minutes. My mother was obsessed with the weight of things, from herself, to vegetables and meat, to porcelain bowls and packed suitcases. So were the rest of my relatives obsessed—and, it seemed, the rest of the people strutting along Orchard Road.

'Got miss Singapore or not?' Everyone asked. 'Got, right? Surely.' When I was young, my mother used to whack us lightly on the head for saying 'got' instead of 'have'. She would then tease, 'Got, got, God in heaven la!' Despite that she still used 'got' in place of 'have'. It was the linguistic rule here: things were not to be had, but gotten, achieved.

'*Zeh zeh*, I topped my class in English this year you know,' my eight-year-old cousin boasted. I used to tutor her before leaving for Melbourne, teaching her to tell the time and reading her tales of *The Magic Faraway Tree*. I tried to lead her into strange lands of dreams where the folk traded in sweets and tricks instead of grades and coins, but still she chose to climb back down the tree to the world she grew up in.

'I topped my class in English this year,' she now addressed her cousin who was the same age but in a different school. 'What subject did you top the class in?'

That girl was swinging in the playground, upside down, with her long hair touching the man-made sand in the pit as she swung up and down. 'Nothing,' she said nonchalantly.

'*Jie jie*, I know how to play *Für Elise* on the piano now. And I'm teaching *kor kor* too,' this girl turned to tell me.

'Really, that's nice,' I said.

'Ya, the pop version,' she informed me, in case I had something else in mind.

Later, the cousins all sat around playing cards, the game of bluff. We were not playing by the rules and the boys were, as usual, taking the opportunity to tease the youngest boy.

'Lex, it's your turn, oi, Lex!'

'Who's Lex?' I asked, puzzled.

'Oh, that's his new name,' one of them told me, pointing to a cousin whose hair was shaped like a sixties Beatle's.

'Ya, didn't you know? He gave himself that name.' Another whispered loudly: 'At his age, who would want to be known by a Chinese name? His friends and teachers call him that.' All the cousins laughed; they called him Lex only in jest, because to them he was always Wei Sheng.

An uncle interrupted our game to talk to me. 'Got miss Singapore or not?'

I suppose I had. Singapore had undergone yet another facelift, and my sister had to translate many new abbreviations (KPE: new highway) and names (Central: new shopping centre). She took me on a mini-tour around our familiar haunts.

'New Starbucks coming up there,' she said as she pointed. 'Thai Express has come here too.'

'Oh! That has replaced the old Japanese sushi counter!' I exclaimed.

'Really? I don't remember.' She frowned slightly. 'Anyway . . .'

I had missed it, of course, felt its lack and absence, and longed for the humidity and company. Everything was the same about this country: she was still so eager to please, and so conscious of her youth. Yet it also felt like I might have missed the point, failed to perceive this country accurately somehow. And why did I feel so out of place, so restless, so bored, so nauseated and constantly sleepy?

'The National Stadium has also been torn down, you know, right?' my sister reminded me. 'They held a farewell ceremony . . .'

We passed the new National Museum. Its new slogan asked me, 'How would you like to be remembered?' I wasn't sure about that; I would be glad if I could only protect myself from forgetting. I made a mental note to ask the pharmacist about that.

'Look! Pass me your camera. I've been meaning to take a picture of the Singapore Flyer ...' my sister exclaimed. That was the London Eye of Singapore, a giant Ferris wheel that went round and round as people watched the other people of the city in boredom. As the taxi passed it by, I felt dizzy again.

Then it hit me: I was now a stranger in two lands; Paul Theroux once warned that it was a result of being away. I felt like a traitor when my thoughts wandered to Melbourne: I found myself missing the things that endeared me to the place—the quirky dress sense, the tram bells, even the piercing Melbourne sun. I then set myself a task: to remember all the things I loved about my country. They might have slipped my mind. She was not to blame; I was. After all, it was not uncommon for things to go missing when one was in the process of moving.

WHEN HORSE BECAME SAW

ANTHONY MACRIS DESCRIBES THE EXPERIENCE OF DISCOVERING THAT HIS SON HAS AUTISM

A*LEX STOOD IN THE MIDDLE OF THE LIVING ROOM*, his toddler's small fingers firmly wedged around the stomach of a toy lobster half his size, its soft, transparent plastic an iridescent orange. As he squeezed the stomach its large claws, weighed down with last night's bathwater, swayed somewhat menacingly, but he took no notice; he was intent on getting it to squeak. Despite his best efforts, it refused: the squeaker had gone silent. He looked over at us, clearly frustrated, and clearly wanting us to do something about it.

Kathy and I were, or course, fiercely proud of him, and reserved the right of all parents, and especially first-time parents, to claim that he was the most beautiful, intelligent and vibrant child in the world.

Development: raising a child was all about development. Gross motor, fine motor, sensory, cognitive, social and emotional: these terms flooded into our lives moments after our first son, Alex, was born, and they fascinated me. A budding human being was a creature teeming with life, with potential. There was so much to nurture, to foster, so much satisfaction to be gained from watching Alex grow and evolve. Yet even if a human being was programmed to develop, this didn't necessarily mean they would. They needed the right conditions. They needed loving parents, stability; they needed a watchful eye, a firm hand when required, or a delicate touch. This was where the challenge and achievement lay: in taking responsibility for the creation of a happy, capable, useful human being. And this was where I felt I was doing something more important and rewarding than I had ever done before.

It's one thing to fully embrace the responsibility of raising a child, but it's quite another to pull it off. As a first-time father I was full of enthusiasm, but without any experience. Kathy, as the eldest of seven brothers and sisters, knew a lot more, but there were things she couldn't quite remember. A major source of help came in the form of one of those parenting guides the size of a house-brick that fill our major bookstores. We'd been prompted to buy one after Kathy and I had had a disagreement over some matter that had escalated into an argument way out of proportion to the problem itself, and which had largely been created by our unwillingness to admit we didn't really know the answer. The book soon became a useful tool that took the sting out of many of our disputes, and turned them into discussions. How long should a baby sleep at six months, at nine months, at twelve months? I had no idea, and Kathy wasn't sure. How high should we let a fever go before taking him to the doctor? We didn't have a clue. The Baby Bible, as it came to be known, gave us basic information we could work with.

It also contained the lists of milestones, the things your child should be doing at any given age. In the evening after dinnertime, Kathy and I would sit on the sofa,

Alex nestled between us, and go through the lists. At twelve months could your child 'cruise'? Cruise? He had already been walking for three months! Could he use his fingers in pincer movement? Alex could remove the tiniest sultana from his cereal with the most dextrous fine-motor movement imaginable. Did he understand, and use, the word 'no'? Of course he could. The very questions were an insult! List after list, at twelve months, at fifteen months, it was clear he was above average. How many words did he have? This would regularly end up in a debate between Kathy and myself. It was clear he had 50 per cent more than the average, but this was not good enough for me. Surely there were more? I'd elicit words I thought he might be able to form, and count them: close enough was good enough. Why couldn't we count 'kah' as computer? Kathy was somewhat more realistic in her estimates, and was also keen to put a stop to what was becoming the kind of mixture of smugness we all know and find so insufferable in parents who think their child may be 'gifted'.

Alex grew, and every day Kathy and I loved him more. It was strange, this new love that seemed to have no limit. It was a love totally different to anything that we had experienced before, and required some recalibration of our feelings towards one another. Before Alex, we lived the cult of the couple, with all its emphasis on personal and mutual fulfilment. But we were no longer a dyad: now we were a collective, one of the smallest that could be imagined, true, but one that called for a whole new approach to our lives.

Once I realised I had these feelings, I was quite stunned by them. They represented a complete reversal of everything I had felt before. The cool rationality towards my most basic feelings that I prided myself on cultivating in my twenties and thirties evaporated. The love Alex had brought with him, this collective love that was very specifically situated in its own three-part system, was breaking me down, eroding my previous independence and individuality. It confused me, this new love that Alex had created. In any given week, on any given day, it scared me, sustained me, entrapped me and liberated me. But one thing at least was clear. I couldn't conceive of life without Alex. If anything were to happen to him, if he were no longer to exist, my life would be unrecognisable to me.

When Alex was around sixteen months old he was given a large, purple plastic crocodile with a xylophone embedded in its back. One mid-afternoon I unwrapped it for him in his bedroom.

The instruction leaflet included a diagram to assist small children and musically illiterate adults (I was one of them) to play 'Twinkle Twinkle Little Star'. It was a song Alex knew well and, following the colour chart, I banged out a passable version for his benefit. Alex listened to a couple of notes, giggled distractedly, then twirled in a circle. This behaviour had been creeping in for some time, but it was not yet consistent. And on this occasion, as on others, I put it down to tiredness: after all, it would be time for his afternoon nap soon. But then he did something that disturbed me. His gaze still somewhere else entirely, he twirled around, picked up the crocodile and, for no apparent reason, hurled it into space. It hit the wall, tearing the wallpaper and dislodging a small piece of plaster. Throwing a toy is something any young child might have done. But there was something very odd about they way Alex did it, and I was too surprised to admonish him. It was as if he did not recognise that it was a toy at all. The object seemed to puzzle him. What was it for?

It made noise. Why did it make noise? What was the noise for? The throwing of it seemed a reaction to this incomprehension, an underlying frustration.

But if he was frustrated, it was only momentarily. I looked over at him to where he was sitting on his bed, flicking through a Winnie the Pooh book. The crocodile seemed to have passed in and out of his world in a split second, utterly forgotten where it lay on its side in the corner, its jaws wide open. It was if it had never existed.

I sat next to him and asked him to pick up the crocodile and put it away. He didn't even look up at me. His gaze was fixed on an illustration of Winnie the Pooh's backside, the rest of him stuck in a honey jar. I asked him again, somewhat sharply.

'Alex, get up, please, and put the crocodile in your toy box.'

At the sound of his name he looked up at me. But his gaze seemed to skitter across mine, as if he wanted to avoid the moment of direct eye contact at all costs, as if it were somehow too much for him.

I picked up the crocodile, put it in the box and left the room.

It was a couple of days later, a Saturday night, and Kathy and I were on the sofa watching television, the volume turned down low. We had put Alex to bed ten minutes earlier, but we knew he wasn't asleep; we could hear him twisting and turning. A thump on the carpet, the scuffing of feet. Wearing only a singlet and a nappy, Alex shuffled into the living room, his eyes pink-rimmed and his face a little puffy. He was smiling and I noticed that his smile was strangely blank, glazed and intense. People can often look very different when they're emerging from deep sleep, and there's always a small shock that comes with seeing the recognisable altered in any way, no matter how fleeting. But this was different. There was a disturbing edge to his smile, as if he had become altered from within.

His behaviour became stranger still. He came to a dead standstill in the middle of the room, then planted his feet on the floor. He paused for a split second, the kind of pause that occurred before a sneeze. Suddenly, he raised himself up on his toes as if some outside force were lifting him. And then it hit him. A wave of sensation coursed through his entire body, a wave that completely exhilarated him. His small limbs trembled with excitement, his face lit up in an expression that verged on the ecstatic, he made whooping noises of nearly uncontrolled delight. He giggled and resumed his toe walk for a little while. And then it was all over. The curiously blank enigmatic smile returned for a while, then lapsed into a glazed torpor. He yawned. He was very tired.

It was at this point that there was a shift in my degree of worry. My suspicion turned to something much more unsettling, something much more concrete. Only later would I realise that it was fear, the deepest fear I had ever known. It tiptoed to the edge of my conscious mind and sat there, watching, waiting for my concerns to be either proved or disproved.

Kathy, too, sitting next to me on the sofa, had witnessed this spectacle of Alex's ecstatic transport. I could sense her worry, but, as if by some tacit agreement, neither of us said anything. Later we would call these spasms of sensation the sea anemone, because it was like watching one of those other-worldly sea creatures have its entire body animated by the current that supported it, totally at one with its environment, with no separation between it and the world.

Soon after this incident, it became apparent that something strange was happening to Alex's language. I was on the way to visiting a friend who had a young son around Alex's age. We didn't have a car, so I was pushing the stroller to the train station. It was a hard job. The Ashfield footpaths around where we lived were narrow and not particularly stroller-friendly, and Alex was big for his age; he was tall, slim and strong, a beautiful boy. He was not helping matters by perching himself on the very rim of the front seat and dragging the sole of his sandal on the front wheel. To distract him, I played one of our word games. It was a simple question-response game, based on his favourite animal book.

'The lion goes . . . ?'

'Raar!'

'The sheep goes . . . ?'

'Baah!'

'The monkey goes . . . ?'

'Baah!'

I was a bit surprised. He knew very well the monkey went 'eep'. He usually didn't make that sort of mistake. I tried an easy one.

'The cat goes . . . '

A pause. 'Baah!'

We caught the train over to the city and walked to a park in Darlinghurst where we were to meet my friend, Paul, and his eldest son Roy. Paul was an HSC English teacher who had taken a year's leave to look after his two boys. We had met ten years earlier, and had been good friends ever since. The park wasn't large, and I spotted Paul and Roy immediately. Roy was balanced on Paul's hip, whispering in his father's ear. I immediately noticed that he was producing what seemed like parts of whole sentences. I hadn't seen Paul or Roy for a few weeks, so this development seemed all the more impressive for its suddenness. Roy was only a couple of months older than Alex, but Alex didn't seem to be at anything like that level. I didn't mention anything, but I was completely spooked.

Throughout the afternoon Alex did not take much notice of Roy, even though Roy would try to engage him. At one point he ran up to Alex to play chasings, but Alex only responded with a kind of nervous indifference; he turned away and went off to a quiet corner of the playground where he could be on his own. Roy was visibly disappointed. When it was time to go I went to get Alex. He had spent most of his time in that same corner. I found him spinning round and round, his faced fixed in a beaming smile. I put my arm on his shoulder to still him. He looked startled, like someone woken from a trance.

On the train home, I felt very uneasy. Alex knelt on the side bench, staring out the window at the passing terrace houses. It was like a depth charge, this kind of worry: it released itself like a muffled explosion somewhere deep inside you, and only surfaced much later. I thought back to the moment, a couple of hours ago, of first seeing Roy speaking to his father. He had spoken in a soft voice into his father's ear. I hadn't been able to make out what he said; all I could make out were snatches of whispers, hushed and secretive because of the presence of someone else. But, on reflection, what struck me more was the expression on Paul's face. It seemed to be lit up by these exchanges, so new, so thrilling; the speech of his son full of new meaning and complexity, the expression of his burgeoning personality made into words. It was as if Roy's speech had become light, a light that passed between them, that illuminated their minds and souls. And I was suddenly acutely aware that I had not yet felt any such connection, such a delicious complicity, with Alex.

Well, Alex was standing right next to me. I could test it out. I turned him away from the window. He was reluctant to leave the view, but did. I stood him up so I could talk closely into his ear. I said, 'So, my little man, you like looking at the houses?' He giggled at my breath on his ear, then squirmed to turn back and look at the passing view.

My little test had failed. It agitated me so much that I nearly missed our stop.

Physically, Alex continued to thrive. He was a little Adonis with his soft golden curls and his slim, sturdy frame. A few weeks after the visit to the park with Paul, Kathy and I were sitting with him in the lounge room, his Lego set spread out before him. It seemed to confound him. When we tried to show him how to join and stack them, he appeared to be at a complete loss. His fine motor movements, so precise whenever he wanted to remove a bit of unwanted food from his bowl, became awkward and tentative when he had to consciously perform some logical task. Kathy suggested we scale back to a simpler toy we had put away because he had mastered it, a set of small multicoloured cups of diminishing size that could be stacked into one another, or also stacked on top of one another to build a tower. Crouched down on the floor with him, Kathy and I tried to help him build the tower. He seemed confused, and needed a lot of guiding just to select a tub. When he did finally get going, he got the sequence wrong, attempting to stack larger on smaller, or confusing the base and the lid. I finally did it for him. He sat and watched me do it and, with a casual wave of his arm, knocked it down. We sat there, all three of us, among the multicoloured rubble strewn across the floor.

'He could do this two weeks ago,' Kathy said, bewildered.

On a mid-summer evening, Kathy and I sat down with the list of 18-month milestones. This time, we opened the book somewhat nervously. Alex had not been talking much lately, barely producing a word, and had seemed prone to long bouts of being distracted and vague. We'd go to the park, and he'd come along happily enough, holding my hand as we went to the swing and did our routine half-hour. But not a sound came out of him, apart from a mixture of babble and jargon with only the occasional word. Also, he seemed to have stopped saying 'Daddy' in any shape or form. For quite a while it was clear he identified me as 'Dah', but now there was nothing. I found it deflating. Also, in certain places he seemed to totally zone out, as if he was either trying to block out an environment he didn't want to be in, or was somehow overwhelmed by it.

As Kathy and I sat down to go through the milestones, there was definitely no atmosphere of unbounded optimism. We worked through the lists. It soon became apparent he'd barely progressed since fifteen months. In fact, he'd gone backwards. A wave of guilt coursed through me, and in Kathy's silence I could feel it go through her too.

What on earth had we been doing? Why hadn't we said something?

But still I couldn't raise my concern that there may be something wrong with him.

'It's only a book,' I said. 'They're only averages.'

Strange how we believed everything the book said when it confirmed that he may have been 'advanced'.

Things started going wrong at child care. Alex had been attending the local centre for two short days a week since he was about eleven months old. The centre was well run and, apart from some very standard settling-in problems, we liked to think that he was happy there. But a month or so after we checked the 18 month milestones, things changed. Alex started to cry as we approached the centre, as opposed to crying simply when he was left. And when it was time to say goodbye, he became fearful and distressed and refused to go into the Twinkles room to join his group. The carers also informed us that he was difficult to pacify once either his mother or I had gone.

Over the next few weeks Alex's distress got progressively worse. His eye contact, now generally rare, was reserved for anguished, tearful looks as I said goodbye to him. Kathy said it was the same when she dropped him off. I began to dread the days it was my turn to take him, and when I got home I was so worried about him that I found it hard to get any writing done.

One afternoon Kathy got home with Alex, and immediately burst into tears. Alex had cried before she dropped him off, but with a degree of fear and anxiety she hadn't seen before. And the carers had told her that he had cried like that, on and off, for half the day. Perhaps they should have called us, but they felt it was a borderline case. When left to his own devices to see if he would calm himself down, Alex retreated to a quiet corner of the playground, and ran up and down. This seemed to pacify him. But they couldn't let him do that all day. They had been about to call one of us when Kathy turned up. He clung to her like a limpet for five minutes, and she had to prise him off.

We both stood in the kitchen, overcome by guilt. Alex sat on a kitchen chair and munched his sultanas from a box, his eyes puffy and swollen, his legs swaying back and forth. His gaze was remote and abstract.

Kathy made herself a cup of tea and sat at the table, staring into space. She was more upset than I had ever seen her before. I was suddenly terribly afraid for two of the people I loved most in the world. I said that I thought we should get Alex checked out. By a paediatrician. There may be something wrong with his development. I used the word 'development'. Not 'him'. 'Him' seemed too direct, too brutal.

Kathy sat at the kitchen table, the tea steaming before her. Her eyes were glassy with tears. She seemed numb. Finally, she nodded in agreement.

Over the next few weeks, Alex's decline became shockingly rapid. It was most noticeable in his language. Words fell away on what seemed a daily basis, and the ones he did still know started to deteriorate: they reversed, scrambled, reduced to a single ill-formed syllable before they too perished. We sat and went through a picture book. 'Flower' became 'walah'. 'Horse', which he could say clearly, became 'saw'.

Sometimes, when he tried to form a word, he added a syllable in what seemed like a struggle to keep saying what he knew. We were out on an evening walk, a mild Sydney evening with a dusty blue sky. Venus appeared, a spark of light. And Kathy asked: 'What is it, Alex? What is it?' pointing up to the horizon. There was a delay, a delay that had grown so incrementally that I barely noticed it. Alex's face was hesitant. He struggled to form the word, put an 'e' before 'star' in order to manage the 's', as if he were speaking in Spanish.

Soon the word 'star' disappeared. The amount of babble he produced increased, the words getting lost in his attempts to form sounds, rather than emerging out of them. Within only a few weeks his remaining functional words were 'no', 'stuck' and 'Mummy'.

Then, finally, 'Mummy' underwent a grotesque reconfiguration. One night Alex stood at the door crying, his mother kneeling before him. She was primped and perfumed, ready to go on a girls' night out. Tonight it would just be me and Alex, the boys at home on their own. He was crying because he knew what was about to happen—the perfume, that extra-special goodbye, filled with its promise of a quick return—it meant mummy wouldn't be around for bedtime, and he got upset. He would settle down soon enough, and we would have a good night, but for the moment he was distraught. Kathy's face filled with concern; she said she should probably stay at home, stay with him, but I told her to leave, that I would handle it. It was easier said than done: after she had gone he continued to stand at the door, wailing. But tonight he wasn't saying 'Mummy'. It had become 'Um-ma', two fractured syllables, a pseudo-word he repeated over and over again with an insistence that unsettled me.

Within weeks 'Um-ma' was reduced to 'ma'. By this stage there was little left of Alex's language. All the words we had given him, the words from the books we got from the local library, from the boutique book stores, from remainder tables, the books given as gifts at birthday and Christmas, the words taught to him as he sat in our laps or snuggled against us at bedtime, all these words were vanishing. In what seemed like no time at all his vocabulary was reduced to the most basic, significant words, the words that designated the things that were most important to him. And then, one by one, those labels too were torn away, until Alex could no longer really say anything intelligible at all.

This period of onset happened so swiftly, with such irreversible force, with such absoluteness, that Kathy and I were stunned. In the days leading up to the doctors' appointments I had arranged, we operated in a kind of emotional vacuum. It was like something in a science-fiction film. The world seems utterly normal, but there is some alien force at work that is capable of penetrating an individual's nervous system and rewiring it, leaving them physically unchanged yet altered beyond recognition. Only it wasn't a film. It was happening to us. To our child. It seemed completely inconceivable. To our child? A child who had been wanted, planned for to the nth degree? A child born out of love? Could this happen to a child born out of love? Wouldn't that alien force know, know how much he meant to you, and leave your child alone?

One night, before it was time for Kathy and I to go to bed, I told her that I wasn't feeling all that tired, and that I was going to do a bit of web surfing: I'd be in soon. Kathy went to bed. I waited until I thought she was asleep before I logged on.

I entered the word 'autism' into the search engine.

THEIR HOOKS FIND HOLD DEEP IN OUR FLESH: PART TWO

AUTHOR Kate Fielding, ARTISTS Elizabeth McDowell and Mandy Ord

The extracts presented in the last, this and following issues of *Meanjin* are taken from a longer work created by author Kate Fielding and artists Mandy Ord, Clint Curé, Elizabeth McDowell and Ben Fox. It was originally presented as an honours thesis in the History Department of the University of Melbourne, and has been subsequently reworked with support from the Australia Council for the Arts.

My brother made me this t-shirt, it's a joke, 'ask a local'. If I was going to make this t-shirt I without his gift for simplicity, would write:

I insist that history is not an abstract, distant exercise — it is instead subjective and political. Thus I feel it is important to engage with histories that unsettle, discomfort or even devastate — because they can also encourage, orient, and inspire. I believe local history is a powerful site for such research. Connections with local places and their histories are emotional, complex and spread over time. They are human. They demand an opinion and beget responsibility. Their hooks find hold deep in our flesh. This engenders a different set of questions, a different relationship to knowledge and information than exists when the researcher seeks to stand 'outside' the history they are writing. What people know about the place they identify with will dramatically shape how they live there, and living there will shape what they know. Local knowledge claims the authority of intimacy; want to know the best fish and chips in town, ask a local! This doesn't mean that local knowledge is true or unbiased; rather it is a specific position from which to write history, with specific concerns and perspectives. When I write the histories of where I grew up I draw on archives, books, museums, newspapers, but I also draw on a textured personal experience of that place, that community, that history. Local histories have the power to be of a human and community scale — in a way that state or national histories struggle to emulate — and for this reason have the potential to create representations of heterogeneity within and between communities. Against a tendency to typify, to categorise, to make iconic and empty, the assertion of specificity can remind us of the heterogeneity critical to our cultural survival. In a global community struggling with diversity I feel this is a valuable task.

In the rural community where I grew up one tale held sway over the historical imagination. This is the story I was told standing on the yellow cliffs above Loch Ard Gorge, whipped by southerlies and warmed by the sun.

On the 1st of June 1878 the ship 'Loch Ard' went down just outside the mouth of that gorge. Cracked like an egg on the line of a reef.

On board were Eva Carmichael and Tom Pearce. Eva was migrating with her upper class Irish family, spending the days of the voyage learning to use a sextant, suncharting her way to a new land. Tom was an apprentice sailor. During the voyage they had never spoken, and now the ship was sinking.

MISS EVA CARMICHAEL.   MR. THOMAS PEARCE.

Flung from the deck, Eva clung to a chicken coop, trying to undo her heavy, snaking skirts to give to a naked sailor.

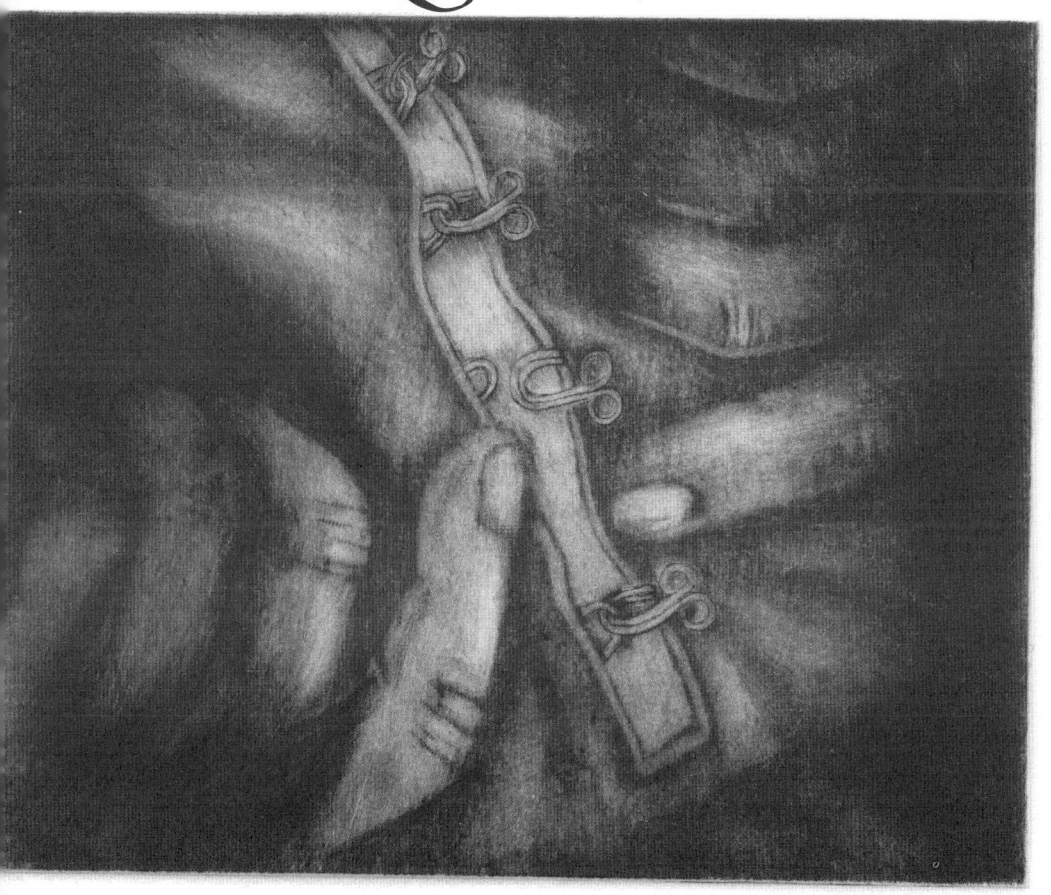

After hours in the
water, Tom made
it to shore. Hearing
Eva's cries he swam
to her, took her clothes
between his teeth and
towed her to safety.

Tom and Eva lay lost on the shores
of a continent unknown to them,
barely covered and bleeding.
Tom found a case of brandy,
and rubbed it over Eva's
frozen limbs, some down her
throat and down his as well.
Tom scaled the cliffs to find
help. Eva hid herself under
some bushes, their unfamiliar
smell crushed around her, the
crash hiss of ocean.

Tom returned with Hugh Gibson, a squatter from the Glenample run and homestead, and his employee George Ford. They clambered over beached cargo from the wreck, stumbling over harmoniums and telegraph equipment cases of champagne and strychnine. Searching for Eva. She heard their calls – 'cooooooee!' – and feared they were 'wild blacks'. When she finally heard a word of English she called them to her – 'I'm dying.'

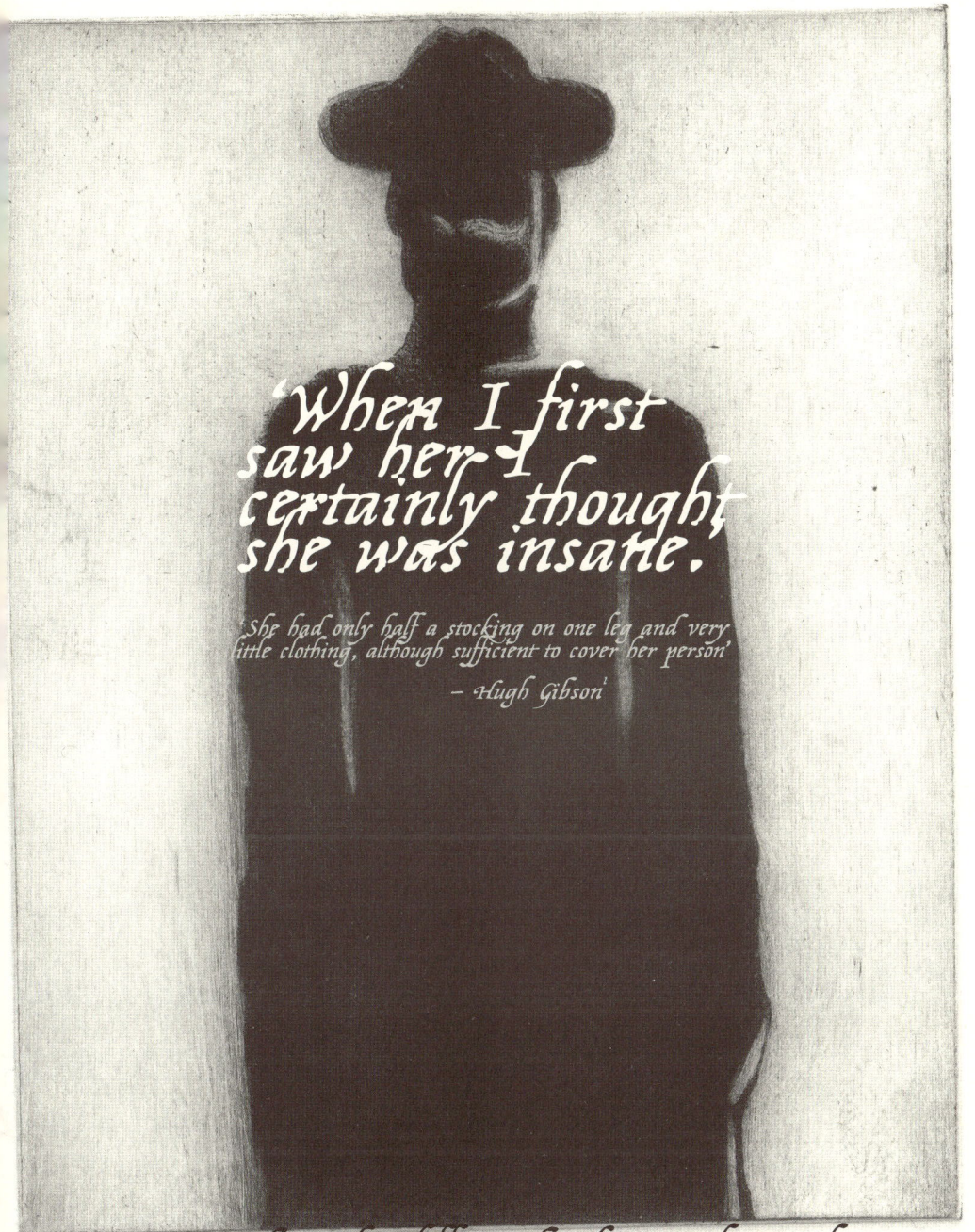

'When I first saw her I certainly thought she was insane.'

'She had only half a stocking on one leg and very little clothing, although sufficient to cover her person'

– Hugh Gibson

Eva was carried up the cliffs and taken to Glenample to be cared for. The bodies of Eva's mother and sister were retrieved, then given to the ground in coffins made from salvaged piano cases. Hundreds of people came to see the wrecksite. The press fawned over Eva. Her survival was regarded a miracle, Tom's actions as brave and gallant.

A second miracle: a Minton's ceramic peacock, almost two metres tall, was washed ashore in its crate. Unharmed save for a chip in its beak, the rich greens and deep blues of its lustrous glaze intact.

The salvage contractors carried it home.

Tom was whisked to Melbourne to have medals pinned to his chest, a grand ball held in his name, poems written in his honour...

Eva convalesced at Glenample, where a local girl, Jane Shields, spent hours brushing tangled snarls from her medusa hair.

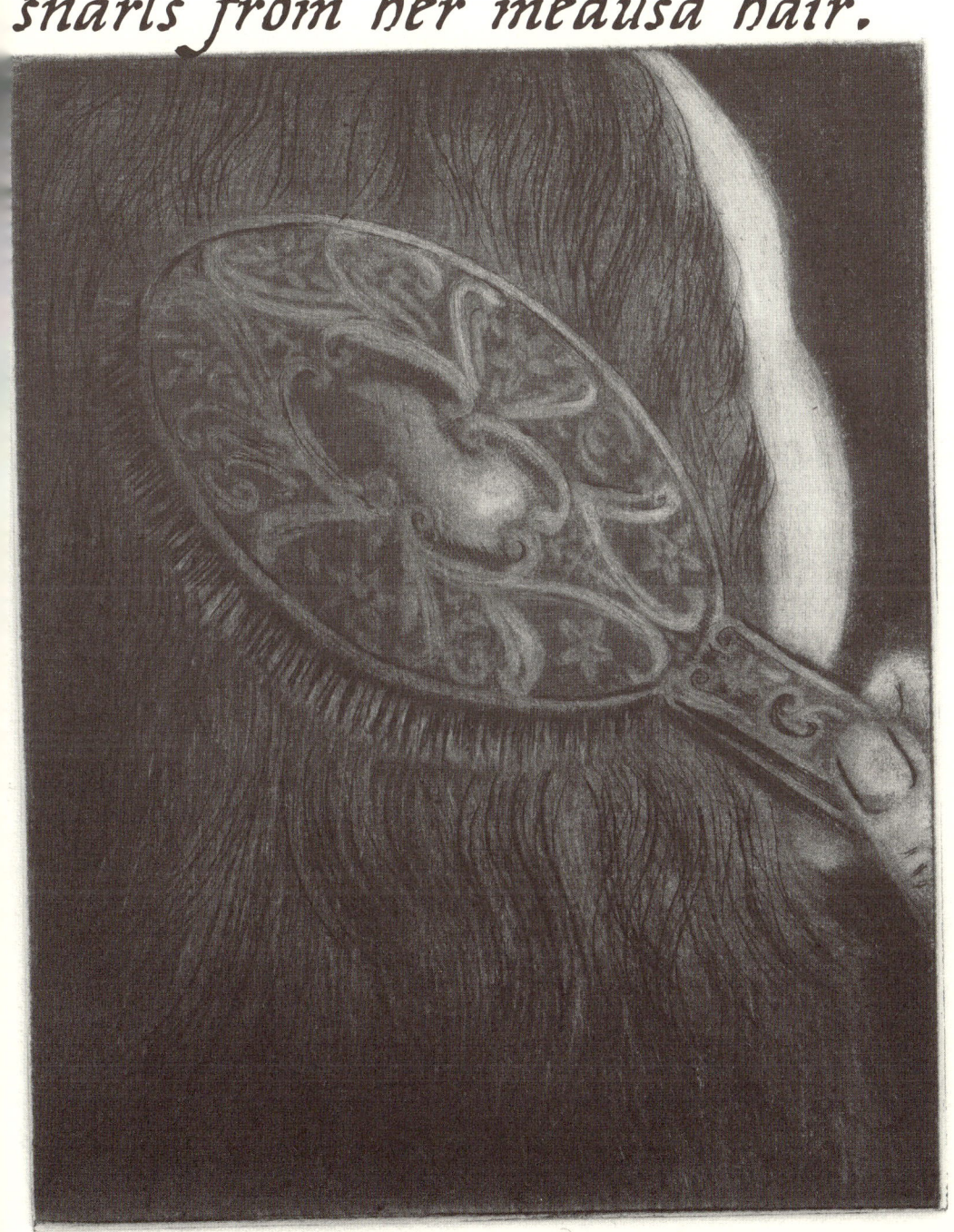

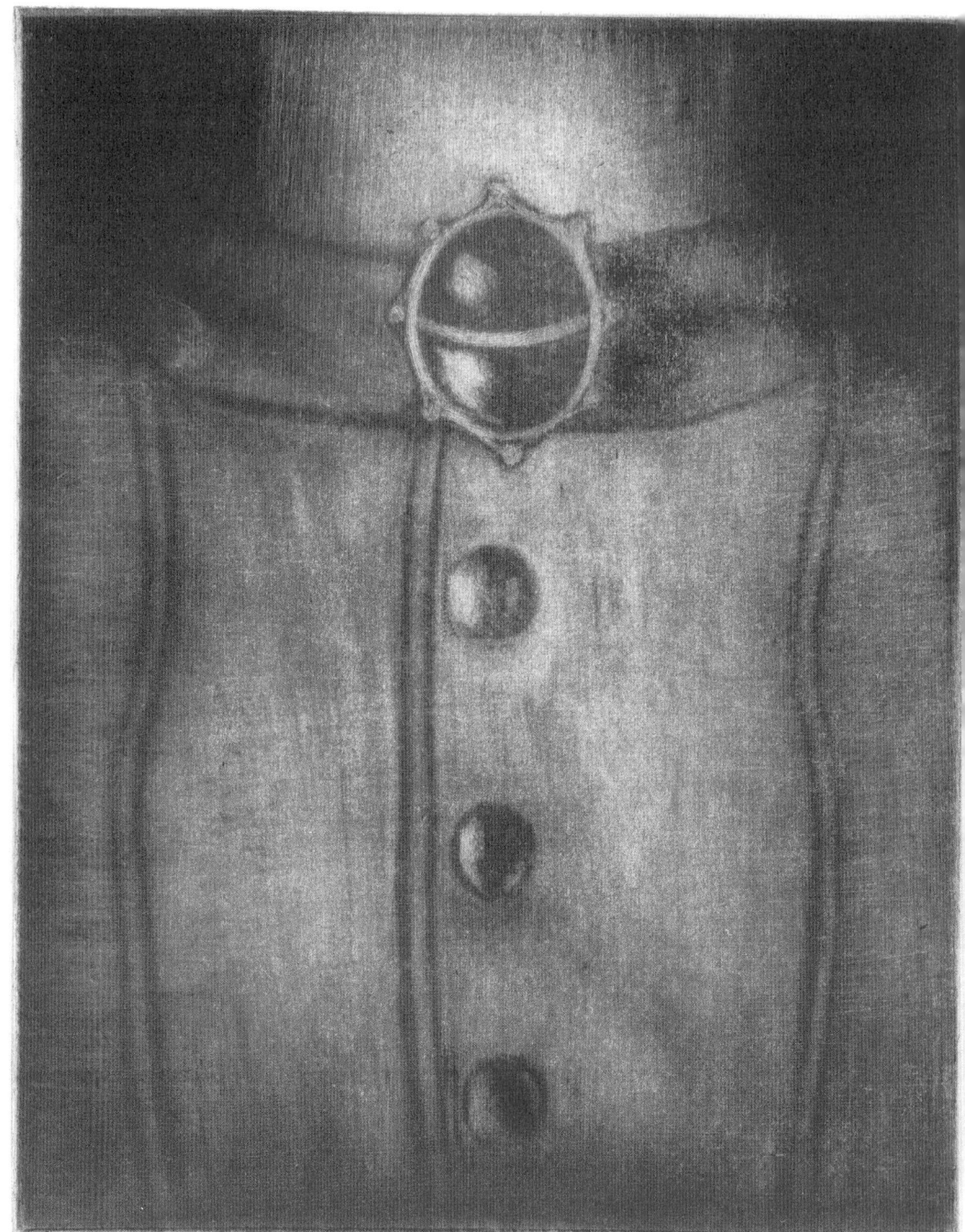

The nation clamoured for romance. Rumours of Tom's broken heart ran through the colony, coupled with whispers of Eva's compromised virtue.
Instead Eva boarded a steamer bound for Ireland, and never returned. Thrice shipwrecked, Tom died on dry land an old man. They did not see each other again.

Many years later, when I had started thinking about that other feature of the coastline, Massacre Point, I began to question the 'Loch Ard' story. At first I wanted to discover Eva a heroine, for her to do something more than be dragged from the sea.

I was shocked to realise that Eva had less than three months in Australia, and barely two of them in the Western district. I wished for a saucy lesbian affair between Eva and Jane to blow the cosy story apart. Instead Eva returned to Ireland as quickly as possible and married a nobleman 15 years her senior.
I hoped for an Indigenous player, as ambiguous and forgotten as Sturt's 'black trackers', a new hero's story to tell.

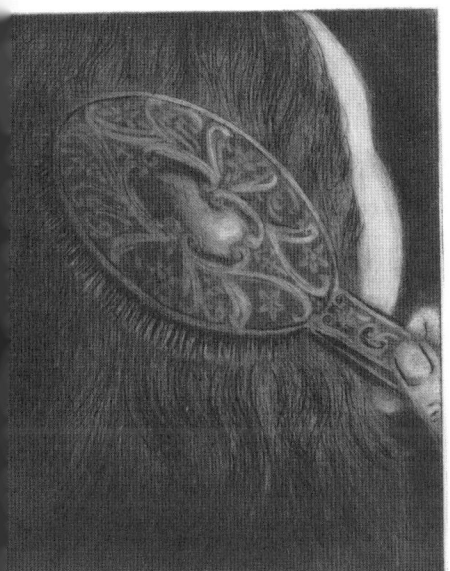

Instead I found the memoirs and letters of Hugh Gibson.

You perhaps would like to know something more of Miss Carmichael, and what I tell you now is in strictest confidence. We cannot make her out exactly. She is a puzzle to all who have seen her.'[2]

The 'Loch
Ard' story was
always pitched as one
of tragedy and heroism. Eva was
its wretched focus, and details of her
response to the loss of her family
abound. Tom was cast
in the saviour role, but
gallantry was attributed
also to Gibson and
Ford for finding
and caring for
Eva. Tales of
heroic white
males rescuing
young, white females
from a hostile environment or dangerous
'savages' circulated widely in nineteenth-century
Australia and throughout the British Empire — it was
this stereotypical narrative from the colony which had
fed Eva's fear that Gibson's 'cooees' were the calls of 'the
natives'. [3]
Everything I was told suggested Gibson appreciated the Loch
Ard wreck for the noble part it afforded him. And yet in
Gibson's 1901 memoirs he makes no bones about his feelings
towards the wreck; 'The 'Loch Ard' wreck accentuated my
difficulties. Selectors increased in numbers, and I had to sell
all the cattle I could muster.'[4] Gibson estimated that 400 people
had gathered at the wrecksite by the Tuesday after the wreck,
and the Sydney Illustrated News reported 'hundreds of pounds
worth of goods have been conveyed away by people who honestly
believe they had a perfect right to all they could lay their hands
upon.'[5] Wreckers abseiled down cliffs to reach beached cargo.
New arrivals to the area — selectors whom Gibson so despised —
obtained much needed material goods from wrecks. Gibson wrote
'...I was invaded by some waifs and strays, who selected bits of
land...not with the idea of cultivating and these people wandering
about make my cattle unmanageable and wild. A shipwreck was
a godsend to these people.' [6] Gibson felt his claim to the land was
threatened by 'unworthy' selectors, attracted and assisted by
wrecks, including the 'Loch Ard'. Accolades aside, the wreck was a
complication in Gibson's struggle to retain land he had squatted.

Suddenly the 'Loch Ard' story was embroiled in the class and land conflicts of the district, a focus of bitterness and vitriolic claims to material goods. Even the peacock, kept covered in a local hallway, was a source of ambivalence and guilty pleasure.[7]

WRECK
OF
THE LOCH ARD!

NO ONE should be **WITHOUT A RELIC** of this **MOST APPALLING CATASTROPHE**, coupled, as it is, with the **DEVOTED GALLANTRY** of the

BRAVE TOM PEARCE!

The advertisement for goods officially salvaged from the wreck sought to couple object and history. It wedded a practical need for material goods in the colony with a sense that such objects were imbued with historical meaning and would enable their owner to be 'closer' to the 'Loch Ard' drama. Though by no means unique to the nineteenth-century, this emphasis on the object echoed a European fascination with objects as symbols of civilisation and progress. The peacock itself was being shipped from England as an exhibit for the 1880 Melbourne Exhibition – one of the many 'Great Exhibitions' mounted by colonial powers around the globe. These 'symbolic battlegrounds on which nations demonstrated their prowess and tested the strength of their rivals' employed material goods, like the ceramic peacock, as expression of national identity and technological development.[8] Ironically the peacock did not feature at the 1880 Exhibition, but was included as part of the 1988 travelling Bicentenary show which pitched the 'Loch Ard' wreck as an important story for Australia. Perhaps the story's enduring appeal lies primarily in this display-friendly relic?

They will also offer the whole of their Magnificent Stock at

SALVAGE PRICES!

GEOGHEGAN & BYRNE,
66. Moorabool St.

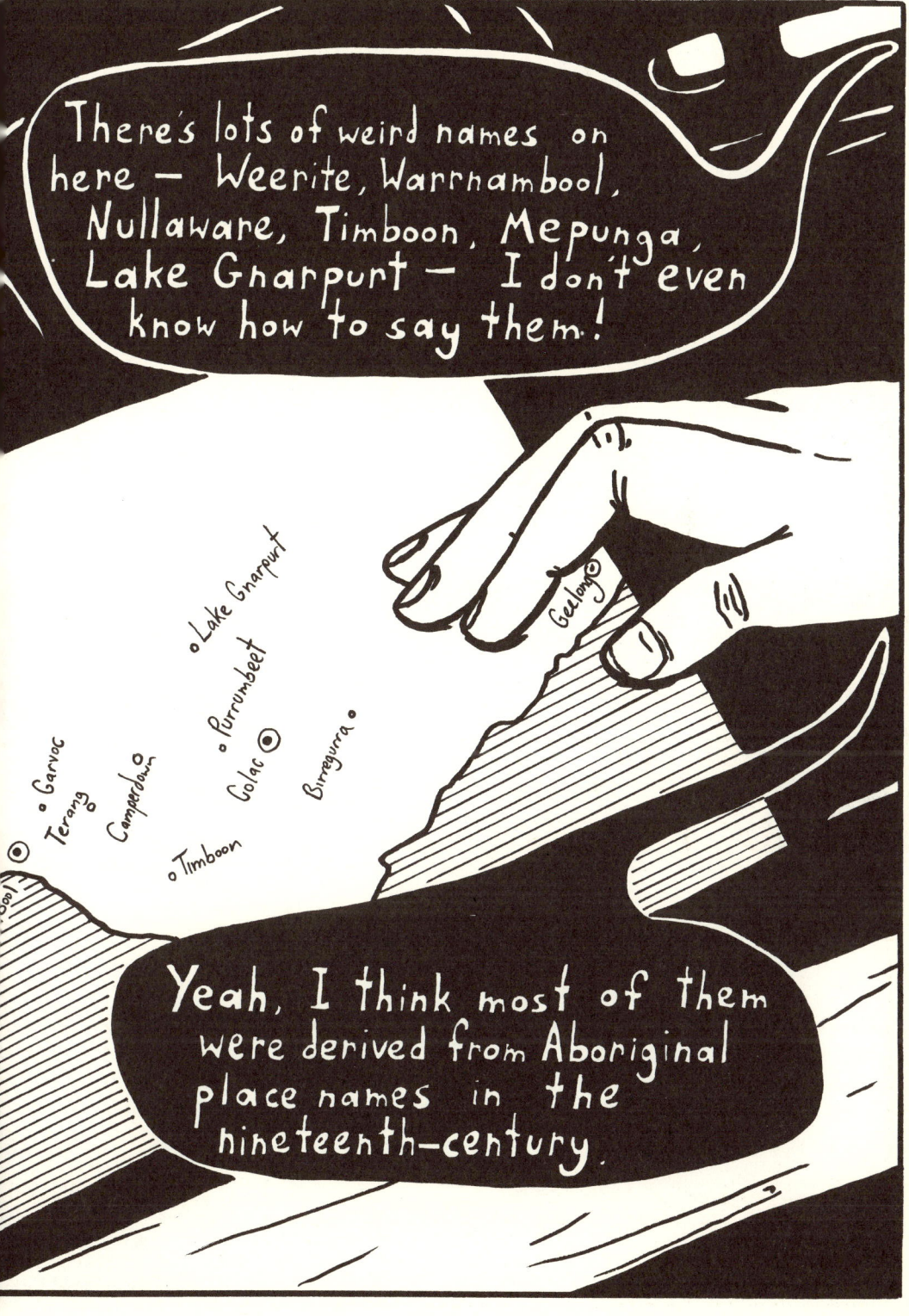

Weird, I thought back then they wanted to get rid of all the Indigenous people and pretend they were never there.

Kind of. I think getting the Aboriginal place names was part of trying to claim the country, kind of pretending that you knew it intimately. Claim the names, claim the land. One of the key surveyors of that area, Major Mitchell, was adamant that surveyors should use Aboriginal names for places. Apparently he used to do all sorts of crazy stuff — kidnap Indigenous people, chase them, get really angry — to try and get names from them.[q]

Last year there was a proposal to give unnamed features around Warrnambool — roads and bridges and stuff — Indigenous names. There was uproar! All this resentment surfaced.[10]

Crazy. People are so scared.

Dya wanna cup of tea?

Yeah....

...ta

NOTES

1. Hugh Gibson, letter to his stepmother, 4 and 6 July 1878 reproduced in Rosamund Duruz, *The Story of Glenample*, Warrnambool Photo Art Printers, Warrnambool, Vic., 1977.

2. Hugh Gibson, letter to his stepmother, 6 July 1878, reproduced in Duruz, *The Story of Glenample*.

3. In a statement given by Eva she notes: 'Before I left England, I heard so much about the wild blacks ...' Reproduced in Port Campbell Progress Society, *Port Campbell and its Attractions—a Brief Historical Sketch*, Port Campbell, Vic., 1937. For an excellent discussion of the potency of 'white woman' captivity narratives see Kate Darian-Smith, '"Rescuing" Barbara Thompson and other white women—captivity narratives on Australian frontiers', in Kate Darian-Smith, Liz Gunner and Sarah Nuttall (eds), *Text, Theory, Space—Land, Literature and History in South Africa and Australia*, Routledge, London and New York, 1996, pp. 99–114.

4. Hugh Gibson, 'Reminiscences, 1901', reproduced in *Victorian Historical Magazine*, vol. 27, no. 108 (June 1957), p. 31.

5. Gibson's estimate in 'Reminiscences' , p. 29. Quote from *Sydney Illustrated News* included, undated, in Donald Charlwood, *The Wreck of the 'Loch Ard': End of a Ship, End of an Era*, Angus and Robertson, Sydney, 1971.

6. Duruz, *The Story of Glenample*, pp. 18, 21.

7. Personal communication, Howard Nicol, former director of Flagstaff Hill Maritime Museum, 14 June 2002. Nicol viewed correspondence held in a private collection in which the narrator describes visiting the house where the peacock was held and comments that the owners displayed guilt about possessing it.

8. Graeme Davison, 'Exhibitions', *Australian Cultural History*, no. 2 (1982–83), p. 5.

9. For a discussion of the methods used to obtain these names, see Gregory C. Eccleston, *Major Mitchell's 1836 'Australia Felix' Expedition: A Re-evaluation* (Department of Geography and Environmental Science, Monash University, Melbourne, 1992).

10. 'Name Change', *The Warrnambool Standard*, 3 June 2002, p.1; 'Residents vote against Aboriginal name changes', *The Warrnambool Standard,* 12 June 2002, p. 4; 'Koori heritage to hit the road—sites will reflect pre-colonial past', *The Warrnambool Standard,* 18 June 2002, p. 5.

INTERVIEW

BEFORE GETTING DRESSED

SOPHIE CUNNINGHAM TALKS TO GEORGIA BLAIN ABOUT LIFE, DEATH, MOTHERHOOD, AND HER FIRST WORK OF NONFICTION

I've known Georgia Blain for many years. We are about the same age and her childhood memories are familiar to me—a decade of educational experimentation (the seventies); family dynamics complicated (further) by the rise of feminism, both parents working and divorce; a certain pressure to be sexually active before one really knew what such matters entailed. Her essay 'Strange Times' begins, 'On the night Gough Whitlam was elected Prime Minister, my parents held a party.' So did mine. But there are many things about Blain's life that are particular and her stunning collection _Births Deaths Marriages_ is about, in part, having lived a life more publicly documented than many. Her father, Ellis Blain, was an ABC broadcaster, and her mother is the commentator Anne Deveson. Deveson's bestselling book _Tell Me I'm Here_ charted her son Jonathan's—Georgia's brother—struggle with schizophrenia and eventual death. Soon after that book's publication Georgia Blain's first novel, _Closed for Winter_, was published. Since then Blain has written three novels—_Candelo_, _The Blind Eye_ and _Names for Nothingness_. _Births Deaths Marriages_ was published in March this year and is her first book of nonfiction. She lives in Sydney with her partner Andrew Taylor and their daughter Odessa.

Sophie Cunningham: I want to talk to you about your nonfiction writing compared to your novel writing. Of the five books you have written, which was the hardest to write?

Georgia Blain: I don't think you can say that one form is harder than the other, I think every book has different challenges. Your first book has the huge challenges of: Can I possibly do this? Can I get to the end? Am I able to be a writer? I think you get technically more adept as you go along, but I don't think your confidence necessarily gets better because you're more aware of the pitfalls in the public process.

SC: And the more you know, the worse it is, in a way.

GB: Yes, so I think that is one of the main challenges. I don't think your confidence in your voice necessarily gets better either, because as you get technically more adept you try new things, things that you're not so confident with.

In terms of whether writing fiction is more difficult than writing memoir, I think the actual act of writing is not necessarily more difficult, but I think the act of going public is a lot more difficult. And by 'going public' I mean even those very early stages of consulting with people who are involved in the story. I'm someone who tends very much to work alone, I don't like to have to talk to people about my work and I hated the fact that I had to, I found that very difficult.

SC: How did you negotiate that process? Did you sit down and work out a kind of ethics policy or did you just follow your gut?

GB: Followed my gut. I wish in retrospect I had worked out more clearly where I was prepared to give and where I wasn't prepared to give. I was probably more prepared to give than I probably should have been. Because this was new territory for me I had to find my way as I went along, and there were key people I had to consult with. Firstly I had to consult with my mother; but I knew that wasn't a problem, because she's a writer herself and she'd written about us and I knew that was going to be okay. I had to consult Andrew [my partner] and I was pretty sure that was going to be okay because he knows the process [from] making films. I also had to consult various people who were at one remove, and there were chapters that I dropped after that consultation process, which is why I say I gave in more quickly than I should have.

GB: No, it was more that I said to them, 'Look, I want you to see this book, as it involves you ... If you really don't want me to do this I won't do it.' And there was one chapter where someone involved really didn't want me to do [publish] it so I didn't do it. There was another one where they didn't say directly that they didn't want me to do it, but I could really tell that it had distressed them so I let that one go as well.

SC: In the case of the person who really didn't want you to use the material, do you think they had the right to make that call or did you give them too much power? What rights does a writer have?

GB: I think ultimately you can just say, oh look, bugger it, I'm going to do it anyway, but in the case of both lots of people we had ongoing relationships that I didn't want to jeopardise. Even though one of the things I let go was an integral part of the book and I would've liked to have kept in there. [But] I'm glad I didn't have to talk about that chapter [publicly] when the people involved weren't happy about it being there.

SC: How did you feel at various points in your life when you were children and your mother was writing about you?

GB: When we were little we were oblivious to it—whatever you have when you're little you take as normal. I write about it in Births Deaths Marriages—that when my mother wrote about my brother I found that very distressing. But in retrospect I'm very glad she did it.

SC: Did your mother write Tell Me I'm Here sooner in your grief process than you would have liked, or was the issue that the book's publication meant that people started asking you about your family?

GB: It's hard to understand now because we have, in many ways, improved our attitude towards mental illness, but at the time this was happening nobody talked about mental illness and it was something you were ashamed that you had in your family. [There was] a long culture of keeping quiet about it and then suddenly [we] were out there—it was incredibly public. So that was difficult to *adjust to. Now I look back and I think there was no shame, and I find it strange that it was difficult [for me] to deal with that.*

SC: *When was Jonathan diagnosed? What year?*

GB: *Probably when he was about seventeen. It was 1980 that he was diagnosed, yes. So it's been a huge change, and I think Mum's book is one of the main movers in that [cultural shift].*

SC: *You've had four novels published, some of which have material drawn from your own life, so why did you decide to move into memoir?*

GB: *First of all I think everybody draws from their own life when they write, and anybody who tells you they don't is lying. I always remember my friend Katrina saying to me she saw Peter Carey at the Adelaide Festival and he talked about writers being magicians who were able to totally step outside their own skin and invent incredible experiences. I think you invent experiences, but I just don't think you ever step outside your own skin.*

    I hit this point where I felt like I was circling around something and constantly drawing from myself. I thought: why not just do it directly, why not just say it directly? And I found the artifice of the traditional novel plot really frustrating. I'd hit this point where it was somehow blocking me from getting to where I wanted to get and saying what I wanted to say.

SC: *I'm fascinated you've said that because I also feel that frustration with the form. Do you think you're expected to be nicer than real life is in a novel?*

GB: *Yes, absolutely. I think you're expected to be nicer, I think you're expected to have resolution, even if it's anti-resolution. I think you are expected to have characters that are in some way predictable and whose motives are understandable, but I don't think people's motives often are understandable and I don't think people are predictable. I think people are multilayered. But then interestingly when it came to writing memoir I thought: I'll throw away the artifice of plot, but there's another artifice that you put on that's very akin to plot because I don't think you can help but make a story of your experience. I set out with the intention of not having a cohesive whole. I ended up with a cohesive whole.*

SC: Nonetheless, a series of essays is a more fragmented narrative. As with linked short stories there is a space between the pieces, where there's an acknowledgement that you are living a life. There's not the same covering up of cracks that there is in fiction. I didn't think that Births Deaths Marriages read too neatly.

GB: No, but I still think you have a clear narrative arc of someone who gradually gained confidence and learned to trust their own voice. I still think you ended up with a traditional narrative arc. I was astounded when I got to the end. It's a bizarre thing, you're writing this happy ending—which I stressed was 'fictional'—about how wonderful and happy everything is and you're editing it on a day when you're shitty beyond belief, and so your life is, as you say, constantly continuing outside the parameters of the story. I felt the only way I could be honest to life was to make it episodic, but also to stress that the 'end' was just one transient point and you could pick any point as the end.

SC: You've told me that several different people edited the collection because individual essays were published in various journals. How many editors worked overall on the book? And how did that affect the shape of it.

GB: Four or five pieces were published in various forms and they were each edited by different editors. Then Jane Gleeson-White read it for me as a friend. She did an initial look before it went to a publisher, and it was fantastic having somebody who was a professional editor and a friend. It was a difficult job for her, but she not only advised me on it as a work but also was able to say [at various points], 'Look, are you really going to feel comfortable about that being out there?'

SC: Which she could only do because she knew you.

GB: Yes. And then it had two editors in the publishing process as well.

SC: Did different editors pull you in different directions?

GB: Not hugely, no. There were moments in the editing where there was a tension between trying to keep it episodic because [some essays had] been edited as self-contained pieces and then they had *to be re-edited so they linked. But I was very determined to resist making it too neatly linked and sometimes there was some tension about that. But ultimately I think it got to a place where everyone felt like it was right.*

SC: *I'm assuming one of the tricky pieces to negotiate was the section when you talk about your feelings both about pregnancy and being a new mother and your frustrations. How old is your daughter Odessa now?*

GB: *Nine.*

SC: *Did you think about her as a reader?*

GB: *Absolutely. When I initially wrote some of those pieces, it was probably before she was a reader, but then as I edited more it became more and more clear to me that she was going to read them.*

SC: *Has she read them yet?*

GB: *No, she hasn't, but the pieces are about my ambivalence about being a mother in those days, and I have talked to her about that. I said to her that a lot of people love little babies and find the toddler stage really difficult, and 'I'm someone that found little babies really, really hard but loved the toddler stage.' You see, I love it. As soon as they start having their personalities and exerting their will ... I completely slotted into being a mother at a time when many of my friends found it very challenging. For me it was very important to talk to her honestly because she's very similar to me and I thought if she has kids she's probably going to be hit like I was hit.*

SC: *Because of genes and personality?*

GB: *Yes, but also I think a lot of women are hit like I was hit, thinking: what on earth have I done?*

SC: *Did you have postnatal depression?*

GB: *I was never diagnosed with postnatal depression. I have been depressed in my life and it didn't feel like it was depression. I wanted to stress that I didn't want the way in*

*which I reacted to be termed aberrant or sick. I actually felt it
was quite a valid response to such a life-changing event.*

SC: *One of my favourite scenes in the book is when you see the guy who's
a bit crazy out on Bondi Beach …*

GB: *Clovelly.*

SC: *Yes, and you're saying to Odessa, 'I think he has schizophrenia' and explaining
that her uncle had schizophrenia and her subsequent curiosity. Her wanting to
embrace him as part of the family.*

GB: *It's a fantastic story for a kid. Kids love gothic melodrama and
there's this person who had died young, who was this tragedy within
our family, who was mad. As a kid with an imagination it's like your
gothic fairytale stuff, so of course she was absolutely intrigued by
that whole story.*

SC: *That must have been quite affirming for you because it made
Jonathan more than a man who had suffered from schizophrenia, and it
gave him a certain kind of spunk.*

GB: *Yes, it was a new dimension and it made me reassess who he
was and it made me wonder what it would have been like if he had
survived the illness and was around now and what he'd be like
with her. [It gave me] an incredibly strong sense that no-one ever
goes, that they're part of the fabric of the next generation and the
one after that and the one after that. And I think probably with
his death, it was such a full-on life and then the absence was so
complete …*

SC: *There's a bigger space because he was such an intense …*

GB: *Yes, that it was only years later that I was able to incorporate
him back into my life.*

SC: *Another really strong essay is the marriage counselling essay, 'The
Final Analysis'. I loved the theatricality of that sequence when you and
Andrew are being watched by psychiatrists from behind glass—it's like
you're in a police station. It felt like a metaphor for being a writer, that
public enacting of self. And then there's a moment where both you and*

Andrew talk about your fathers' suicides but with a certain reluctance because you don't want the counsellor to latch onto those events, but of course she does and so does the SWOT team behind the glass. How do you deal with the fact that people often talk about your life story in terms of the tragedies—your brother, your father—rather than, say, your struggle with being a young mum, which is a more common struggle?

> GB: Obviously both those tragedies are a part of who I am, but I do feel strongly that they're not all of who I am. I wanted to incorporate other pieces that dealt with more ordinary daily stuff, like dealing with the dog, the daily dynamics of just living and the stuff about becoming a mother. It's all part of the fabric.

SC: It's also part of resisting that narrative shape to some extent, isn't it? Because you could have written a memoir in which the peaks were your father's death and your brother's death, alongside the love story with Andrew.

> GB: Yes, I could have written a traditional memoir of growing up with mental illness in the family and I really didn't want to do that.

SC: Did your dad have the same illness as Jonathan?

> GB: No, I don't think my dad did have schizophrenia. I wouldn't be at all surprised if my dad now were diagnosed as being OCD.

SC: Let's talk for a moment about the essay 'The Germaine Tape'. It is both funny and terrible—you're listening to your father's interview with Germaine Greer thirty years after the event and you're embarrassed by his old-fashioned sexism. Children are always humiliated and embarrassed by their parents and this was that writ large.

> GB: My mother always downplayed her own success. She always said, 'Oh but your father is a better interviewer than I am.' So I think I always thought he was a wonderful interviewer, and it's probably not fair to judge him on that one interview but he really ... I mean, Germaine Greer was a media performer long before ...

SC: She had him for breakfast, basically.

> GB: Yes, she ran rings around him.

SC: You first wrote this collection as part of a PhD, didn't you?

GB: Yes but the Germaine Greer piece was written a long time beforehand and was almost like the centrepiece. I built backwards from it and forwards from it.

SC: Is that because that's the moment where you had a very clear sense of distance, of observing your parents?

GB: No, I think because that was the first time that I tackled writing about myself and it was probably the piece that I found most difficult to write because it was the first time I did that ... but I loved doing it. And I had that incredible narrative gift of having Germaine Greer in the interview there.

SC: How did you deal with autobiographical material in your novels?

GB: With my fiction there really isn't much of my life in there, in terms of facts and things that happened, but in terms of the emotion there is a lot of my life in there. What I find curious with Births Deaths Marriages *I suppose is how I feel looking back at it. I don't really reread my work for a long time, if ever, because I can't really bear looking back at it, but I think ... am I going to look at that and ask: 'Is that me?' I don't know whether it's me, if that makes sense. Whereas some of my fiction I might look at it more and think, oh God, that's me. Curiously.*

SC: Is that because you were being clearer about not letting people in because it was writing from life?

GB: Take Closed for Winter. *I look back on it and—I can't bear to look back on it actually—but I would think it was very much how I was when I was depressive. So I see a part of myself in there so very strongly, even though it's not my story in that sense of the word. Whereas* Births Deaths Marriages *is ostensibly much more me, but it's a much more crafted me, it's not a raw me.* Closed for Winter *is a raw aspect of me.*

SC: I got frustrated with the characters in my novel Geography *because they grew to some extent from life. I find you're more judgemental of characters who have grown up that way, the way you are quite hard on friends who've behaved badly and the way one can be hard on oneself.*

GB: *That's an interesting one actually because I think when you're writing about life you feel more of an obligation to write about the more generous, positive side than you do with a novel. I felt much more of an obligation to try and bring out the finest in people in how I portrayed them in my work than I would have in a novel, which is a curious thing.*

SC: *How was the reading of this collection for Andrew—the reading of the essay 'Close to the Bone' on the death of his father? It's a very sad essay.*

GB: *Look, I think it can't have been easy. He's a person who believes in letting you do whatever you need to do, so it would be very rare that he would say, 'Don't go there, I don't want you to do that.' It was very difficult to write about him because the relationship with him is a constantly changing dynamic and so it's a very hard thing to fix it in a time and place. I found it more difficult to write about him than I did to write about anyone else.*

SC: *In a way what you do in that essay is give him space. You write about physically giving him space and standing back. You don't presume to know what's going on for him.*

GB: *I guess it was more that the way in which I saw how he reacted to his father's death was a constantly changing thing. I saw it in one way at the time when we were in the midst of the grief and then I reinterpreted it later on. I reinterpreted it again and again, which is what the whole book's about, that life's constantly open to reinterpretation.*

SC: *I'm interested by the idea of the writer as therapist. I'm not talking about a book being therapy for you, I'm talking about reading a book being therapy for other people. You have used quite intimate material. Do you find that people want to engage with you in a particular way?*

GB: *After this book there was a period where everyone was saying to me, 'I feel like I know you,' and my immediate internal response is, 'Well, you don't.' But of course I can't say that because it is one aspect of me ...*

SC: *But the real you is changing constantly.*

GB: The real me is changing constantly, and it is very much crafted as an intimate voice. People say I was very hard on myself in the book, but I actually think it's the nicer side of me. The thing that I was really anxious about was the people who know me vaguely, the people I have passing acquaintance with, who are more likely to conflate the book and me and to put me in that prism.

And some material is confronting. Take the essay about losing my virginity. Usually women either do the brazen act of saying bugger this, I'm showing you everything and it's a political act, and it's out there, you're going to get it in your face, bang! If you're not doing that it's much more difficult territory to negotiate. I felt there was a huge dearth of pieces about a female experience of losing your virginity, but there's a hell of a lot about boys.

It is as if it is very unladylike to reveal that side of yourself, it is a pornographic act. To me one of the only films that ever really talked honestly about that was Somersault. Men hated Somersault, women loved Somersault. Women really understood that awful stage of having sexual power and not knowing how to use it, of confusing love and sex and it being this terrifying land where you put yourself in danger. It was frightening.

SC: What are you working on next?

GB: Absolutely nothing.

SC: That's not a particularly inspiring end for our readers!

GB: I feel like I have finished a phase. I feel like I'm a different person to the person who wrote all my previous work. Different things interest me and different things concern me and I don't feel capable of writing until I have some perspective on this new person.

SC: I find it very weird how different we feel at different phases of our lives.

GB: Do you find you don't even really remember ... you think, who was she? How did she think and how did she feel?

SC: Sometimes I think you write things and you don't realise how brave they are. I don't know if you experienced that with Closed for Winter. You just write it and you're maybe unaware of how intense an *experience it might be for people who love you. You don't think that when you're writing it because you probably couldn't write if you did. There's a certain wilful naivety to writing, I think.*

GB: Which you have to have to be able to do because …

SC: … otherwise you don't do anything.

GB: I think you have to close yourself off from what anyone would think or … almost the entire outside world in that act of writing. I almost feel like the process of editing is a kind of slowly getting dressed to leave the house.

FICTION

Chagall's Wife

by

ABIGAIL ULMAN

I HAD NEVER BEFORE bumped into a teacher on the weekend. But there he was, sitting at the counter in the window, and I slowed down to take it all in: the face that looked more relaxed than it usually did, the late breakfast in front of him, the hardcover book in his hand with the library tag on its spine. Through the glass I saw him slide something off his fork with his mouth. I felt his eyes land on me the second I took mine off him. I drew in a breath and sauntered in.

I took a seat next to the wall and sipped my juice through a straw, flipping through every page of a magazine without taking my eyes off his back. Dressed down for the weekend, he was wearing a pair of faded black jeans and a khaki jacket, and his dark hair, usually as neat and orderly as the jars that lined his desk, was ruffled on one side as though he hadn't even checked it before heading out that morning.

When the waitress came to collect his plate, I saw her brush her arm against his as she reached over him, and he looked up and smiled and said something before going back to his book.

Under the fluorescent lights in the toilets I rubbed some gloss into my lips. I yanked my hair out of its ponytail, ran my fingers through it, and arranged it over my shoulders. It was dirty blonde, and dirty. I tied it back up. My jeans were good and new and tight but the grey hoody that showed a stripe of stomach kept going from daggy to sexy and back again. I narrowed my eyes at my reflection. Whatever you do, I told myself, don't mention tampons.

'Mr Ackerman.'

'Sascha, hello.'

'I saw you earlier, when I walked in.'

'Ah, yes.'

'You saw me, too. Why didn't you say hi?'

'I don't know. I suppose I thought you might have better things to do on a Saturday than chat to your daggy old science teacher.'

'You're not daggy.' I lap-danced my eyes over his weekend stubble, the grey T-shirt, his right hand, which was tugging at the leather band of his wristwatch. 'What's that you're drinking?'

'An affogato.'

'What? Like the vegetable?'

'It's a coffee drink. Kind of like a spider for grown-ups.'

'I see.' I leaned one hand on my hip and sucked my bottom lip under the top one until it disappeared. Mr Ackerman looked down to the floor, where one of my runners was standing firmly on top of the other. Then he blinked around the room, at the smattering of people reading newspapers or quietly chatting to each other, and back at me.

'Would you like to try one?'

I perched on the stool next to his and leaned my elbows in front of me. We kept our eyes on the street. It was early afternoon in the middle of autumn, and the sun was bright but stingy with its warmth. A woman walked past pushing an empty baby pram; she was talking on her mobile phone. Our silence was long and expectant, like the minutes between the snooze button and the return of the alarm.

'So,' I spat out. 'Sorry about the tampons.'

'Oh, don't worry about that,' he said. 'You've done your time.'

Every year, since year seven, a nurse had come to science class to talk about periods and menstruation. We were never warned beforehand; it was always sprung on us at the beginning of the lesson. They'd schedule it for first term so the weather was still warm enough for the boys to go play sport with Mr Ackerman on the oval, while the girls were forced to sit again through the same embarrassing question time; the same video with the same girls wearing eighties hairstyles and wardrobes, back when it was really the eighties and before it was cool again.

This year when the boys returned after the talk, Sam Kinley and Sam Stewart had snatched my box of complimentary Tampax off my desk, and I was too embarrassed to ask for it back. While Mr Ackerman was out saying goodbye to the period lady, the boys had taken the tampons out and wet them under the tap, and then thrown them up at the ceiling where they'd stuck; hanging down above us for the rest of the lesson like the stalactites we'd learnt about the year before.

Later that afternoon, the tampons had dried up and started dropping one by one onto the heads and desks of Mr Ackerman and his year seven students. I wished I could have seen it. We were halfway through English class, and the boys were excused and the girls told to produce their tampon boxes right then and there. Of course, I was the only one who didn't have mine so I got dragged to Mr Ackerman's office, where I stood in front of him and told him with a straight face that I had got my period that day and had used them all up already.

'All of them?' he'd asked.

'Two at a time,' I'd said.

Unfortunately for me, Miss Varnish, the swimming teacher, had been keeping track of our cycles so we couldn't use the same excuse every week and, when consulted, she had divulged that I wasn't due for another fortnight. I wasn't about to dob on the Sams, so I'd sat through detention every Thursday night for a month.

When my drink came, I started eating the ice-cream out of it with a baby spoon. Mr Ackerman told me in his class voice to stir it in so it would sweeten the coffee. I left it to melt and reached for the sunglasses sitting next to his book and keys.

'Are these yours?' I asked, putting them on. They were too big for me. The arms reached way beyond my ears and I had to press the lenses to my face with my fingers to stop them falling off. The world looked blue from beneath those glasses, like science fiction. 'They're so bling.'

'I don't know about that.' He smiled for the first time, his face stubbly and blue now, too. 'I've had those since I was in high school. They're probably as old as you are.'

I kept them on while I tasted my coffee. It was still bitter and black and it made me cough so hard my throat stung. I pushed it aside. By the time we stood up to go, the ice-cream had floated to the top and was sitting on the surface, solidifying.

Mr Ackerman was shoving his wallet into his pocket when he came outside to where I waited on the kerb. 'Well, thanks for the company.'

'Thanks for the coffee.' I took a step closer. His eyes veered past me to the traffic in the street. 'You don't have to worry about being spotted by someone. I don't know anyone who lives on this side of town.'

He looked down at me with a small smile. 'I live on this side of town.'

'Oh, really? With your wife?'

'No, with my parents. I'm just here temporarily. On Charles Street.'

'Is that where you're going now then? To your mum and dad's?'

'No, actually, I was planning to go over to the NG—'

'I could come,' I cut in, lowering my voice, my eyes still on his. 'I've got nowhere else to be.'

On the tram, I sat down while he went to buy himself a ticket. When he came back, he stood across the aisle from me, and tilted his head to look out the opposite window. I looked too.

'Think it'll rain?' I asked without caring, and he shook his head.

'Nah,' he said. At a tram shelter outside, a group of girls were laughing and backing away from another girl, who was sitting on the bench, pulling off her jumper. She was red-faced, and laughing, too. A bird probably shat on her, I thought.

'Where are your friends today?' Mr Ackerman looked over at me.

'Uh, Amy's at drama lessons. Nat's babysitting. Courtney's at home, she's still got glandular.'

'And your family? How come you're out by yourself?'

'My parents are in Sorrento. We've got a place down there.'

'Ah, yes,' he said, as though he'd known that already. He had his sunglasses on his face now so I couldn't see his eyes. More than half the seats around me were empty but he stood the whole way there, his arm reaching above his head, past the swaying handles, to hold onto the rail.

The security guard and I played the game: he pretended not to be checking me out while I pretended not to notice. My teacher went to the cloakroom and I stopped at the first picture and checked my reflection in the gold frame. Why, I wondered, couldn't I have just drunk the stupid coffee?

'A monogamist.' Mr Ackerman had come up behind me.

'A pardon?'

'Chagall. He loved his wife very much.' He leaned in close to the painting. 'That's her up there, see? She's flying. And there he is, on the ground below, waiting for her to come down. Hoping to catch her. He put her in all his work.'

He walked on to look at the next one and I watched him go. For a science teacher he seemed to know a lot about art. I, on the other hand, didn't feel like learning school-ish things on the weekend. I dragged myself from painting to painting, ignoring the essay-long inscription next to each one, staring at the colours till they blurred before my eyes. I made inkblot tests of them all. Instead of a tableful of angels I saw a close-up of a mouth with teeth falling out; I turned a juggling bird into a woman belly dancing; a bunch of doves in a tree became soggy tampons just hanging there.

But it was true what Mr Ackerman had said, about the guy's wife. She was all over the place. First she lay draped naked over a tree of roses. Then she was dressed as a bride with a long veil and holding a baby. And later she wore a housedress and the two of them floated together above the orange floor of their kitchen.

I finished the room quickly and wandered back out to the foyer. That's where Mr Ackerman found me fifteen minutes later, sitting on a cushioned bench with my legs tucked under me, staring at the floor and pressing the pad of my thumb up onto the roof of my open mouth. He sat down beside me.

'I don't get what he saw in her,' I said. 'I mean, she was nothing special, as far as I could see. She had no fashion sense whatsoever and I'm sorry but her arse was gigantic.'

'Maybe Chagall liked substantially sized women,' Mr Ackerman offered. He laughed when I rolled my eyes at him. 'You've had enough, Miss Davies. You want to go home.'

'I want to eat.' I dragged myself to my feet. 'I haven't had anything all day.'

He knew a place in Southbank that was nice and quiet, with white tablecloths and waiters in half-aprons. He furrowed his brow over his menu like he did in class when someone gave a wrong answer, and he chose my meal for me because I couldn't decide. Then he asked me what had brought me to the 'wrong side of town'. So I told him about the formal dress, and the sewing lady at my dad's factory who had put straps on a strapless gown and how I wished I'd just gone to Chapel Street and bought something off the rack like all the other girls had because now I didn't even think I should go to the formal because I'd probably be the only one in straps. He was silent through all this, looking around the room at the empty tables, the waiters chatting near the kitchen, then out the window at the river.

'What's wrong?' I asked him.

'Oh. Nothing. It's just a little strange, I suppose, sitting here.'

'Do you want to go to the food court?'

'No. I just—I haven't eaten out in a restaurant for a long time. But this is nice. This is fine.' He looked at me. 'You're hungry.'

'I'm ravished,' I said, and he smiled and nodded down into his bread plate.

Halfway through our risottos, I finally got up the nerve to ask him if he was married. He had been, he told me, for three years, but it was over now and he didn't say why.

For a while after the divorce, he told me, he had stopped reading books. He couldn't sleep properly any more either. For the longest time, he said, he would go to see movies, dramatic movies, and keep his eyes closed the whole way through. Just so he could be moved by the music. I asked him why he didn't just stay home and listen to CDs in the dark, and he said he liked the ritual of buying the ticket, smiling at the popcorn sellers in their vests, and sitting among the couples and groups of kids who didn't bother turning off their phones before the main feature. He said he liked the way the score kept up throughout the whole film, dipping and rising, like someone's chest as they lay sleeping. It was cathartic, he said.

'What, like churchy?' I asked him.

'No,' he said. 'Like healing.'

'So now you read books again?'

'Yes, I've started to. And I guess I'm becoming more social.'

I had waited through the last few hours for him to tell me something about himself, something personal like this, but now that it had happened, I didn't know how to respond properly to any of it.

As he talked I found myself imagining the scene at home when I got back. The quiet that would greet me once I'd shut the big door behind me. The laughter of my sisters coming from somewhere in the back of the house. I saw myself going to the pantry and standing there, surveying the shelves full of lunchbox food: Le Snaks, fruit leathers, apple purees, and twelve-packs of Twisties. Leaving the kitchen without taking anything, I would sneak upstairs to my room unnoticed and lie on my bed in the dark, fully clothed, with my school books open on the desk, Natalie Portman grinning down off the wall, and the duct on the ceiling slowly exhaling its heat into the room.

'Excuse me, Sir, this card's been declined. Did you want me to try it again or use an alternative method of payment?' The waitress stood beside him with her hands behind her body. The two of them looked down at the insolent card that lay on the tablecloth, silent.

'Uh, give me a second.'

'Certainly, Sir.' She unclasped her hands but stayed where she was. Mr Ackerman fumbled through all his pockets.

'Shit,' he murmured, and I bit down on the inside of my lip. I shouldn't have eaten a main course, should have insisted on a soup or salad. I shouldn't have said I was hungry in the first place.

'I have some money,' I said. I took out thirty dollars and handed it to him.

'Thanks, Sascha, I'll pay you back. I have the money, it's just in a different account and I haven't transferred it yet.'

When the waitress came with the change, neither of us touched the five-dollar note lying on its plastic tray. The kitchen staff were loitering near their window, looking out at us. What are they thinking? I wondered. She's too old to be his daughter, probably, and too young to be his sister. I wondered what conclusion they'd reach.

Outside, a chilly afternoon wind had started blowing, and the clouds over the city were threatening something worse. We walked among the Saturday shoppers, all searching the sky for a sign of what next. By the time we reached Collins Street it had started to spit and I tried to lead him into a shoe shop.

'Don't worry,' he told me. 'It'll clear up any second.' But a few blocks later it was aiming at downpour status and the wind was so furious it was sucking people's umbrellas up into tulip shapes. 'Here.' He pulled me into a building and we stood inside the door, staring out at the water thrashing onto the road. We looked at each other, the rain streaming down our faces, and laughed.

We had walked into the foyer of an old school theatre. There were a few people sitting along the wall, reading or staring out at the rain, paying us no attention. There were posters behind them advertising films I'd never heard of, and the candy bar consisted of a basket of mixed-lolly bags selling, the handwritten sign told us, for $1.50 each.

The woman at the box office was glaring at us as though we should be paying for the privilege of taking refuge in her dingy little foyer. As though he agreed with her, Mr Ackerman wandered over and asked her when the next session started.

'There's one just started at four,' she growled at him. 'Or the next one's at half past.'

'Should we hide out 'til the rain stops?' he asked me and they both watched me nodding.

'One adult and one child?' She coolly met his eyes.

'Student.' We both reached for our wallets. 'One adult and one student.'

The movie was a foreign one, old and black and white, and as we sneaked in he whispered that he'd seen it before. The plot was nonexistent and there were no effects or celebrities; it was just people talking. I ignored the subtitles and studied the main girl, who had cropped hair and sold newspapers on the street. I wondered if he found her attractive. Probably, but why? I was yet to work out exactly what it was that guys found sexy in women but I knew whatever it was, I had it. My body was still boyish and small and straight up and down, but I knew that it was interesting to men, not necessarily the guys from school, but other men. I'd known this fact for two years now since the day on the train.

I had felt them before I saw them, the man's eyes on me. I had been sitting across from him and his family and looking out the window behind them at the back fences and side streets and the lights being turned on in small office buildings. Then, with a snap like a rubber band, I felt the heat of his gaze and shifted mine until we met.

It had been a Tuesday evening and I was twelve years old and heading home from school with my mind on homework and netball and *Big Brother* and then suddenly this man had found me, my reflection in the window, and held me there. His arm was thrown around his wife's shoulders and she fussed with the two small kids beside her.

'Don't do that!' She slapped the toddler's hand from its nose and the man smirked at me in the window and raised his eyebrows.

I don't know how long we sat like that for. My house was pretty close to school so it couldn't have been longer than five minutes but I knew as I sat there in my uniform, my nipples growing hard, my cheeks hot, the terrible secret passing between me and the stranger, that I was being admitted into a new world, that I was growing old or dying or changing or something. A sensation passed over me then, like insects crawling around on my back.

That was the first time. Since then I had started a list in a notebook in my room of other things that gave me that sensation. Like 50 Cent clips on MTV. A car crash I saw happen on Glenferrie Road. An article I read about peacekeepers and refugees in Africa. Being on a tram without a ticket when the inspectors climbed on. The faces of people waiting outside nightclubs on weekends. A porn site I'd found open on my dad's computer when I was checking my e-mail in his study one night. And standing in front of Mr Ackerman in his office and lying to his stern face that I had been shoving tampons up into my vagina, two at a time.

And so today, walking down Smith Street, when I'd glanced up from the footpath and seen him sitting there in the window, looking both strange and familiar, like photos of my parents when they were young, I had felt it—the heat, the hardness, the insects. I had turned into the café without missing a beat, as though this were a movie and I was only just now being shown the script. I had had the sudden and full knowledge that there was a reason I had been admitted into this new world, that here, today, later today, sometime, Mr Ackerman was going to take this feeling to its real and necessary ending.

In the flicker and dark of the movie, I closed my eyes. There was no soundtrack but I listened to the up-and-down lilts of the language as though it was music. I leaned my head onto his shoulder. His jacket still held the cold of the rain and it smelled like outside when I breathed into it. Mr Ackerman put his hand on my hair and stroked it. I felt dizzy and humid, like I was flying above myself in the dark. I imagined him standing below me like that painter guy, getting ready to catch me before I hit the ground.

'Mr Ackerman,' I whispered, my teeth against his jacket.

'Are you tired, Sascha?' His mouth found my ear and he took his eyes off the screen. 'Or do you want to go somewhere else?'

The Face of 1970

by

MARK DAPIN

I PARKED THE KINGSWOOD outside the motel across the road from the Commercial pub. She coughed as she braked and sighed when she stopped. Frankie said she sounded like she was slipping away. Frankie is supposed to be my driver, but he does not see so well after Singleton.

The car door swung open like a gate in a gale. Frankie said he had to do something about those hinges. A fat man watched us from the motel, with fried-egg eyes. Frankie opened the boot and tugged at the amp, but he could not lift it out. I reached over to help him, and between us we hauled it onto the tarmac. Frankie's back is not what it used to be since Singleton, and I guess I am my own roadie now.

The fat man saw us struggling with the gear, so he lit a cigarette. I heard music from the pub, a bass that bounced under the pavement.

The fat man showed us our room, which had only one bed. It smelled of sweat and chicken. I said we asked for two beds. He said the motel was full, but we had passed half a dozen rooms with open curtains and folded towels. He said a coach party was due in later on. 'Maybe they're coming to see your show,' he said, and he made his mouth twitch at one corner. He crushed his cigarette in the ashtray under the mirror.

When Frankie has dreams, he jerks and he thrashes about, so I unrolled my swag against the wall. Frankie said I ought to take the bed, but I know his bones ache more than mine. Frankie tuned my guitar, because it was something he still could do, while I splashed my face with cold water and tried to think of the last time we played this town. I thought it was four years ago, and there was a red-haired woman with grape-green eyes.

Frankie played the opening chords to 'Mandy' and howled like a wild dog. I laughed, like I always did, because something about Frankie puts me in a good mood.

If you remember any one of my songs, it would be 'Mandy'. It was the Christmas hit of 1970. Your sharpie dad probably felt your virgin mum's breasts while 'Mandy' played on the Dansette. It is about a girl who stows away with a sailor, and is based on the true story of what did not happen to me when I joined the Royal Australian Navy and shipped out to Vietnam. The real Mandy left me for Jack Reynolds, who got a deferment to study animal dentistry. I opened her letter in Vung Tau, and counted the kisses.

We dragged the amplifier over to the Commercial Hotel. Frankie carried my guitar on his back. It was seven o'clock and the bar was half full. There was nobody wearing an admiral's hat, but sometimes they hide them in their sports bags and do not bring them out until I come on stage.

The barman offered us a drink, and we both asked for a beer.

'Six bucks,' said the barman.

'We're the band,' said Frankie.

'That and six bucks'll get you two beers,' said the barman.

He wore black tattoos. He wouldn't even have been born when I was the Face of 1970.

'Where's the dressing room?' asked Frankie.

The barman covered his smile with his hand. 'Most people come in here already dressed,' he said. 'But then, we don't get too many international acts.'

'We had hits in Japan,' said Frankie. 'And Germany, New Zealand . . .'

Frankie plugged in the amp while I smeared gel though my hair, checking my reflection in the base of the foil ashtray. A guy with food on his face wolf-whistled. His mate, who could only stand if he held on to his stool, blew me a kiss.

It was not always like this. In 1970 they called me 'the new Digger Ronnie Blake'. Digger Ronnie Blake had six top-ten hits in 1969, including 'The Girl I Left Behind (Was the Woman who Waited for Me)', which also did not happen. The girl Ron left behind ran off with his bassist. I had her later, under the tarpaulin at the Isa, her warm hands pulling hard on my hips, her painted nails carving bloodlines into my shoulders.

I came back from Vietnam with a medal for killing. I was drinking in a navy bar with Jim MacLean when the Viet Cong tossed in a grenade. One minute I was talking to a man with a nose and a mouth, the next I was looking at a burning, screaming piece of meat. I chased Charlie into the street and hit him with a broken bottle. First I caved in his skull, then I dug out his eyes. Most nights, I dream of featureless men clawing at my eyes, trying to take them for themselves.

When I got home, my brother-in-law introduced me to his accountant, Izzy Berger. He came to watch me and the boys play at a club in Kings Cross. At the time, we were the Jacob Goldman Band. Berger said the name made us sound like some kind of rubber-lipped nigger jazz quartet. 'You should call yourself Lucky Jack Gold,' he suggested, and I thought he was talking to me.

I did not want to make a big thing out of the Navy, but Berger said we needed something to make us stand out from the other bands. I thought that could be my songs.

Berger told me I was a war hero and, just like Digger Ronnie had his slouch hat, I should wear a navy cap. This was at the end of the sixties, and somehow that little white cap grew into an admiral's hat. Berger tried to talk me into wearing an eye patch.

The first Lucky Jack Gold record was 'Sail On'. It was supposed to be about me saying goodbye to a girl who was leaving for England, and wishing her all the luck and the love she deserved. You could hear it another way, though. Some people thought I was telling Australian battleships to sail on to Nha Trang or somewhere, and the RAN kind of adopted the song.

As I sipped at my schooner in the Commercial Hotel, a bloke my age slapped my back and said, 'Sail on, Jack. You won't be buying another drink tonight.'

Frankie called 'testing one-two-three' through the microphone. The guy with food on his face applauded, as if it were a song.

As soon as I finished my beer, the barman brought another to my table.

'Courtesy of the old fellas,' he said. Life's not so bad, really.

Frankie warmed up the crowd with the same jokes he has been telling since 1968. Nobody was listening and I was the only person who clapped. Frankie, who could not tell where the applause was coming from, beamed and bowed. He has lost a lot of weight. His biceps have collapsed and his veins jumped out of his skin, but he still wears a white, sleeveless T-shirt with 'Lucky Jack Gold' in stardust across the chest. Berger threatened to sue him, but Frankie says it is the only shirt he's got. His suitcase is stuffed with them, all neatly pressed and folded. They hang from his shoulders like curtains.

'And, now,' Frankie bellowed weakly, 'ladieees and gentlemennn, you've truly "struck gold" tonight, because right here, on stage, for the first time this millennium, it's the boy who's worth his weight in bullion, the singer from St Kilda with the Midas touch, the one and only *face* of 1970, Lucky . . . Jack . . . Gold!'

Berger would have Frankie's arse if he heard him talking that way.

Frankie turned on the backing tape, and I wandered up to the stage. A couple of drinkers shook my hand. Two pretty girls left the bar.

I opened my set with 'Mandy', and as soon as I finished 'Mandy' I went into 'Rebecca', which is pretty much what happened in real life. I did a medley to get the crowd warmed up—a bit of the Beatles, a snatch of Motown, a couple of choruses of Digger Ronnie Blake—then dived into 'Sail On'. I did not have all that many hits, so I generally play every song twice.

Frankie stood at the front, whooping and cheering and yelling, clapping his bony hands. When I sang 'Sail On', he rubbed tears into his eyes.

'Hello, Sailor!' shouted Food-on-his-face a dozen times.

In the old days, Frankie would have leapt across the floor and pushed the man's pig nose into the back of his bowling-ball head, but he lost his fight in Singleton, left his punch on the town hall floor.

The war was a waste of two years of my life and all of Jim MacLean's life. I didn't like the way 'Sail On' was misunderstood, so I wrote 'Don't Go'. It was a love song, like 'Sail On', but this time I was telling the girl to stay put and not go overseas. It was number one for five weeks, before it was knocked off by 'Angie'.

Nobody got the message, so I had to tell them straight. At the Christmas bush dance in Singleton, which we used to play every year, I introduced the song with a bit of a speech. I said, 'Don't go following orders. Don't go following officers. Don't go to Vietnam.'

The town hall was wriggling with toey conscripts just finished their training. At first, they just booed us, then they threw bottles. Frankie picked one up and hurled it back, and it was on for one and all. The drummer got his head put through the bass drum, the bassist had his teeth knocked out with his own bass heads, and three Queensland boys held me up against the wall and took turns to bash my skull against the bricks. Frankie flew in and floored every one of them. And when Frankie knocked you down, you did not get up. The problem was, there were four guys in the band—and Frankie lugging the gear—but thirty boys from the base. They had us all on the ground in the end, but they really took it out on Frankie. The last thing I remember, they had made a circle around him, kicking him in the head.

These days I sing 'Don't Go' without an introduction. People can take it any way they want.

We couldn't get a gig anywhere after Singleton. Our label dumped us, and Berger broke up the band. We never made any money for ourselves. Most of it went on management fees or expenses, or an investment Berger made for us in phosphate mining in Kiribati, where there isn't any phosphate.

I went solo, and played in pubs around Western Australia and the Northern Territory. Frankie stuck with me, although half the time I could not pay him. In 1973

I was served a writ from Berger, who said I could not keep performing as 'Lucky Jack Gold' because he owned the name.

I yelled at him from a phone box outside the Battery Hill hotel in Tennant Creek, asking whether he wanted to call himself Lucky Jack Gold, Chartered Fucking Accountant.

He said no, because Lucky Jack Gold was not the name of any one person, it was the name of the band. He had thought of it and he had registered it, back in 1969. He said Lucky Jack Gold had re-formed without me, and the new singer was called Simon Monahan. If I wanted to keep playing their songs, I was welcome, but I had to do it as Jacob Goldman's Lucky Jack Gold Show. Also, I had to pay Berger royalties, because he owned the publishing rights to the songs I had written.

Frankie wanted to kill him.

When I turn up at a pub under the new name, most people expect a tribute band, playing Lucky Jack Gold covers. They think Lucky Jack Gold died in a car crash near Broome, but that was Digger Ronnie Blake.

I was the face of 1970, but you wouldn't recognise that face now. It's got lines across the cheeks like a map of all the roads I have driven with Frankie, working this big, empty country from St Kilda to Port Hedland.

Sometimes I tell stories about the old days, just to break up the set. I knew everyone in 1970. I drank whisky with Hans Poulsen, played poker with the Mixtures, had Liv Maessen in the back of a truck—but nobody remembers those names now. It's like 1970 has been forgotten. You never hear about it. It's always '1967' or '1969' or '1974'. I don't know why. It was a good year.

At the Commercial Hotel, I did the yarn about Lionel Rose and the trapeze artist. It got a laugh, because everybody loves old Lionel, and everybody knows how much he likes a drink. I think the crowd warmed to me, because they clapped during the second half of the set, even though I was just playing the same songs again.

I finished with 'Mandy'. Food-on-his-face-and-hat-on-his-head came onto the stage and sung with me, his heavy arm around my shoulder. He wanted me to come down and have a drink with him and his mates. I said I had to help Frankie load up the stuff.

'Fuck off, then,' he said, 'you stuck-up cunt.'

Back at the motel, I was about to lie down on my swag—Frankie was already asleep—when I heard a soft knock, like a cat bumping against the motel-room door. I picked up Frankie's baseball bat, and held it lightly against my leg.

I opened the door slowly, and there she was, in a tight sweater and a skirt that showed her knees. She was carrying bourbon from the bottle shop, and she reached for my hand.

She led me through the forecourt, over the railway track and past the cenotaph. We kicked off our shoes and ran barefoot across the bowling green. We turned on every light in her house, and made love on the couch.

Afterwards, she rolled a joint.

'That was to thank you for such a beautiful song,' she said.

'Which one?' I asked.

' "Rachel",' she said. 'I used to pretend it was about me.'

Actually, 'Rachel' wasn't one of mine. It was a hit in 1971 for Digger Ronnie Blake, but as I kissed Rachel's breasts and ran my fingers over her thighs, the digger raised a glass to me in heaven.

Faith

by

SANDRA WHITE

M Y SISTER KILLED MAX on good friday. She believed in resurrection on the third day, Easter Sunday, just like Jesus. But I could've told her that cat wasn't coming back.

My sister's name is Charlotte but we've always called her Charlie because she was never going to be a Charlotte. The cat's name was Maxine, after Maxine Brown, a sixties singer my mother said was underrated. But we've always called her Max.

My sister's got an apocalyptic vision of the world: you know, the rights and the wrongs of the world, fire and brimstone, thy kingdom come. She veers between the Old and the New Testament, depending on what day it is.

They stuff her full of it at Sunday school. I won't go any more. My father only sends her there for babysitting, free child care from God, but she wants to be there anyway.

The other night she came out of the bathroom with her hair slicked back and swept down her neck.

'Just like John the Baptist,' I said.

'Don't patronise me,' she said. 'You're always patronising me.' She's got some big words for a ten-year-old.

'I'm not always patronising you.'

'You are.'

'Am not.'

This went on for a while before she said: 'I'm as deaf as a post and I can't hear a word you say', which was really annoying because I started that game and now she'd stolen it. When I tried to say something she put her hands over her ears and sang La-la-la to drown me out. Then I pushed her, which made her so mad she knocked me to the floor and started bashing my face. That hurt, so I biffed her one. She yelped and ran to her room crying.

She didn't tell. She's not a dobber. Anyway, she never says anything about anything any more, except for the God stuff, which I've told her I don't want to hear.

Most of our arguments are settled on the living-room floor, 'The Ring', we call it. Even though she's small, she's wiry and strong. Just talking about it, I can almost feel her foot in my crotch, her favourite place to kick me when her back's against the wall. My father says it's not gentlemanly to hit a girl, but he doesn't know her I like I know her.

Anyway, it's for her own good. With her temper she'll be in fights for the rest of her life. Now I'm doing karate, I hide behind the door and practise sudden moves on her. I use the element of surprise to get her in a headlock. 'Hey, sis, get out of this one.' This makes her go mental, and even though she's younger than me, and a girl, sometimes I can tell by the look in her eye that it would be better to let her go.

Then there's Dad. In court they call him the 'Hanging Judge'. After a day of sending drink-drivers to jail, he loves celebrating with beer, whisky chasers and his boozy friends. When he's thoroughly relaxed he catches the 'blue light taxi', which means some young copper has to drive him home.

These days he's even drunker and later getting home. After Mum left, everything fell apart. She went on a day Dad was meant to be collecting us from the babysitter's, only he was at the pub. Mum was supposed to be at art class, but she wasn't. She was getting picked up by Dave, who was younger than her and had scruffy hair and wore shorts all the time. Dad refers to people like that as 'long-haired louts', but obviously Mum saw something in Dave because that day she got in his car and that was the last we saw of her.

The cat took Mum leaving as badly as we did. Max was Mum's cat: chosen by Mum, named by Mum, abandoned by Mum. After she left, Max would come into the house and look around distractedly, as if something were missing but she was unsure what.

'I don't know how any child of mine could have turned into such a God botherer,' my father has said more than once, and loud enough for Charlie to hear it.

'Keep an eye on her,' he says, even though I've tried to explain that it's a thankless job looking out for that girl.

Last weekend while Dad was out, there was a horrible yowling sound in the bathroom. I rushed in to find Charlie holding Max tightly and wrapped in one of my old T-shirts. She was pouring water over Max's face as the cat protested loudly.

'What are you doing?!'

'Baptising Max.'

'What?'

'She won't go to heaven if she's not baptised.'

'That's people—not cats, you freak. And you're crazy if you believe people go to heaven . . .'

'That's not true. You're insulting my religious beliefs. Say you're sorry!' Charlie was demented, which gave Max the chance to struggle out of her arms and scramble off, the T-shirt dragging behind.

I nodded my head in the direction of the retreating Max and grinned. 'And Max agrees . . .'

'Shut up! Shut up! Say you're sorry!'

'Sorrr—' I began.

'Say it properly!' She was hysterical now.

'Sss,' I hissed.

Her face went red. 'You think you're smart, but you're not,' she screamed, then ran up to her room. She called down a moment later: 'And remember, the meek shall inherit the earth . . . arsehole!'

This morning I heard the front door slam and I knew Dad was back. 'Anybody there?' he called upstairs.

I didn't answer. I got as far as the door, then hesitated. He thought he could just turn up after ages and call and I'd jump? He thought wrong.

There was no sign of Charlie. She was probably down at her secret cubby-hole, which she'd made me swear on the Bible that I wouldn't tell Dad about. She was becoming more and more distant, and sometimes I wondered what thread was holding her to anything at all. There was no sign of Max, either. I hadn't seen her since the baptism.

'Tom, Tom!' My father's voice was more insistent. Ignoring him was not an option.

'What?'

'Come downstairs, please.'

He was standing in the kitchen wearing his 'uniform' of white shirt with rolled-up sleeves, khaki trousers and brown lace-ups. The shirt needed ironing and the trousers, even by my standards, needed a good wash. He might've been paying Mrs McPherson to do our washing, ironing, cleaning and cooking, but if he'd bothered to ask me I could've told him he was not getting his money's worth.

'Where's Charlie?'

'Dunno.'

A flash of irritation crossed Dad's face before it settled back into distraction. 'We're going to visit Aunty Liz and Uncle Bob and we're going to give them some Easter eggs,' he said. 'Then we'll look for Charlie.' Aunty Liz used to be Mum's best friend. She's married to Uncle Bob, in theory. I didn't know why I had to come along. Maybe because it was Easter Sunday, since Dad usually visited her by himself when Bob was at work.

Before I knew it, Dad had pushed me into the car and started the engine. Dad swung out of the driveway and his heavy old bomb jolted over the dirt road. Because it'd been dry lately, every pothole was a killer. As soon as we were there, Dad wasted no time getting in the door and saying to Uncle Bob, 'Happy Easter, mate, we thought we'd drop by some Easter eggs for you.'

What's this *we* shit, Lone Ranger? I asked myself.

Aunty Liz thanked us but had a strange look on her face. Uncle Bob had an even stranger look on his. Aunty Liz went into the kitchen to make some coffee. I liked Uncle Bob and Aunty Liz, but I wasn't happy with Dad, and I showed it by slouching and staring out the window.

We sat in the sunken lounge, surrounded by bricks and shag carpet. There was a pot plant stuck in the fireplace, because the weather was way too hot for a real fire. Aunty Liz put the coffee down on the table in front of Dad. She must have misjudged the distance because the cup banged down hard on the glass table. 'Thanks, Liz,' Dad said too loudly, not looking up. I'm sure he'd have preferred a beer, but it was eleven o'clock in the morning and he was trying to impress.

Uncle Bob was going on about some new tower block he was designing and Dad was pretending that he was interested. The windows in the room were huge. Looking down at the river, I could see the tide was going out fast.

Aunty Liz was busying herself in the kitchen. It sounded like she was washing the same plates over and over. Dad's eyes kept flicking towards the sound of the clattering plates.

Maybe my sulk was having the right effect, because Dad asked, 'Tom, would you like to go and look for Charlie and take her home?'

'Not really.'

'It's not really a request,' he said.

I gave some rocks a good kick along the way, thinking about how Charlie refused to get in the car with Dad any more because he was always crashing into things after he'd been drinking. Charlie's new hard-line attitude must have cut him up. Charlie had always been his favourite, but now she was AWOL all the time and as mad as a cut snake to boot.

Further away from Aunty Liz and Uncle Bob's house the river was quieter. With the tide going out you could see the roots of the mangrove trees exposed on the muddy bank. It smelt like rotting plants, with a few mozzies and sandflies about. As I got closer the mangrove started to thin out. The rocks there were large and jagged, with big pools of water between them. The headland was rough and windswept and I felt almost inhabited by the wildness of Charlie. I could see why she liked it there. This was a place where she knew she would be alone—a wide open place. I helped her to make this hideaway in the rock cave by the sea but as the tide roared closer I knew it had been a bad idea. I crept towards the entrance of the cave.

Charlie was there with Max. She must have carried her there in a basket or something because there was no way Max would've come this far by herself. At first I wasn't sure what was going on. Then I saw the splatter of dried blood down the cat's chest.

'I'm sorry, I'm sorry,' she was saying over and over.

The tide was coming in. I got Charlie and held her close, the dead cat crushed between us. Then I led her away. She clutched the cat. We didn't speak.

It was very quiet when we got back to Aunty Liz and Uncle Bob's. Dad was on his own at the back door. He was pale, and paler still when he saw us, Charlie holding Max tight. He guided her to the car without a word. 'In the back,' was all he said to me.

The drive home seemed much longer. I wound down the window and let the empty air rush over my face, the deserted Easter streets streaming past.

I don't remember much else. I remember thinking about Mum and Dad, Charlie and Max. And thinking, if this is what faith is, then it must have taken a lot to do this. If there's one thing Charlie's tried to keep, it's faith.

Salem Lodge

by

ALEX MILLER

W AS THERE EVER SUCH A THING as a memory that was inviolate and which could not be corrupted? 'Sit on my knee, Michael,' his father said and patted his knees. Michael scrambled onto his father's knee and his father placed a hand to his back to steady him. Michael looked out at the London traffic framed by the narrow side window. He breathed on the cold glass then rubbed away the misting of his breath with his fingers. They were in the back seat of the car, so it was probably a taxi, or maybe the people had sent a car and a driver to pick them up. He had never been in a car before. He could smell the leather and the warm tobacco smell of his father's clothes and he was not afraid. When they arrived, his father held his hand and they walked up the wide steps together. A large woman dressed in grey stood at the top of the steps above them. She opened a big glass swing door for them and admitted them to the foyer, which was deserted and chilly… His father had gone. Michael's nose was bleeding, it was pressed against the wall, the shiny green tiles cold against his skin, a sharp stink in his nostrils.

The screen of Michael's memory went blank after this. He had always referred to the institution as Salem Lodge, but his mother corrected him when he did so in her presence once and gave him the correct name. He did not retain the correct name of the home, however, and persisted in referring to it in his mind as Salem Lodge. While he was growing up, living with his parents in the flat in Downham and attending the local secondary modern school, he seemed to forget about the home. The episode was never referred to in the family, nor did he speak to his school friends about it. After he had left school and was working as a labourer's boy on the farm in Somerset—which was probably the happiest, or at least the most innocent, period of his life—he and Morris, the labourer with whom he was living, were eating their lunch in the woods one winter day. Morris had never been to London and was curious to hear about Michael's life there. For some reason Michael found himself telling Morris about being sent to the children's home when he was a small child, recounting the shard of memory of Salem Lodge—even though he knew that was not its real name—which was all that remained to him of the experience.

He and Morris were sitting on the stumps of trees they had felled for timber in the spring. They had spread sacks on the stumps to keep their breeches from melting the ice and getting wet—their brown corduroy breeches and leather leggings were identical. Michael always did as Morris did, and was careful to model his behaviour and his dress on those of the older man, but discreetly and with respect, so that Morris probably felt flattered. Where they had cleared the leaves back, the ground in the wood was frozen and the nails on the soles of his boots rang like hammers against it when he swung his legs. The wood pigeons cooed in the branches of the leafless elms above them and Morris listened with attention, pausing in his eating until Michael had finished telling him about Salem Lodge. Morris was silent then for a long while. At last, and with a considered gravity that offered a certain respect to the story he had just been told, he said, 'The experience of being sent away to a children's home at such a tender age would have left its mark on you, Michael, and that mark will stay with you till the end of your days.' Then he added this: *Like a brand on the hide of a beast.* Which was typical of his way of speaking. And it was something that stuck with Michael. *Like a brand on the hide of a beast.* There was no harm in repeating it.

He could not remember ever speaking to anyone else before this about the home. After telling Morris, Michael often thought of Salem Lodge and of what Morris had said, and when he was lying awake in his bed at night he sometimes relived the experience of travelling to the home in the back of the car with his father, then finding himself alone and pressed against the green tiles in the corridor, his nose streaming blood down the front of his green pullover. It disturbed him to think of the home, and no matter how hard he tried he was never able to add to his fragment of memory. The loss of memory, he knew, must have been enormous. What was down there? What had happened to him at Salem Lodge? He would love to have known. But, truthfully, he was afraid too of what it might be and was not altogether sorry he had forgotten. The words 'Salem Lodge', along with the unpleasant smell of the place, stood in his mind for the meaning of evil, but he did not know why. He wished he had been able to ask his parents their reason for his temporary exile from the family. But that had not been possible. And now they were both dead it was too late.

He was fishing with his father one summer day at Keston Ponds—the memory of that day suddenly came back to him now. His brother David was still a baby at his mother's breast at the time, so he, Michael, must have been seven or eight years of age. His father baited the hook for him with one of the soft pink earthworms they had dug up together earlier in the garden. The worms were still alive and moved slowly over each other in the jar, tying knots of themselves. His father handed him the baited rod and then unfolded the portable stool he carried with him on these occasions and Michael sat beside him. While Michael fished, his father made a number of pencil and watercolour sketches of the scene. It was quiet there by the pond and the June sun was warm. They did not speak but each attended to his business. Then, quite suddenly, and for no reason, Michael asked his father, in a voice that was calm and quiet and not at all agitated, but as if his question were of little consequence to either of them, 'Why did you and Mum send me away to that children's home that time?'

His float bobbed and he struck but failed to hook the fish. When he drew in his line he saw that the fish had taken his bait. He turned around and began to rebait his hook with one of the worms in the jam jar. He saw then that his father had his head in his hands and was weeping. Michael put down his rod and put his arms around his father and stood close against him. His father was shaking with sobs that tore at his chest. Michael was too shocked and too afraid to speak. From that day on he placed his question in a deep hole far inside himself and closed the hole over with a landscape of his own invention, and he never again asked his father or mother why they had sent him to Salem Lodge. It was too much.

After his brother's visit and their long talks by the fire during the evenings, and the suicide of Karen, all this, which had left him in peace for many years, came back to Michael and tormented him with uncertainties about himself. He woke very early in the morning, while it was still night really, when he should still have been asleep, and was assailed by the black thought of Salem Lodge and Morris's words, *Like a brand on the hide of a beast*. He could not see what any of this had to do with Karen's death, but he did feel guilty at having avoided her when she had tried to speak to him. He had avoided her because he had sensed that she was deeply troubled and in need of the kind of help he knew he was incapable of giving her. But he still felt guilty. They had once been lovers after all, and that should, he knew, have given her the right to appeal to him. There seemed to be no obvious connection between these two events, however, the one that had happened so long ago and the other that had happened so recently. Except, of course, the obvious connection that he united these two events in his own private history. As the weeks went by he was troubled and unable to shake off a sense of futility and increasing helplessness.

He went up to town on the weekend and he and Alice went to an early movie at the Nova then had a meal in a restaurant in Lygon Street. It was a small and rather unfashionable restaurant, and perhaps was not really a restaurant at all but a café with a certain reputation for its evening entertainments rather than for its food. South American music was played there and some of the evening crowd spoke Spanish. Michael saw that the two women who ran the café—for that is what he had decided to call it—had not consciously intended to give their patrons the illusion of being travellers in South America, and were oblivious to this side benefit. They had merely done at the café the one thing they had known how to do. The café was a replica of one in their own home country of Argentina, to which they had added over the years elements of Chile and Peru and Guatemala and Bolivia and some photographs of Mexican children and old women. But nothing from Spain itself. Michael sometimes drank a Bolivian beer there with a friend or a colleague when he was not with Alice. He liked the modest style the women had adopted. Unlike the hundreds of Italian restaurants and cafés along the street, the Argentinian women did not make any attempt to market themselves, but just went along being themselves, as if it had never occurred to them to think that this would not be enough to satisfy their customers. The café was often completely deserted at lunchtimes, but the calm and cheerful attitude of the two women remained the same. It was as if they thought to themselves, Well, life has to be lived and there is nothing to be done about it, especially not worrying about things like a lack of customers when everyone else along the street is pumping out pizzas as fast as they can and is still not able to satisfy the demand. *We don't do pizzas*, they said and smiled whenever someone enquired. *But molettes and tortillas we do*. Of course nobody knew what molettes were, especially when pronounced with a thick Argentinian accent that made it sound like *moyettay*. Was it that? So interest was slight, as it is well known that people go for what they already know and are not interested in stuff they don't know.

The café was a haven of calm and Michael often went there for coffee or a meal when he was in the city. The coffee was always hot and strong and he never had to ask for it to be that way.

Alice and he both ordered steaks. The larger of the two women brought them a bottle of Chilean white wine and said good evening to them. They drank the wine while they were waiting for their steaks. The film, which was French and had been shot in black and white, had started promisingly from a good idea that seemed to suggest something mysterious and interesting going on between a beautiful and rather sad woman and a man twenty or thirty years older than her, but the director had not been able to work out what to do with his idea and after the first very beautiful and suggestive scenes he had kept elaborating on the idea until he finally ran out of time and brought the movie to an abrupt end. Alice said, 'That director couldn't find the end of the story, so he just gave up and stopped.' Michael thought this was a pretty fair comment. But even though it had not taken the initial idea anywhere, he had enjoyed the film. He did not tell Alice this. It was the kind of film during which it was possible for him to dream about other things than the film while enjoying the images on the screen, as if the film were a safe way of looking at his own thoughts. And, anyway, he didn't as a rule care about endings in films unless they were old Westerns, in which the endings often held all the meaning of the film. He usually forgot endings, and indeed whole films, minutes after he came out of the cinema.

When their steaks came, Alice said, in a slightly put-on voice, as if she were trying not to give too much meaning to her question, 'So are you staying in town tonight or going home?'

Michael spread hot English mustard on his steak and thought about her question. It surprised him. He was expecting to stay at her flat as he usually did when he came to the city.

She put her hand on his. 'I didn't mean that to sound the way it did, Michael. I just wondered. That's all.' She smiled and called the thin woman over and ordered a bottle of the Chilean red.

Another couple came into the café and sat at a table across from them and they talked in low voices and leaned close to each other and every now and then they looked across at Michael and Alice but they did not offer any kind of greeting or eye contact.

Michael cut a piece of steak and put it in his mouth and chewed. The meat was tough and overcooked. The soft Latin music was fine though. He did not care much about food. He did not know how to answer Alice's question.

She said, 'I like coming here with you. I don't know anyone else who comes here. You always find unusual places. When I mention this place, no-one ever knows it.'

He was sure that what she really meant by the word *unusual* was that her steak was tough and overcooked and the wine was not very good. She was wearing a white blouse and small green earrings, her dark hair cut short and only just reaching the collar of her blouse. She looked very smart and petite and attractive. Her lipstick had worn off. She had begun to look older lately and he thought it suited her. She was thirty-five. Fifteen years younger than he. Almost, he sometimes thought, another generation. There were times when he felt they had nothing in common and had never really met but had only pretended to meet for the sake of sex and each other's companionship now and then, their deeper realities always elsewhere and held back out of sight from each other. He was thinking about Karen's class paper and her suicide. Suddenly, without meaning to, he began to tell Alice about it.

She stopped eating and looked at him and held up her hand. 'Please!' she said, appalled by what he was telling her. 'Please don't tell me! I don't want to hear.'

He apologised and said no more. She had not known Karen anyway.

Alice said, 'I just can't bear to hear anything tragic at the moment.'

He apologised again. Then he said, 'I gave her a mark of 100 per cent for her class paper.'

Alice stared at him, horrified.

'I've never done that before.'

Alice shook her head and the little green earrings shook and her short hair shook. 'Michael, please!' she begged him. 'Can't we just eat our dinner and be happy?'

He apologised again. 'Sorry,' he said. 'I haven't really been able to tell anybody, that's all. I keep thinking about her. We were lovers years ago. It took a lot of courage for her to enrol in my class. A lot of courage.'

Alice said, 'Perhaps you should see a counsellor.'

He laughed. It was not a laugh of amusement but was sudden and rather wild, more like a bark or a shout, as if someone had trodden on his foot. The other two customers looked up at him quickly, as if they expected something eccentric to happen. 'I won't stay the night if you don't want me to,' he said.

'I didn't say I didn't want you to stay the night,' she said and she sounded a little haughty. 'I just asked, that's all.' Then, after a moment, she added, 'Sometimes I don't know you.'

'Sometimes I don't know myself,' he said. He tried to keep his voice and his manner light and cheerful, but did not quite succeed.

She looked at him as if she wished to let him know that she had no time for this sort of thing. She cut the last of her steak into two neat cubes then put one of the cubes into her mouth.

As she opened her mouth to take in the cube of meat he felt himself mimicking her, opening his own mouth slightly and tilting his head the way she tilted her head, like a bird taking a titbit. He saw the raw pink membranes of her gullet. Skeins of mucous and a number of chewed shreds of steak clinging there. He pretended to cough and looked away.

'You just seem to want to keep things secret sometimes,' she said. 'I don't know why you do that. You know I don't like secrets.'

He drove out along the empty freeway. The night was clear and there was a nearly full moon. The wide landscape of paddocks and wooded hills was bright, empty and still. Since his brother's visit he had felt as if his life had begun to erode—he imagined the foundation stones of a building beginning to crumble to dust while the building remained upright and unscathed and as solid-looking as ever, then suddenly the whole thing collapsing in a heap of smoking rubble. He didn't think he was being fanciful. A big old male kangaroo sailed over the fence and crossed the freeway ahead of him. The graceful creature was like a ghost from another world, grey and silver and silently gliding through the moonlight as if the freeway was not there, following some archaic pathway inscribed in its mind, seeing another landscape. He thought of his youth in North Queensland, tailing a mob of quiet cattle through the great moonlit savannas of the Gulf of Carpentaria. A few kilometres further on, a carcass of another kangaroo lay sprawled and eviscerated in the lane in front of him. In the moonlight it looked like a Francis Bacon portrait. One of Bacon's gay friends.

Perhaps Alice was right and he should see a counsellor. But he knew he would not ask for help. Even if he needed help he knew he would not ask for it from someone whose job it was to help people. There would be more dignity in suicide. He realised how greatly he admired Karen for doing it. Taking her own life. Taking it from herself. He had been no help to her. A hundred per cent had not been enough to give her confidence. She must have thought he was . . . He couldn't think of the word. A couple of kilometres later the word floated up: *insincere*. Well, he was. Was it possible to be sincere? About other people?

When he got home he went out and stood in the back garden. The night was still and quiet. He liked to hear the steady humming of the great looms at the carpet factory and imagined the workers toiling through the night in the great weaving hall, seeing them as if they were figures in a nineteenth-century engraving, an allegory of how man is dwarfed by his machines. He envied them their lives. He had been born into the working class. Why had he ever left it? The round prison tower on the hill stood clean and solid in the moonlight. He thought of Karen's question, *I wondered if Rilke himself had ever been an inmate in an institution for the insane*. He didn't know the answer. The whole of Paris, he seemed to recall, had been for Rilke an institution for the insane. His telephone was ringing. It was three in the morning. He hurried into the house and picked up the receiver. It was Alice. She was crying. 'I'm truly sorry, Michael. But I just can't bear it any more.'

He could hear someone moving about in the background of her flat. He felt chilled by what she said. 'I'm sorry,' he said. 'I didn't realise we were having so much difficulty.'

She sniffed and said, 'You just don't seem to realise *anything*.'

'No. I'm sorry. I've been preoccupied since my brother's visit. I'm not sure why.'

'Oh it's not just since your brother's visit!' She sounded angry now, as if the tears had been merely a plea for his sympathy. 'It's you. You just don't notice what other people are feeling. You never have.'

He waited, listening to the odd background sounds. 'Why did you ring me at three in the morning?'

'It's over, Michael. Surely even you must have realised that tonight.'

He asked, 'Are you on your own?'

There was a long silence. Then she said, 'After you left I couldn't bear it and I called Andrew.' There was a pause, then she said, 'Goodbye, Michael.'

He stood with the dead telephone in his hand, then he slowly replaced it. He had not put the light on in the kitchen, but it was flooded with moonlight. He had expected to stay in town and so had not lit the Rayburn before going up. By morning there would be a frost. Karen had said, *I just want to know that I belong.* Wasn't it what everyone wanted and no-one could have? To be free and to belong. How could it be done? He thought of getting her photograph out of the manilla envelope his brother had left, but decided not to. He was cold and tired. He went to bed.

Guerrillas in Your Midst

by

LUKE STICKELS

Who can thwart the global system?
Certainly not the anti-globalization movement . . .
–Jean Baudrillard, 2002

S OMETIMES YOU DO THINGS **you thought you'd never do.**

I went to the meeting with Amber because she convinced me that people are stronger together than apart. I went because she talked of an immense beast, so destructive in its myopic focus and in its callous disregard that it must be brought to heel. I went because I've been masturbating about her twice a day for the last week. I went because Jonie's been doing her own thing lately, so my nights have been freer than I'd like. I went because I was still seduced by the idea of resistant communities. Because I thought: this is my last chance.

Amber had said, 'No-one can do it alone.' I knocked back the last gulp of a long black and attempted nonchalance. I left her there with her bike lock on Smith Street, walking away with hackles raised.

A few days later we met again and headed off down Lygon Street together in the warm evening air, noting the longer days and both vibing off the very recent memory of seeing each other get off. I'd told Amber it was a one-time thing, and was only a little embarrassed when she chuckled in her low-pitched way. She knew all about Jonie. We never discussed it, but she still asked me why I kept looking over my shoulder.

'No reason. Bit chilly.'

'It's twenty-three degrees…'

Our goal was Trades Hall, that proletarian bunker. Amber led me up rickety wooden stairs to a small, crowded room that smelt of dust and sweat. Five minutes in I knew it was years too late for me to come to a meeting like this. It was like turning up to a party in that shirt that never quite seemed right. Amber said a quick warm 'Hi' to her mates. They struck me as lacking the cold severity that usually rattled me at parties, that would most often kick start a vicious cycle of mutual diffidence. They clasped hands and grinned, with smiley eyes, because here they were fighting the good fight, and no-one else could really understand that. Me least of all.

The meeting began with a seminar by a battle-weary, first-wave boomer feminista with a grey bob and plain dress of no actual colour droning on about the bosses and the revolutionary spirit that was about to sweep through the working classes. For her this meant the tradies and technicians. I thought of the techies I knew, as well as the printers, fitters and turners—all massive stoners—and winced. I peered around the room to see how her speech was being received, and worked harder on my poker face. During the discussion that followed, I spoke and admitted to a certain naivety, before asking how we were supposed to negotiate the tiered reality of modern Australian capitalism, a complex system in which bosses are often workers and vice versa. How was that meant to fit into the revolutionary equation?

The room froze and the grey feminista's nostrils flared, until the young, mousy but otherwise competent chair branded it a Good Question. Hands went up and Amber exhaled. A crazy old man used the opportunity to launch a vitriolic attack, soaked in expletives for a full two minutes, against what he called 'smarmy academic arseholes'. Others were clearly still coming to grips with all the permutations of Marxist rhetoric, unable to find any recognisable shape or argument. Everyone referred to various episodes in revolutionary France but never episodes in Australia. No-one responded to my question, no-one referred to real life and no-one else seemed to get the joke. I found the whole thing hilarious. A nervous young guy stuttered his way through a diatribe that had precisely nothing to say about the ruling class and the passion of the masses. He then timed out with his non-point left hanging. The masses in the room listened patiently before politely ignoring him. I mocked him privately, until I realised: that's me. It probably all made sense in his head too. What we're fighting here—this Leviathan, being everywhere and all around us—is notoriously difficult to see in its entirety. In fairness, I wasn't letting my new comrade off the hook, but rather condemning us both.

All the boys wore hoodies. One of them faced me directly as he spoke, explaining with large, splayed hands and the nervous hint of a smile why the moral bankruptcy of mass profits for the country's privileged few was indisputable, no matter what terms you used. I nodded respectfully and returned the nervous smile. If we were samurai I might have bowed. After a while I thought something about the glint in this dude's eyes seemed familiar. The masses rose up around us, one at a time, and I listened on but it was all seven shades of bullshit.

I must have wanted Amber to say something, because I was disappointed when the discussion moved on without her input. I wondered if I'd pissed her off or embarrassed her. The meeting's agenda continued to unfold, and various discussions sprang up on practical matters: impending rallies, several seconded motions about whatever, future campaign ideas and hotly contested debates on the most effective strategies to communicate a consistent message. To whom? Dunno. I wondered about the structure of the assembly: an obvious elevated sub-stratum of committee positions, project coordinators and leaders, setting various priorities. I wondered if the chair for each meeting was elected or rotated. Was this a massive contradiction within a group that advocated for non-hierarchical social orders, or did I simply fail to fully understand the subtlety of their values and ideas?

As soon as the official meeting ended I was swooped upon, as people crowded in to assess this new face in their midst. Amber said 'He's with me' in her lilting drawl, and I waved like an idiot. They seemed to relax.

We headed upstairs for a beer and I was grilled about what I considered to be my compelling yet humorous question. Everyone seemed to agree that such questions were inevitable, given how new I obviously was to Marxist thought. I looked up to the massive portrait of Rod Quantock and thought, Jesus Christ. I tried to keep my mouth shut, but once the beer started flowing I may have dropped a bomb or two about their language being comical and obsolete. 'A-ha!' they said, taking up my objections as though we were ancient philosophers in sandals on the steps of the Parthenon.

The familiar-looking blond guy with the big hands said 'I know you' and I said 'Huh?' and he said 'We went to the same election party.' I squinted my eyes like I was looking at something far away, recalling his random but snappy one-liners.

Eventually I said, 'Oh yeah—the ham-on wry guy.'

'What?'

'Nothing. I remember—Alex.'

Amber looked vaguely worried by my new friend and touched my arm reassuringly as she moved off to find people she needed to speak to. I continued to get stuck into those backward pseudo-intellectuals and they continued to get stuck into me. My main point was that if Marx—in my excitement I may have referred to him as Marky Marx—were around today he wouldn't talk about bosses and a ruling class because that's not how modern capitalism is organised. Someone said there was little difference between workplace conditions now and the mass-production factory conditions of Marx's era. I didn't know enough to disagree. I thought of my old call-centre job at Auto Electrical; those confining partitions on the one hand, and the multidiscipline structure of skip-level meetings on the other, in which every supervisor is open to scrutiny from those above and below.

To the assembled amber pints and flushed faces I pointed out that no-one had actually answered my question: who were enemies and who were allies? I told them it was stupid and naive to make heroes and devils out of the workplace. I asked them why they couldn't just advocate a system that regulated profit and accountability— through taxes and transparency, for instance. They said I'd been sucked in by ruling discourses on money and power. I said, 'If only I could be.'

I tried to out myself as a middle-class brat and they insisted that, because of my call-centre background, I counted as working class. I asked who else in the room had a private school education and a tertiary degree. They didn't get it. Then we got into an even more obtuse argument comparing different kinds of jobs. The grey feminista who gave the seminar rolled her eyes at everything I said and eventually told me to go home and read more. They told me reform wouldn't work—the whole system needed to be overthrown. I asked why they bothered with posters and picket lines. They said revolution had to be peaceful. I threw my head back and laughed. I asked them to take a look around at the systemic levels of force and paperwork that held society together. I said Socialist Alliance was a speck of dust sticking to the windshields of the planes that ripped through the twin towers. The grey feminista spat that I was my own cartoon, that if anyone committed an act of revolutionary terrorism in this country we'd have an instant police state.

'Good!' I said, adding that wide-scale oppression was the only thing that was going to shake the Aussie populace out of its many forms of apathy. The grey feminista said Australians weren't apathetic, they just lacked education. I said they were plenty educated, they were just dumb selfish bastards. And another thing: Marxism's optimism about the sharing, caring revolutionary human spirit is a load of steaming coils.

Amber returned at the tail end of this and began a round of hurried goodbyes. Alex followed us to the door and I explained in more restrained terms that I was worried they were alienating themselves from the wider community, with their outdated terms of reference. I gave him my spiel on the strategic safety of self-marginalisation to boot.

'So are you saying we're too extreme or not extreme enough?'

Amber was silent but paying close attention; I could feel her watching me, gauging how I either did or didn't fit in. She seemed coolly amused but worried I would overstep the mark with her friends. And fair enough.

'Look, that's a good question. I don't know, to be honest. But someone should be doing something, and you guys are . . . '

Alex waited by the door for me to finish, and I realised the creeping smile was less nervousness than concealed arrogance. 'But?'

I faced him with furrowed brows and both hands clinging to the scarf around my neck. 'I think that before you can reform the world, you need to reform yourselves.'

He nodded and said, 'We could all use some reform. What are you doing tomorrow?'

And I was happy to find an ally.

Amber warned me about Alex on the way home.

'He's a good guy, a smart guy, but he tends to cycle through people pretty quick. Be careful.'

'What's he got planned for tomorrow?'

She shrugged. 'I thought you'd discussed it already.'

I shook my head. She let out a soft, sceptical 'Hmmm'.

She asked me what I thought about the socialist love-in, and I gave her a modified version that was polite and a bit too earnest. I guess I was trying to impress her on what I presumed to be her level. I asked her what she thought of me back there.

'Bombastic and ignoble . . . you might just fit in after all.' She leaned into me as she said this. Or perhaps that's how I remembered it later.

'You always pay them out, you know, for being so full on and macho . . .'

Amber shrugged. 'Yeah. That's them. They are.'

'But there's such a balanced presence at the meeting . . .'

'The boys keep their head in at the meetings. To be honest, most of the projects are coordinated by women. But the rallies and the boozy events bring out the bravado and the cocktalk. It's ugly, and revolutions need cool heads.'

I asked about extremists.

'Some would say there's a vigilante fringe but it's just enough talk for white punks from the suburbs to feel good about themselves.'

I kicked a paper bag towards the gutter. 'Yeah.'

Walking north in the dark, Amber described how Socialist Alliance interacted with other activist groups, giving me a sense of the collaborations and cross-purposes that contributed to that cliché of the fragmented left. She said I'll see some of it at the next rally if I go, prompting my own sceptical 'Hmmm.'

We joked about political schizophrenia, and I mentioned Greg from the Napier: a homocidal ex-con we knew, who didn't stand a chance against our middle-class conceit.

Amber laughed, saying it wasn't the same thing. I wondered aloud if living against the cultural grain required or resulted in an element of madness.

Her brows flicked up dismissively. 'Compared to more socially acceptable versions? Political schizophrenia is the US government flying the Bin Ladens out of their country after September 11.'

She hounded me to come to the rally next week. I explained that I would never join an activist group. Because of the fantasy such communities create and work so hard to reinforce.

She said, 'What about your own fantasies?'

'I guess if I never articulate them, they're indestructible.'

'And you'd still never have to win.'

'Maybe.'

We finally reached my doorstep and I invited her in, trying to maintain a happy medium of self-deprecating confidence.

Amber appraised me sidelong—just long enough to warn me against assumptions, then perhaps for a little longer. 'Sure.'

Sometimes you do things you thought you'd never do.

Alex told me to wear dark clothes, including a beanie. He'd take care of the rest. I met him late on a Wednesday at Rue Bebelons for a couple of warm-up drinks. A good thing too—two weeks before Christmas but tonight was a cold one. Rue Bebs was a cosy place that heated up quick; even faster with a couple of whiskies.

He wouldn't show me what was in the backpack, but it was busting at the seams. He seemed a bit edgy but it could have just been that awkward manner of his.

He said: 'Where we live, people like us are a dime a dozen. But not enough of us are actually doing anything.'

We talked about how difficult it was to sort through all the posturing party talk and soft-left wankery: liberation, freedom, democracy, justice.

I said: 'No-one understands what these words truly mean.' But then I would say that. We talked about how tough it was to find the right strategy to stamp our mark on the country's cultural fabric, woven for us before our eyes, even as it excluded us.

'We should insist on representing ourselves.'

'I'd do anything to voice my dissent.'

Anything.

'Right. But at the same time—fuck. I mean, look at us: clinging to the edges of what's acceptable: legal, moral and decent.'

'Meetings. Posters. Demonstrations. Allowed because they're redundant.'

'We cling because we're scared . . . '

'Dissuasive legal penalties: with a criminal record your life is fucked.'

'Without fear, what new options would we create for ourselves?'

Before long I was halfway up a ladder on Lonsdale Street passing up ungainly stencil templates that were even more difficult to handle because of the light smattering of rain. Alex's arse hung ingloriously above my head. I was wearing his backpack across my chest so I could reach easily for the templates, tape and spray cans.

We were up the side of the Sensis building. The smooth, bright logo stood for the first bold step in privatised telecommunications. Bold, because by outsourcing national directory information services, a number of free services now had to make economic sense. Bold, because they expected their new, exorbitant call rates to be swallowed whole by a passive consumer public. Bold, because that's exactly how it played out. In a globalised corporate heaven, the meek inherit fuck-all.

And like all good global citizens, Alex appreciated the value of information flows, so he made these stencilled numbers—the new call rates for what used to be free. Because his mates are all talk, just like mine, he needed my help to market his project effectively. That's what we were doing, him with his arse in my face, me with a pack full of basic art supplies: bulldog clips, superglue, a couple of spray cans, electrical tape, stencils.

There's a certain ritual of blokey camaraderie that goes with physical teamwork. It's a multisensory exchange of nods, squawks, winks, yelps and grins.

'Yep yep yep yep yep yep . . .'

'Almost . . . Beautiful. Perfect.'

'You right? Cool, cool . . .'

'Ah! Hold up, hold up . . .'

The ladder came from Alex's neighbour in Coburg, an eighty-year-old retired roof repair guy. We were suspended over a narrow cove of stairs, the ladder feet perched on top of a handy retainer wall. The ladder started a full two metres up from the stairs beneath us, and we were another three metres up the ladder—any slip would be messy.

Given the rain, attending paramedics would conclude that we were morons. What we were doing was illogical and foolish on many fronts, but as we went up the ladder we agreed this wasn't about logic, it was about belief.

Alex said: 'All logic is supported by belief anyway . . .' with a mischievous grin as he tested the first rung with his boot for stability.

At that moment I decided Alex was ballsy as hell.

A fair while later, I also decided he was also fucking slow. I craned my neck to the street as he strained above me; it was really remarkable how little attention people were paying us. Maybe they stopped looking at the world after one in the morning on a school night, even in the lead-up to Christmas. Maybe they thought we had a legitimate purpose. Maybe they couldn't bloody see us in the first place. There wasn't much traffic, but our luck wouldn't hold forever.

'Dude! Hurry up—this rain's not easing off and we are perched on a wall. The revolution will not be televised from the casualty ward!'

'Right, right! The wall here's mostly protected by the overhanging structure, but the stencils are wet—this ain't easy!'

After a few more minutes he signalled to come down, shaking his head in frustration. The perilous descent was worse than the climb. We were both relieved to be back on safe, wet land.

The two of us stared up at the key space beside the Sensis logo.

'Too wet?'

'Maybe. The wall here's mostly protected by the overhanging architecture, but I'm not sure what the paint will do on the wet stencil.' He looked across to me. 'It's worth another shot.'

I nodded. We checked that the legs wouldn't slip on the retainer wall yet, and went back up that fucking ladder.

Alex was faster this time. His hand came down for the spray can and a fine black mist floated around us both—I felt guilty for being so relieved that my clothes were already dark, but also glad I hadn't worn the Mooks jacket.

Then we got hi-beamed! The ladder jerked suddenly as Alex schitzed out above me. The spray can dropped past me and bounced off the stairs below. Our collective weight teetered to the left: to the street, then to the right: to the top of the stairs, and either way we seemed to be, well, fucked. We were still working together on relative stability when I glanced down and for a split second thought it must be the cops, but instead it was a security guard in a ridiculous yellow shirt, with a spotlight on us, speaking quickly into his walkie-talkie.

'We gotta go, dude!'

Alex swore loudly. 'Go? Go where?'

'To the stairs. Jump off before we land, bro!' I leant us to the right. We teetered, and Alex screamed obscenities at me. And fair enough—he was moving faster than I was because he was higher up the ladder. We jumped and both landed at the same time, him at the top of the stairwell, me halfway down. I bounced awkwardly a couple of times on my ankle.

Adrenalin kicked in and we tore off. The security guard was calling out behind us. I guess he was having to navigate the ladder clogging the stairwell, but he was still on us as we rounded the corner into the lane towards Swanston Street.

There's always been less going on in the CBD late on a Wednesday night than at any other time in the week, but it still spun past us in a multi-stream of fluorescent lights. We turned into Little Lonsdale; a favourite café of mine hurtled past us, the Myers walkway floated over us, and we crossed Elizabeth Street then continued to pelt into the darker corners of corporate Melbourne. The security guard was nowhere in sight.

'Slow up.' Alex's breath was short. 'Hide in here . . .'

He led me off into a lane—the kind that makes locals fall in love with their own city. We rested in the shadow against the wall, taking in big gulps of air, trying to bring our pulses down. My head was throbbing with energy and blood.

At any other time we'd have been full of bluster, but right then the best way to apprehend the moment was, again, without words: heaving breaths, creeping smiles and looks exchanged from the corners of eyes stretched wide in alarm and elation. I flexed my ankle and it felt okay for now. My hands were shaking from the adrenalin, so I guessed it might be sorer later.

I was pushing to hit the street again.

'You wanna get caught? I think we should stay put.'

'You wanna act scared?'

'It didn't work out like I planned . . .'

'Don't be dejected, brother. How much did you get painted?'

'Not enough to make any sense. They'll cover it for sure.'

'It doesn't matter. Fighting's more important than winning. They got the message.'

So we emerged from our cosy shadow, and our skulking evolved into a boisterous jaunt. I didn't feel invincible so much as confidently adaptable. Alex was taking events a little harder. This west side of the city was Melbourne's corporate epicentre: all banks and law firms, lots of grand marble stairs, columns, fountains, heavy-handed sculptures and those huge floor-to-ceiling, plate-glass tinted windows.

'I hate this fuckin' place.'

I told Alex stories about life in the corporate underclass.

Alex seemed to feed off the contrast. 'You know what, dude? Who cares if the jam didn't come off—another sanitised rebellion at the end of the day; costs them a bit of money to clean up, gone in a day, the world rolls on.' He sent a bottle skittering enthusiastically across the street. 'But it shows them they're not bulletproof. And it takes control, if only for that one day, of the war of images. Never mind reds under the beds, man. Globalisation and terrorism—the new culture wars in this country.'

I nodded ruefully in agreement; my stories had helped Alex's spirits at the expense of my own! He said we should get a drink and call it a night.

'I'm not done controlling the image yet.'

I found the skip we passed earlier, and vaulted inside. Smashing and scrunching loudly through its contents, I sorted through a couple of concrete lumps, a cement block and some light iron rods, before finding something suitable. I crawled over the side dragging a thick metal pole behind me. It had a rough clump of cement attached to one end, where it had been ripped from the ground. It was almost too heavy to lift.

We dragged the pole through the alleyways and backstreets, anywhere it didn't stand out like dog's balls.

Eventually we broke cover on William Street, dragging the pole up the steps towards the entrance of one particular building set in from the footpath.

'I thought you were taking us to the Magistrate's Court down the way . . . '

'A worthy target indeed, but this one's special.'

Alex's teeth flashed in the moonlight. I stared up the face of the building with my mouth open, remembering that sinking feeling of rolling in with the deodorised, clean-shaven rush at eight-thirty each morning (eight thirty-five, eight forty-five). I remembered thinking: this is it.

I hefted the pole a few times without success. Alex and I brainstormed the angles for a bit. I tried facing to the left of the giant automatic doors, with the heavy end resting on the ground, winding up a three-quarter circle, going the long way around and bringing up the cement clump for the final third. It slammed into the glass, dead on. But no.

We could have been laughing among the dust and flecks of cement that sprinkled out before the doors, riding the adrenalin and hysteria of aimless, adolescent vandalism. It could have meant nothing to be here. Instead, my brow sat heavily on my face—I could feel it pushing down on the rest of me. Alex was up against the door, flush to its edge and looking sidelong, increasingly desperate to figure it out.

We tried it a few times each.

'I want to break this so bad . . . '

'It's strong.'

'Maybe too strong.'

'We just haven't found its weakness yet.'

We sat down to nut it out. It wasn't fun any more. I nearly said 'Let's go home.'

Alex stood up. 'We want to scare them a bit, yeah?'

'Yeah.'

'So we don't need to break it. Gimme the pack.'

Alex dug out another spray can, shaking it hard as he swaggered towards the doors. His mouth was a thin line.

When he stepped back, my old building now had 'The Terrorist Gains What the Writer Loses' scrawled across four panes of glass, in blood red.

'It's beautiful.' Alex had captured my imagination.

'It's Don DeLillo.'

'They will shit their dacks.'

'Blah-blah-terrorist-blah-blah . . .'

We hid the pole in a nearby side street. For the benefit of the morning papers, we both took photos on our phones. Eyes trained and a soft blue light reflecting onto his face, Alex murmured: 'Let the journos chew on the exact same fear they created for the rest of us.'

I couldn't decide if I felt giddy or a cool calm.

'Honey,' I said. 'Let's go home.'

Stripped

by

CAROLINE LEE

One: Sophie in the city

THE LAST FEW MOMENTS ARE ALWAYS THE BEST. Every movement in the dance is slow, agonisingly slow. The music quietly pulses. The room gets quieter, as if all of them, all of those hundred or so men, are holding their breath, not daring even to blink, caught in the delicious moment between wanting and not wanting; wanting the revelation, the release, the final moment, and yet not wanting anything to change, to come to an end.

And yet come to an end it does, with the last slide of my fabric, the last twirl and stretch.

As I walk off the stage towards the back of the room I feel a draft. Laszlo must have opened the door for me. All the fine hairs on my arms rise as if to meet the breeze. I wrap myself up in my gown, the soft silk cool on my flesh, and make my way slowly down the back stairs to the office—what we call our dressing room. As I descend, the sounds of the room, of the men cheering and talking and moving around, of Laszlo and the other security guys telling everyone to leave, float down after me. Soon it will all be empty. The men will have shuffled, stumbled, slunk into the street, eaten up by the movement of the city's morning.

4

My legs are tired. I feel them as I go down each step, the muscles lean and hard, pressing against my skin. When I reach the office, it is empty. Unusual and wonderful. All the others must have gone home, thank God. I put on my jumper, grab the illicit keys and go up to room no. 14. I can't sit in the fluorescent light of the office, surrounded by the debris of dancers, not even for a moment. It's been a long night.

My muscles complain as I go up stairs this time; these ones covered in carpet, dark red like the rest of the club. I get there and unlock the room. The air is full of that powdery smell, thick: of cigarettes and sex. No-one comes here much, except me. It's old, like me.

I push open the fire escape and the morning sun falls in. Straightaway I lie down in it, on the carpet. This too is a familiar routine. The sounds of the city waking up drift in through the door: building sites, traffic, people coming into work. The sun creeps into my body, soothing, relaxing, and unravelling the accumulated crustiness of the night. Oh yes, this is what I've been waiting for.

Although it's not entirely working this morning. I can feel a hardness, a tightness lingering inside me. But there's also something trembling. How long can I hold on? Keep the lid on it? And why is it so particularly hard now? I think back through the evening. Was he there at the club tonight? Any of them? And then I remember, I saw Lillian yesterday, on my way to work. For the first time in three months. The one person I could properly talk to about what happened and the one person I can't. She made that very clear at Christmas time.

She slammed her hand on the table. Heavy and hard, like an encyclopaedia. It was such a definite sound, cut through the crassness of my story like an axe.

'Enough!' she said. 'You know what? I'm sick of all your filth. I'm sick of all the crap that comes out of your mouth and I'm sick of the fact that you think we need or want to hear it. You are coming from this incredibly teenage position of thinking, still thinking, Sophie, that it's a smart or relevant or exciting thing to do to stick it up all of us with your knowledge of the dark side, your contact with evil or death or sex or whatever it is. Well I'm here to tell you that you don't do any of those things except perhaps to reveal to us, in technicolour, how pathetic you are, how little you really understand and how sorry we are for you. You wound us, not with your knowledge but with your lack of knowledge, and with how ugly and uncaring and insensitive you've become. I'm sorry, but I can't listen to you any more.'

5

She got up and left the room. We all sat there in silence, Mama, Peter, Daniel and I. And the silence stretched on and on and on. I was waiting for Daniel—Lillian's husband—to break the ice, to squeeze my hand or wink at me: not that I looked at him much, just a glance or two. But there was nothing. Everyone just looked at their plates.

That silence was hard. Lillian's words were hard but the silence harder. Because I knew then that they all agreed.

I got up from the table and went to my room. I lay on my bed and I cried for a long time. And then I packed my bags and left. I didn't know where to go but in the end I went and stayed in an awful Gold Coast hotel for the night. Then I changed my ticket, went back to Melbourne the next day and returned to work.

My boss was really pleased to see me. Good old Bernie, no questions asked.

A few days later I realised I was angry. The fucking bitch. What gave Lillian the right to stand in moral judgement upon me? To influence other people's opinions about me in that way? What gave her the right? So I hadn't called and neither had she, and we hadn't seen each other. Then it happened, the incident at the club and I've been trying to forget it, to get over it and move, on but it comes to me in dreams, and I can't get her words out of my head, berating me, stripping me bare. It's not me who's ugly and uncaring and insensitive, it's those arseholes who trapped me, played their little games with me. And then out of the blue I saw her yesterday, caught a glimpse from a distance.

It was about four o'clock. It was windy and I could see her fighting against it, hunched up tight. She seemed little. Her dark suit and charcoal-grey coat blended in with the Supreme Court building and the expanse of road. But her hands stood out, pink from the cold. Lillian has always spurned gloves, even when we were in Europe. It drove Mama wild.

She made her way towards the station, a tram went by, and she was gone.

No-one's ever been able to baby her. She came out of the womb like that. Mama says she got it from Bruno, our grandfather; he too was small and tough and uncompromising.

And that's how she was at Christmas, slamming her hand. It's difficult to work against such a sound.

It's useless. I can't relax. I get up, leave room 14, go downstairs, gather

6

my things and go home. Maybe I'll be able to coax my body into a couple of hours of sleep.

Later, at home, I wake up and it's already morning. The sun is spilling across my bedroom floor, glinting on the floorboards. It looks like a beautiful day. I get up and feel the warmth of the sun under my feet as I move into the kitchen. As I fill the kettle I look out the kitchen window and then I see that it is actually night-time. It is the middle of the night outside. No moon, and definitely no sun. What's going on? I check and it's definitely night, the streetlights are on and the headlights of the cars are shining, but inside it's warm and light.

Then I hear a small thud on the windowpane and there it is, the green glove, plumped up as usual, fluttering against the window, like a moth trying to get into the light.

I feel a couple of drops of sweat roll down my spine. I watch the glove bumping and rolling against the window. I wonder how strong the glass is. Will it break? Will the glove get in, get to me, as it always does? I can't move, am caught staring at the glove.

But as I watch, I slowly realise that this time it actually doesn't seem aggressive. Perhaps it's simply attracted to the light, because it seems content to stay there, bumping and knocking, then flying a bit and then bumping again. Every so often it stops, just touching the glass, and at one of these moments, which is longer than the others, I lean a little closer towards the window. The glove stays there, almost as if it's watching me. I move even closer. It launches off again and I tense, in case this time it is going to come through the window, but no, it just flutters and bumps a bit and then comes to rest a little further along.

I move in again, close enough to look at it, carefully, through the glass. Its skin is covered with lots of tiny red lines, which at first I think are veins, but as I continue looking I see that they are not veins, but more like lines, little gashes, and then as I get even closer I see that they are not gashes but tiny mouths. And they are all different, all in different shapes, in different positions, some smiling, some sneering, some beautiful little rosebuds, some thin and serious. I don't know whether I want to laugh or vomit.

Then I notice something else. It's wearing a little collar with a bell on it, around the wrist, and I can hear the little bell tinkling, just faintly through the glass. Then someone is banging on my door. I wake up, I'm in bed, and there's a

7

party next door, people are banging up the stairs. I half get out of bed and then I realise that they are banging on the next-door-neighbour's door. I can hear a woman laughing, someone yelling at her, and music.

I get up and go to the window. It is night, inside and outside the flat. There is no glove. I feel that weird feeling you get when you go to sleep in the daytime, in the afternoon, and wake up in the night-time. Mama used to say it was bad for your soul. I look at the streetlights and the headlights of the cars. Oh yeah, there's trouble in my soul, no doubt about that. And then I see my phone. There's a message from Lillian. She wants to talk. It's an indication of how strung out I am that for a few moments I think I might cry.

We meet in the city for lunch. I come into the dining room at Syracuse, she's already there of course, sitting quietly at a table with some papers in front of her. She stands up to meet me. She looks the same, absolutely the same. I don't know what I've been expecting, signs of stress, of anger, a few more crow's-feet around her eyes? She smiles, but not fully. There, in that slight reserve, is Christmas: my dirty story, everyone's shock, Lillian berating me with her cutting words and her banging hand, then the long silence.

But now we're here, looking for all the world like two city workers doing lunch, only there's a few more pauses and a lot more tension. We chat. I'm looking at the patterns of the wine glasses on the back wall, the way in which the roundness of the body of the glass contrasts to the sharp flatness of the tops, and then I hear Lillian take a breath, as she does when she's about to say something important. I brace myself. But she launches into a story about work, and once she starts she just can't stop talking.

'I've just been in Sydney. There was a special tribunal held up there. You see, I'm part of this group here in Melbourne who advocate on behalf of refugees, and we've taken up this woman's cause, you know the one who died recently in prison? A lot of people are pushing to have an inquiry into her death, because she was a sex slave, so there had to be this preliminary hearing. So I went to Sydney, well, I wasn't going to go at first, but get this, they couldn't find anyone in Sydney who would take the case. No-one. I mean it was short notice and pro bono and all that, but still. And so they rang and asked me. And even though it's early days and I've only just got my own practice, I thought it would be great experience, and I decided to do it.'

8

What? What's going on? Is this supposed to be some kind of moral fable? Am I supposed to be getting some kind of message from this? I can feel my legs starting to jiggle, but I don't want to have a fight so I keep looking round the room, try to enjoy the European chic of the surrounds. But my thoughts keep going back to the club. And Mr Alan, what he did to me. And if I am or am not a sex slave.

'But oh my God it was tough. It was really tough. The judge was so resistant. I mean it was a civil case, not criminal, but still he really went for me. "Ms Deluca," he said on the first day, "my advice to you is that as you don't have much experience, you shouldn't do anything to complicate matters unnecessarily." But the thing was, there were people there from the Department of Immigration, from the detention centre and from the Health Department and it seemed to me that all they wanted to do was to hush everything up. I had to fight, I had to use everything I had, complicated or not.'

What makes a sex slave? Do you have to be downtrodden? And what makes a sex slave worth defending? With brains, time, money? Would she defend me? How big does the trouble have to be for Lillian Deluca to think it's important? Would she stand up in court and look those men in the eye and defend my rights, my honour, my . . . I think I need another glass of wine.

'So I couldn't just sit back and let them do all the talking and not ask questions and at least aim to get some recognition of what had actually occurred in this poor woman's life. I was determined that her death would not be in vain. This woman should never have been in a refugee detention centre, she should have been in a hospital. And that's why she died. It was so terrible, Sophie, that after so long of holding herself together, working as a sex slave and, you know, living at the place too, some disgusting old hotel in Kew, she should finally get up the courage to escape and ends up being locked away in a prison.'

She's always done that, brushed away tears as if they're nothing, just an annoying activity that her eyes engage in, separate to the rest of her. She's kind of shaky. Maybe she's telling me this by way of an apology. Or a hint? An opening? Maybe she knows that something's wrong. Sometimes our Slavic inheritance seems to make a surprise appearance. Grandma used to swear that one of our distant ancestors was a fortune-teller. Maybe she wants to help me? Maybe she would defend me. If it came to that.

9

But then, as Lillian keeps talking, I understand. I can be a bit slow sometimes. Or, yes, utterly self-obsessed. It's about her, that's what it's about. She has no idea what happened to me. This is about her and her vocation. The remarkable coincidence that she's just been defending a sex slave and her own sister is a kind of sex worker seems not to be registering at all. Although, of course, I'm not a sex slave. And that makes all the difference. Apparently.

I watch her talk. She just doesn't even make the connection. Yet she realises something is up, because she's nervous. And Lillian is never nervous.

'Anyway, when I was up there I hardly slept. At the end of the first day's proceedings we went back to the hotel and pored through the evidence and everything that had been said by the other side. I was exhausted, but I forced myself. So in the end I was able to cast reasonable doubt. On the last day we were called in to give a summation and the other side just did a basic reiteration of their evidence but I had actually prepared a list of recommendations and was able to make those recommendations in my statement.'

'Uh huh, so . . . what recommendations?'

'Well, you know, that there should be a proper inquiry into her death, and that more importantly there should be an inquiry into the whole issue of sex slavery in Australia. Then we adjourned for lunch and the judge asked to see all the material and when he came back he said that he considered that the evidence was in support of an inquiry and that there absolutely should be an inquiry. So that was, of course, a complete victory for us.'

'Oh, well. Yeah, that's fantastic.'

Lillian pauses. She stumbles over her words. 'Yeah . . . yeah . . . and . . .'

Where would I start? What words could I use? Lillian is looking at the tabletop. It's one of the marble ones, they're always so cold, seem to generate coldness. A blotch of red has appeared on the side of her neck. She puts her hand to her mouth. Just holds it there. I want to hold her hand. Like when we were little. A drop of sweat trickles down the side of her face. It moves down the edge of her hairline, then slowly past her ear. It disappears round the corner of her jaw.

Then she says, 'Well, I just felt incredibly proud of what I was able to achieve. I mean, I know it sounds corny, but that kind of thing is what I did law for.'

I feel my legs lift me up from the table. 'I'd better be going, Lillian.'

'Oh really?' She looks at me, finally quiet. There is a pause. 'Yeah, well I have

10

to get going too, actually. All of a sudden I seem to be inundated with work, it's crazy. Karma, I guess.'

We are standing, fiddling with things: coats, money, bags. She looks at me again, but I can't speak, can't tell my story now. I feel so old; messed-up, useless, broken. My shoes need polishing.

'I'll fix the bill, your turn next time,' she says.

And that is what I'm holding onto as I walk away, that tiny thing: that at least there will be a next time.

Two: Daniel washes it all away

Ooohh yeah . . . the best thing about the morning is the shower. And Lillian. But not today. She's still asleep. A work day. The site in Broady is coming along pretty well, although those boys from Mitchell's are bullshit. Lazy as they come. All they wanna do is sit around on their arses, drink coffee, smoke, crap on. It's better if you just work. Get on with it. Get home. That's where it all happens.

Better get out. The water. Lillian knows it, even in her sleep, if I waste it.

The power lines are swinging outside. And there's the sun. Just starting to show above the horizon. It's windy. There's gonna be more sitting around on the site today.

The barbecue. Tonight. What was that about the sausages? Lillian freaked out, and she doesn't do that. Not about sausages. And fuck, I checked with her, they were the right sausages. They were the ones we were supposed to have and which didn't have too much fat because now everyone's going on about fat. And the meat? That was okay. The butcher at the market was not the best, no way, not as good as the city market, but still, he's all right. So, the sausages. Should I have got pork and rosemary sausages? Or was I supposed to get something in case people didn't eat sausages? But people can have salad.

Look, whatever it is will be all right, because she has a sense of humour. Thank fuck. She rolls her eyes and she tells me off, but in the end whatever that wrong thing is will pass.

I go down the hallway to kiss her goodbye. It's still dark in here. I go slow. Don't want to wake her. Our room is still, like a chapel. I go slowly to her, don't want to step on anything.

II

'Lillian? I'm going.'

She wakes up enough to kiss me back, full on the lips, like she mostly does in the morning. And like it mostly does, it makes me hot, makes me wanna get back in bed with her and wake her up, properly.

Nope. No can do, gotta go.

A piece of paper. It was lying by the side of the bed when I came home last night. I stood on it. Can't see it now. Bloody work function and then those few beers and when I'd finally got home Lillian was in bed. Nothing wrong with that. Nuh, there was nothing wrong there. She's got a big week at the office this week; it's crunch time with that huge case, there was nothing wrong with me going out with the blokes and having a beer and she had never said anything was wrong with that. When I came in I was quiet, as quiet as you can be with a few beers inside you.

She's back to sleep already. Must be exhausted. I'll call her later. Because if I've done something wrong with the sausages that's probably gonna ruin the barbecue tonight. Well, not ruin it but it could be just one of those things where—how does she put it?—the balance of the meal could be messed up.

I kiss her forehead, I love to kiss my darling. Better go. At least I've shaved, in the shower, which according to those gay guys on TV is something, yet another thing, you really should not do. But anyway, I'm done now, shaved and moderately clean. It's not lookin' good, this day, already, but I reckon at least if I make an effort to resolve the situation about the sausages then I can move on with a clear conscience, and I can be pretty confident of avoiding disaster.

Three: Martin's heart's in his boots

Moving up and down the pool, quite fast, pressing through the water, trying to reach the calm, but I can't today, not quite. Jane's still in my head and all that stuff from last night is waiting for me, at the edges of the calm, still seeping in. Why did she have to push it? It's been good. I thought she was smarter than that. Tougher. I can't have her stay the night, it just doesn't work.

If they stay, they always want something. She did. I could feel her energy pressing against me, wanting. Wanting even a cup of tea in the morning,

12

wanting to see which books I read and which CDs I play and why do I keep my CDs in alphabetical order on my shelf and what's the thing about female vocalists anyway? Those are the sorts of things that really make me mad because what business of theirs is it anyway what I do with my life and my things? I don't want them dragging on me. There is nothing so heavy nor so malevolent as the dead weight of a needy woman. All men know that. Whether or not they admit it, all men know that.

It limits the possibilities, I know. She's a good one, this Jane, she's smart and sweet, but not too sweet, and she's sexy and not uptight. But they can't deal with it. The women I want rarely accept those terms, or at least not without a fight; and the other women, the ones who accept my terms, are pretty frightful, really; I have rarely encountered more alarming specimens of humanity. So, what: relinquish sex? Get on with life, with the job? No. No way. That hunger's not going to go away.

And so the pool, the swimming. And so too, the strip clubs.

I like the echoing sounds of the pool. They make everything disappear. There are all sorts of sounds and they lie in layers, in ordered layers. There are splashes and other sounds of water—water being broken and cracked and thrown—then inside that the sound of my body and my blood, pushing through the water, fast and solid and strong.

Forty laps is my usual. That usually works. But it's not really working today. So tonight it will have to be the strip club. I'll wear my new boots. You can wear anything there—for that I've often been grateful. Can wear a suit if necessary, if I go for a quick visit on the way to somewhere else; or anything really, jeans, leather jacket, tracksuit pants—although I haven't ever worn my tracksuit pants. There is a certain amount of my mother I don't ever want to leave behind.

Late in the night; walking through the city streets to the Midas Club, my favourite of the many on offer. Run by simpering, weaselly Jeff. He's good, Jeff, a man in whom nothing is as it seems. Plays low status but has power. And his mix of girls is good; slightly different to the other clubs, there's a different feel. There are older women, as well as the usual young blondes, bottle or otherwise, and also troubled women, damaged women. Yes, yes, it's a cliché but they're more exciting. Women with a life. With lies. Women who have loved.

13

I do love women. Despite the best intentions of my mother.

Walking down Little Collins Street, feeling great in my boots. How often is it that I get to feel this way: never, never. You know, people in the office will think: well he's a wanker, look at that, and I know boots like this open me up to scorn, I know that people can look at me and laugh, what's a journo doing wearing boots like that? But I don't give a damn, they can think what they want. Yeah, I'm tall and clumsy and so what?

I have to admit that it was partly the fuck that did it. Right after that, I got the boots. And I knew that it was coming to an end with Jane, knew that, but oh my God it was good, it was really good. Yeah all right, whatever, maybe it wasn't just sex but what can I do with that knowledge? What can I say about it except that we both know, being intelligent people, both know that I am . . . whatever. What would she prefer? That dumb space of everything being okay and everything being nice? Damaged. That's what happens to your car. Walk, walk, walk it off, let the cool air and the dark night do their work, brush it off.

Oh, great, what do you know, outside the club there are two buses and a huge crowd of footballers. Fuck that, I'm going to the Men's Gallery, round the corner. Haven't been there for years; let's see what it's got to offer me and my new boots.

I pay, go in, and decide to start upstairs with the proper dancing. I walk up slowly, feeling the solidity of my boots on each step. I love it, I am strong. A string of pink lights around the door beckons me. Through that doorway is bliss.

I step in, look towards the dancer up there on the stage in the centre of the room, and suddenly I realise I know her. I know that body, that body with not much left covering its pale skin. It's Sophie, Sophie Orlovsky.

I've got a photograph of them in my wallet. Sophie and her sister, Lillian. God knows why, I'm not sentimental like that. It's old and torn. How long has she been doing this, how many years of her life, how many thousands of hours has she spent up there performing her dance to the gaze of men, men like this? I can't help but watch her, just a bit, watch this body I once knew so well. But then she slows down, softens and yields, then finally starts taking off her suspender belt and knickers. It's all too much. Too fucking much. Not what I had in mind for me and my boots at all.

I get out of there. Quick smart.

$1\frac{1}{4}$

Four: Sophie dances up a storm

Midway through the dance, I catch a glimpse of someone's watch. Five o'clock. Fabulous. Nearly time to go home. The room is still quite full. Of working men, mainly. That is, real workers, not office workers. There are a few boys. And a few women. Strange, the sorts of women who come here. My eighth time up this evening, and nearly finished. Down to my camisole, suspender belt and knickers. A man comes through the doorway. He is silhouetted by the soft red light. I think I know that shape, but I can only make out his form, not the details of his face. He is tall. Time slows down, I straighten up, still looking, no longer continuing to peel off my remaining pieces. I step slowly forwards, towards the edge of the stage; it's like I'm walking on sand. Martin, it's Martin. But then the men at the edge of the stage start to notice that something is different, especially Ross Miller, that fuckhead. He's been standing back, as he often does, but now he moves forwards, staring. But I can't help myself, Martin is watching me dance. I turn my head to the left and tilt it a little, softly, and then continue on with the task of undoing the ribbons on my camisole and giving the men what they've paid for. Oh yeah, professional, consummate, in every sense. That's what they say.

I'm so slow. I didn't realise I could move so slowly. I turn, half as fast as the music. My eyes move to the ground, I turn my shoulders. My breasts can now only be seen obliquely, from the side.

It appears that Ross finds this incredibly exciting. As do the other men. They go quiet; this is something the like of which they've not seen in a long time. My back curves, I feel the lights above me; my skin is warm and glowing. The men are getting hot. Looking at my spine, my buttocks, my long, muscular legs. I am allowing them in. That never happens. Slowly, so slowly, I undo the first clip of the suspender belt. Martin is still standing there, in the doorway, watching, I can tell from the way the light is still altered by his presence. The men begin to sigh, tension and excitement are beginning to enter the atmosphere of the room, an atmosphere that with its unimaginative depiction of bordello usually kills real atmosphere altogether. But now, there's frailty, real emotion. It's alluring.

I finally come to the last moments of the dance. The music finished about a minute before, but everyone is spellbound and virtually silent. I gently turn

15

around to the front of the room again, still curved. I feel like a swan. I brush my hand across my skin and finally straighten up, looking towards the light; but he's not there any more. The doorway is empty. Martin has gone.

The next morning is beautiful, clear and sunny and warm. On the spur of the moment, I call Mama.

'5572 7314.'

'Hi Mama, it's me.'

'Lillian? Is that you, darling? How are you? How's—'

'No, Mama, it's Sophie.'

'Oh.'

There is a cat making its way across the parapet of the building over the road. The light is so bright outside I can even see its collar, blue against the grey fur. 'So . . . how are you, Mama? What have you been up to? How's Peter? Is he away at the moment or is he around? Have you—'

'You took your time.'

'Sorry?'

'You took your time to ring. You are ringing to apologise? For that last phone call? And for Christmas? I'm actually very busy, Sophie, and—'

'Mama, I am sorry, I—'

'Yes, I looked after you girls all alone, all by myself for all those years. In that terrible city and through that terrible cyclone and when that terrible man, your father, upped and left and went and did his own thing. Not that it did him any good. Yes, I went through so much for you, Sophie, I mean I went grey because of you, and so I'll say it now because you didn't let me say it the last time we spoke on the phone and I need to get it off my chest, I don't appreciate it at all that my daughter who I looked after for every hour of the day, every day of the week, every week of the year, for so many years, yes, could ever, ever, ever speak like that at my own dining-room table. A dining-room table full of food that I cooked with my own two hands.'

What else did I expect? Nothing; this is exactly what I expected. I suppose it's better than silence.

'Now Lillian, Lillian would never do such a thing. And she was embarrassed, Sophie, we were all embarrassed. Embarrassed and humiliated.'

'I'm sorry, Mama, I—'

16

'I mean I wouldn't have been surprised if that had been the end of things with Peter. A new member of the family, one of the first real Christmases he's spent with us and you had to start on with such terrible stories and such awful, awful language. Do you want something? Is that why you've called? Money, is it? Is that what you're after, because I don't have any, Sophie . . .'

The cat comes to the edge of the roof and looks down, watching the street.

' . . . and your auntie hasn't been well. It's been very trying actually, because I wasn't able to get away and meet Peter on his last trip because—'

'What's wrong with Rosa?'

'Oh, she just had one of these terrible flus that all of you southerners bring up to the Gold Coast with you. I mean she's all right, she's certainly playing it for all it's worth. The doctor said she had pneumonia, made her stay in bed for two weeks and you know how hard it is to get her to stay in bed. Peter said he was just trying to get more money out of us. That's what they do up here, you know, the doctors, yes, they prey on all the oldies. It's a known fact. They drive around in their BMWs . . .'

Suddenly I think of Grandma's hands, lying on top of the blankets on her bed. Those precious hands, right at the end. Hands that held, and soothed, and smoothed. It's Grandma I wish I could ring.

'How's Lillian? Have you seen her?'

'Yeah, we had lunch a few days ago.'

'I had a weird dream about her, it was quite unsettling. She had a rabbit with a broken leg. She was nursing it, and it was getting better, but it had become attached to her, and it wouldn't let her out of its sight. It was an ugly thing. Yes, I thought maybe it meant some terrible criminal type is stalking her. Oh, I've been so worried! Peter told me not to worry but I haven't been able to get it out of my mind. I tried to ring her and it took me three whole days to get through to her. She said she was busy, but I think something's going on. I think something's going on and she's not telling me. Did she say anything to you?'

'Mama, there's nothing going on, you always think—'

'Or maybe she's pregnant? Yes, is she pregnant? Did she tell you that?'

'No, Mama, she didn't but I'm sure she'd tell—'

'Oh, you girls never tell me anything. Keep everything to yourselves, even leaving home, you didn't bother to tell me about that, did you?'

The cat has gone. Off on another adventure. Breakfast, perhaps.

17

'Look, Mama, I'll ask her, okay? You want me to do that? I'll check with her and I'll let you know.'

'Well don't take three weeks. I'm a busy woman and I can't afford to be worrying unnecessarily about you girls. You should be old enough to look after yourselves now and as for—'

'Okay, all right. I'll ring her soon and if I find out anything I'll ring you back.'

I put down the phone.

Lillian. It's always about Lillian.

THANK YOU:
Carolyn Fraser, Chris Womersley, Dr. David Thomas, Jenny Kemp, Kate Beattie, Kate Wakelin, Keren Barnett, Melissa Cranenburgh, Olga Lorenzo, Dr. Penny Schofield, Dr. Simon Wein, Steve Wide, Toni Jordan, The Marion Eldridge Award and Sophie Cunningham

18

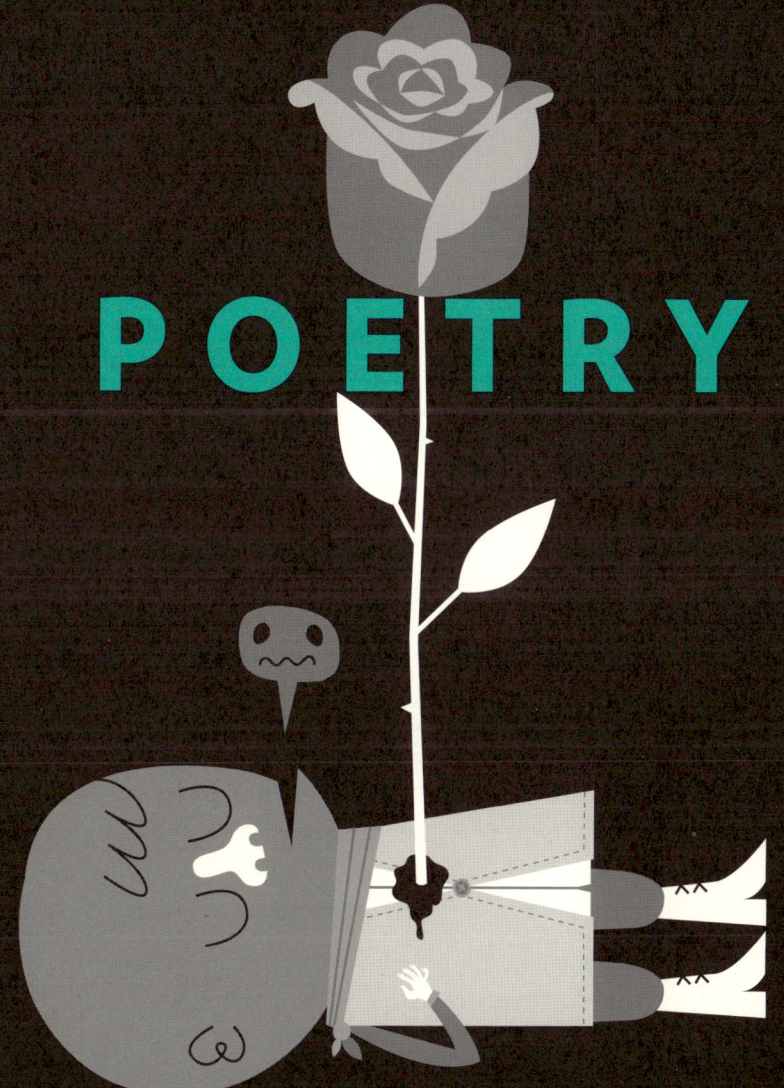

POETRY

EUCALYPT

She is one of Webster's women: gorgeously capricious,
allegiances about as stable as the bark that peels away in fringes

or flaps like an unanchored pocket on her heart.
The common lime has wrapped his cloak around her

as she backbends by his side; brother, or Brachiano—
either way he holds her. All month he cradles

and constrains her, fingers stiff with opportunity;
until, like the White Devil, she hangs dying.

She was the colour of death before death caught her.
Is she acting?

*

Evergreen, immune from drama, the fumble-fingered
succulents are drawn up like a chorus

that has seen men list like trees, extend the full length
of a neck and die on the autumn wind.

LOTUSES

If you had seen them rising from their leaves, or watched
the folded buds picked and angled into a pot;

if you had known their stillness, or attended to a single pod,
a cup replete with seeds, and caught in its archaic shape,

clumsy and touching, a ripeness like an undertaking to arrive
(if you believe Confucius, you could say 'to be wise') at seventy—

this is a way of asking if you had listened to the meditative
rhythms of your mind rather than your disjoint heart, auricles,

atria pulled one against the other, taut with the illusion of balance—
might you not have held them as no more than simple fissures,

those griefs that split the structure of your heart?

Diana Bridge

THREE TESTAMENTS TO APOLLONIUS

For Czesław Milosz

—*Non, je ne regrette rien*. What was required of me
is what I attempted: simplicity, always
simplicity. When we were children, who was to say
the Argonauts never stood beside the Vistula
preparing a sacrifice to their shrewd gods or scheming
to steal our national myth? We grew up
jealously behind city walls, imagining the erotic
pleasure of creation. The Greeks had raided
everything they could find: the mannerist prosody,
the epic fatalism. Their schoolmasters
bullied us into becoming poets. We knew what
ethics was and did our duty.

—I always suspected your words, which you called
silence. If the future exists, why should it listen
to our private misgivings? our furtive dialogues
with all those we could not love or save? our bad faith
at having been condemned in absentia by what
we could not write? War and occupation were our
normalcy. They bred their own language
that never could become our property, to be stuffed
in a book and goaded from time to time with
sentiment. Our childish gods were officially dead,
exposed to indifference, or sold off for the sake
of a footnote to History.

—Soon our sweet movie comes to an end. We rise
from the dead again and everything begins,
exactly as it was meant to. It was enough to know
that someone must also have thrown the last stone,
that images do not belong to words, that we
alone know what a horizon is. Life takes its toll.
A mechanical dog laughs and perhaps it is us
it is laughing at. An old grammarian with his
mental puppet show, rehearsing the great show-
trials of the Slavic poets. One by one they are
snuffing out the conjectures; on our heads they are
reconstructing the old borders and checkpoints. Soon
they will not need to prohibit us.

Louis Armand

WHAT IS BROKEN

What is br
oke
n is broken. W
h
at is br/oke/n is broken. W/h/at is br/oke/n i
s broken. W/h/at is br/oke/n i/s broke
n. W/h/at   br/oke/n i/s broke/n.
         is

br/broke/n. /h/is/ /s/i/n/ W/oke/ /at

Joel Deane

CANTO OF THE MOTHS

The rains have come and winter
is not as far away as it was looking,
though beneath shadecloth

and over the glistening white sand
of Timmy's sandpit, hundreds
of moths are staggering

through the air, falling to sand
to fly up confused again. In dull
green light they are tiny angels

without entries or exits,
and following them with our eyes
we grow giddy and confused.

Their wings heavy with rain,
dust is running off like sludge.
The terrace of sand a desert

of the drowning and drowned.
Plastic buckets and shovels,
rakes and rubber balls,

compact earthmovers and bulldozers,
starfish and castles, all tombstones
where there should be no markers

of the real. In a place where shadows
filter through shadecloth onto sand,
late rains have altered the rules:

angels, like spent nuclear fuel,
toxify in their different forms,
boomerang back into sacred lands.

John Kinsella

INARTICULATE

It's true the full impressionable weight
And placed articulation of those limbs
Are gone for good and only in the whims
Of dream and memory investigate
These retrospective chambers for the date
In which the foot is flexed, head turns, mouth prims
Before the compact mirror, gloved hand trims
The rose stems, tongue has fancies to relate.

But still among your clothes for a little while
In some few fully human cells will issue
The scent of you in the scent you would apply,
And in your purse, imprinted on a tissue,
Your red lips waiting in a folded smile
Will show themselves as lost for words as I.

VOYAGER

Out here where light becomes an apparition
Dispersed and flecked among the turning pattern
Of dusts and crystals and ice-crusted shards
That form the heaven-haunted rings of Saturn,
This frail scintilla brushes in its arc
Their powders and records them and discards
A wake of earthbound signals through the dark
That hides the passage of its boundless mission.

Fainter and fainter, ever more delayed,
The messages return out of the sky
To Earth. And Earth exhales to outer space
Its own intelligence, not in reply,
The mortal messages that are conveyed
Out of the world and leave no earthly trace.

Stephen Edgar

SUGAR
Åhus, 2005

My grandmother pours cold milk in her coffee.
We are at her kitchen table, facing each other.
The room smells of Sun dishwashing liquid;
sometimes small bubbles escape from the bottle
and float through the room.
She sees them and I see them.

The clock on the wall is ten minutes fast
so that she won't miss the news. Everything else is slow
in here, and I, too, do things at a different pace.
It is all one long afternoon,
putting on the coffee, taking a nap,
setting the table, having dinner,
putting on the coffee.

She takes a lump of sugar
out of the brass bowl.
She holds it in her right hand;
in the palm of her left hand
she snaps it in two.
It makes a sound like dry bones breaking.
As a child I always looked at her fingers,
making sure they were whole. Now,
I turn away. She stirs until the sugar is dissolved.
'Once,' she says, looking out the window,
'when I was working up north . . .'

And I sit here, waiting for a story that never comes.
The clock ticks loudly and I can hear
a plane far away.
'What?' she asks
when she sees the questioning look on my face.
'Nothing.'

The milk has formed
a thick grey skin over the coffee.
She pushes it to the side and fishes it
out of the cup with her spoon.
On the white saucer it looks like wrinkly hide.

The bubbles rise from the bottle,
and drift towards the ceiling
like frail little souls.
They break against the plaster
with a pop.

Maria Freij

ON THE UNDOING OF BUTTONS

Pray you, undo this button
—Shakespeare, *King Lear* V iii 307

But no, I mean button-heads
creaming nameless slopes,
that blur at railway sidings,
whites, yellows rippling alps

to echidna satin. Heads too small
to turn heads, everlastings we say.
Yet do not, do not undo these
subtle threads rethreading

stream, muscle, sinew, nerves
of earth. If you drift into sock-
burr grass and bend to see,
you may jolt at abrading air,

query lace-wings, plash of eel,
corroboree frog, gone where?
bacteria, fibre, moth, wing,
hammering sky mute of birdcall.

Desert claws at snow gums,
ploughs burrows tuned to
fur, to moist and cool—
fires the red unravelling.

And Earth *will* shrug us off,
Turn dryly to her punctilious sun
Warming to next time round.
No tragedy will play.

Elizabeth Lawson

UNTITLED

I

If not for oneself, leave me a carton (a garland that holds
of idle black blossom   in the garden where you walk

I peel you upside down from the vase unaware you are naked
                underneath   skin bowed—talk of sunlight, pollen   attacking your
eyes livid, fingers blue
the ink of asphodels   trembling   still   in the lines
of your hand   and aside
from shiver & pace swans threading
a second horizon   and aside from them
pond of nothing

except perhaps a willow   lipped in perspex stone, or costume
artillery   only in the silkiest   had we a stencil of sky-coloured leaves—
audible
& leaping   we would read notes from the gallows & float
in light of
idioms
but a centipede away
you crack only a vertebra of silence
at the afternoon, dig a hundred
quivering heels into socks
of red quilty mud

*

hairpins of rainwater gaining behind me, beat of a drum
of fawn-green leaves
the passage of itinerancy malformed in hibiscus

                we drift downstream

Tsvetaeva weeding banks of the Styx, her moulting heart a periscope
into the persimmon lights of Prague

language clear & water weary, she cuts our orbit piecemeal—
ducks coins you fire into lamps to keep the sun from shining

we enter the vase from behind the rosebush—fingers fall away and you,
injured still, coil
into a swallow dive   (paisley underbelly, tinsel-tipped, wing-singed
                one-sixth of a drachma falling on your lips
swift, flapping, shadowful,

it is not
that you will not return (today, yesterday, tomorrow
but that the thimble you gave me is as appalling for rowing
as for drinking

II

.... reddened by rime & rot   rose leaves arch and turn amid fingers of
second winter
—I bend around a corner
scuffle of pigeons harrowing a bread roll
grey dog in a window slanting a gouache eye   bowl of hot purple mussels
hands waving paper-cuts into an aviary of *goodbyes*

we weave dishevelled
beneath windmills gnawing sky into tethers
      of cloudweb

a tinderbox peddling spider love opens   onto the rift
of twelve soft   vein-cheeked women who glide,   glide   (black & white
back
& forth   murmuring always   (in unhurried motion
the same eight bars of *Peter*

and the Wolf—
night folds away with

(stay
he exits fierily   disappearing majestically into eyelets of brick
wearing the carpet
in-
to warbles of thunder

*

permafrost down the window
tongue lolls into calamine, rolls over shoals
rocks, coals
and sandbars pink-purple shells   a-clap   a   clap   (full of thought and
civilised commentary

a thing once called midnight   glimpses back in the dark   wind   blowing
across an utterly black pitch of saline
crosses fissuring gold sparks and
mud and stars, mud and
stars, mud
and stars
and lightening
and a stranger who opines to neither stay nor leave
but squats inside the acorn tree within the orthodoxy of a cape

invisible chaos into a flotilla of spears, impression of salt hammers
openly hewn—   cannot wash ghost from gist of the daffodil

III

See how deeply I dive, clutching seaweed in my hands.
—Akhmatova

5th February   such little *bonheur*
        in the half-present moment
        instead brouhaha
        velcro stars   verse cracking winter
        full of tinsel bees   a flame smudging wax across
a gunpowder sky

        voice from the fountain came and said come
        grey deer woman picked us an oversized heart
from the moat of twinkling aspirin in which our oily eyes
        had been swarming   amorous   like drunken carp
perhaps because you   (recognised
        the forked eternity in her gesture &
        harsh unhurried
        caught nape
        my
        backwards
   (in the quick of your hand
        until the imprint   of fingertips   had been transferred   until the up-
   turned grave I had hitherto forgotten   roused the barb of wasp-whispers
howl
of nothing   ruffle of half-moons tucked into hunting eyelids

        decanted throat   loosens
        bands of neck-tie   and touch-   words stumble   (errant   madly
   in the gorse of your hair

shadow of baobab tree leaning into broken paths   saluting ceremoniously
shades of false white

        you look on   as I speak   (reflecting
        the law of sandbanks
pulse pressed turbulently   palpably   into the corners of my tidal
dress

Claire Potter

RAIN LOOP

a cross a stolen landscape spreads
avenging wings of screeching dust
patrol the parking bay's forecaster
retreating into the bluffing clouds
scour record shops for a rain loop
winterlong living on neenish tarts
purple storms on beige buildings
slapping feet the patchwork quilt
roads forgetting moisture pasture
memories swirl with locust winds
one drought at a summer time as
my prayers for rain bring no cure
lying in a darkened room I heard
sounds of a rain loop in my head
not a cold or humid rain but airs
wet with healing & humane tears
looping through the night as rain
should slapping against that roof
frogs gurgling in the mist & wind
reconciling against my glass pane
walk down the slope to riverbank
green see spirits there afloat with
hope & generations of new birth-
rights respect truth dignities that
loop endlessly horizontally sweep
the floods & the rain gauges away
forgotten snow seeding stockpiles
wet eucalyptus covers a continent
rain loops replacing the earworm
droughts of our commercial radio
barren plains of hoarse whistling
gone flushed out shouts drowned
shrill shriek of parched politician
shrub with no foliage greenery in
the deep bowels of an empty dam
echoes with the rain's new refrain

David Prater

HUNGER

Picture this: two women
one small child. Whose baby
is this? Whose need, whose hunger?
While one has skin like a ghost gum
       the mother is cinnamon dark—

but her child lies across
the other's pale knee. Both women
weep: silent tears glitter
on their cheeks. They do not
look at one another, but stare

at the camera's accusing eye.
The child is passive, silent.
Her thin limbs flop against
her new mother's body, her eyes,
unfocused, stare up

at the courtroom ceiling
distant and hot as the sky.
The fans rock and whirr, rock and whirr
but do not stir the child's thin
cotton frock, or dry the weeping sores

a necklace of staphylococci
      ringing her throat.
               One mother leaves
cradling her newfound child; the other
stands on the courthouse steps
bereft.

Ron Pretty

FACEBOOK

Veronica is painting her nails.
Jordan is buying a new TV.
Kate is at work.
Tom is having issues.
Chen is in Coorain.
Noah is beginning to suspect the meaning of life might have been inside that fortune cookie he ate.
Harriet is waiting for inspiration to strike.
Jasmin is procrastinating.
Geordie is discombobulating.
Mia is wondering who tried opening her door at four a.m. last night.
Denise is realising her parents were right all along.
Zoe is wishing the phone would ring.
Hannah is somehow less than she once was.
David is waiting.
Anna is alone.

James Bradley

STRIPED MARSH FROGS

the first stars
after so much rain
and the frogs are going off like popcorn

each note
a fingernail flicked on a paper drum
they tap the patter
of rain arriving

my garden's energetic
invisible typists—
if I come close
they know me for a sort of wading bird
and fall silent

then cautiously begin
again their transcription,
their morse-coded words,
tapping the glad rambling
letters of the rain

Pam Schindler

THE ECONOMICS OF SPRING

I

Midnight is a parliament of frogs. The ground vibrates with their shrill
contentions, the various factions of their self-belief, and my breath smokes
the black air, inventing galaxies
                                that spread and atrophy
before I can breathe them back again. The night smells like any one
of a dozen childhood camps, in which the present has pitched her tent.

II

The trick is to fall asleep beside your sons at eight and sleep
them to sleep till ten and wake and stalk the sleeping house till twelve.
These are the hours the rest of your life
                                        spins around and nothing is impossible
and nothing has to happen. And in the morning the news
I have reached the shed reaches me as I reach the shed, and it all starts over.

III

By noon, the sun is in recession and the future is in cloud and the day is cold
in its boots. The wind comes off the road bringing news of every passing car.
So the fallen world goes.
                            One's work in it, a purgation.
A steep and necessary climb under friendly fire. The price one pays
for loving too well the imperfect world is the imperfection of the world.

IV

Trees, those ossified spirits, quicken in a rising wind. They circle me,
pleading their silent cases when I leave the shed to pee.
Winter loosens the world's grip on itself;
                                        it stands our slender inner lives
out in the weather. The black cat, who's wandered into our care like a saint
into retirement, climbs two arthritic steps ahead of me and falls into the blue

V

Chair. White-cheeked rosellas bright as drag queens in the morning rain;
the easterly air and the daffodils the children planted, pushing up out of winter,
and the wood-ducks on the river:
                                this is how it always went. In the beginning
was the world. And in the end. The words came in the middle. The world
gave them to us with no particular end in mind. And what shall one give

VI

In return? I sit here writing poems like cheques, wondering
if they'll bounce, when the phone rings, and I drop my best pen,
nib down, and it doesn't.
                          As oracles go, that's blunt. We're speculators,
my friend the painter tells me; we back what's in our heads;
we float our souls in a deregulated market, helpless as lovers,
                                        hopeless as drunks.

VII

I sit in the ebb of winter writing fifty-dollar poems at a thousand-dollar desk:
the story of one's life. My desk is made of railway sleepers
which I sit here, morning on morning,
                                        trying to wake. This is no way to prosper,
but that's not what it's for. I'm doing what the ironbarks did
before they felled them; I'm doing what the fettlers did after that.

VIII

You do what you must. The work at hand. You stand; you fall; you give
beneath the profane rhythm that travels you daily, in which you are told,
but only obscurely, why. As I walk
                                to my shed and hear the cows across the river,
I think I'd rather be going down to work as hard to do and as easy
to define as men once did down here. But I stop wanting that at the door.

IX

Tim from downriver came to the river when the bottom fell out of the valley.
I didn't want to keep doing, he told me, *for twenty-seven cents a gallon
what had been hard enough at fifty.*
                                    And now his neighbour's spoiling the river
to carry a road to his new subdivision in what Tim had mistaken
for his view. Landscape—another deregulated market.

X

When I say to Tim, conversing as neighbours do, at dusk by a river,
Same thing happened to poetry long ago, he laughs at whatever he thinks I mean
and shows me the ruins
                              of the old bridge where the cattle used to traffic
between the now doomed paddocks of the middle distance and my shed.
The future's going the same way the past went. Only sooner.

XI

I was born empty, and each morning I wake empty again.
Who you are is where you've slept and whom you've slept there with.
This morning, then, I am three children
                                        and the Osage Orange at the door;
I am the ice on the windshield and the summit of world leaders come to nothing
up the road. In flood by nine, I walk to the shed to empty myself making phrases.

XII

And it's one kind of sin to stay indoors today, spring coiled in the morning's bed,
parrots limning the ends of winter. It's another kind to leave one's work undone.
No way out, no way back,
                          I throw wide the shed's door and compromise.
The outside walks on in; the inside out. My deaf and dilapidated muse sleeps on
in the reading chair, like one of the saved. White blossoms open on my fingertips.

Mark Tredinnick

INFORMATION ~ ABOUT ~ SUBSCRIPTIONS

In recent times *Meanjin*'s subscription rates have barely covered production and postage costs, so our prices need to go up. The slight increase per issue is still cheaper than buying *Meanjin* in bookshops and, if you subscribe before December 2008 you'll get 5 editions for the price of 4. We are also looking at the introduction of online subscriptions in the near future. *Meanjin*'s new subscription rates are set out below.

To subscribe contact the *Meanjin* office on (03) 9342 0317 or visit out website at http://www.meanjin.unimelb.edu.au.

SUBSCRIPTIONS RATES
Individual – full: $80
Individual – concession: $60
Schools: $80
Other institutions: $125

OVERSEAS
Individual: $105
Schools/Institutions: $150

8 issues: (individuals only)
Regular: $145
Concession: $120
Overseas: $180

12 issues: (individuals only)
Regular: $190
Concession: $165
Overseas: $240